CROWN OF STRENGTH

THE HIDDEN MAGE SERIES

Crown of Secrets

Crown of Danger

Crown of Strength

Crown of Power

And set in the same world:

THE SPOKEN MAGE SERIES

Voice of Power

Voice of Command

Voice of Dominion

Voice of Life

Power of Pen and Voice:

A Spoken Mage Companion Novel

CROWN OF STRENGTH

THE HIDDEN MAGE BOOK 3

MELANIE CELLIER

ISBN 978-1-925898-55-2

Luminant Publications
PO Box 201
Burnside, South Australia 5066

melaniecellier@internode.on.net
http://www.melaniecellier.com

Cover Design by Karri Klawiter
Editing by Mary Novak
Proofreading by Deborah Grace White
Map Illustration by Rebecca E Paavo

*For Genevieve Rachel
who is an utter delight*

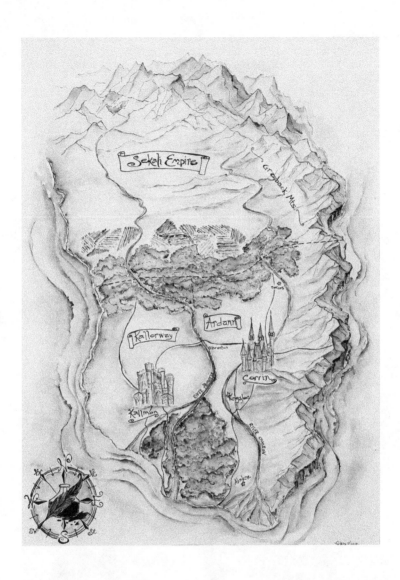

CHAPTER 1

I woke abruptly in the darkness, startled awake and disoriented. Where was I? And what was that noise?

The rustling and creaking came again through the night as I slowly recognized my surroundings. Bookshelves cast shadows through the dim room, reminding me I had been reading in my family's personal sitting room—a room my parents had turned into a small private library. I must have fallen asleep, the mage light winking out at some point in the unknown hours that had passed since then.

I squinted at the moon out the window. It must be nearing dawn from the faint hint of deep blue in the night sky. I groaned and stretched, sore from the hours spent slumped in the armchair.

A soft gasp made me sit up straight and peer around the room. I wasn't alone.

Two frozen shapes, darker than the rest of the night, caught my eye. They stood near the small door that opened into the palace grounds.

"Who's there?" I asked sharply, my hand reaching for the protective compositions I kept stored in my pockets.

The second gasp sounded so fearful that my muscles relaxed slightly. It was hardly the noise of an attacker, creeping into the palace with dark intent.

"It's only Verene," a voice whispered at the softest possible volume.

The words were clearly meant for other ears, but it was so quiet in the room I easily caught them. And I recognized the voice.

"Stellan?" I stood up and tried to peer harder through the darkness. "Is that you? What are you doing here?"

An exasperated sigh sounded, and a second later a light flared, illuminating the room.

"What are *you* doing here?" my younger brother asked. "You do have a bed to sleep in, you know."

I ignored the question as I examined the two people revealed by the light. My sixteen-year-old brother looked irritated, but underneath it I detected a hint of real fear.

I frowned, a new wave of anxiety flooding me. What was Stellan doing creeping through the palace in the dark? And why was he afraid?

His companion looked outright terrified, and I had the over-whelming impression she was barely refraining from clinging tightly to Stellan's arm. I didn't recognize her from court, and her clothing suggested she was a commonborn. But what was my brother doing with an unfamiliar commonborn girl? A girl who looked around his own age and whose wide eyes and plain clothes did nothing to mar her beauty. A sense of foreboding swept over me.

"Stellan, what is going on here?" I asked, although my eyes didn't leave the girl.

Her long black hair had been braided and pinned to her head, the effect almost regal, despite her plain outfit. Her golden skin and high cheekbones reminded me of our Aunt Saffron. Had she also come from the northern city of Torcos? Perhaps Stellan had met her through our aunt.

"Nothing to do with you," he said, making my frown deepen. My brother wasn't usually so combative.

"I'm Verene." I kept my attention on Stellan's companion, introducing myself since he didn't seem inclined to do it for me. "Stellan's sister."

She immediately dropped into a curtsy. "Yes, of course, Your Highness." She faltered a little, casting an anxious glance at my brother before adding, "I'm Elsie."

My eyes dropped to her wrists, but her skin was clear and unmarked. If she was a commonborn, she wasn't one of the fortunate sealed, able to read and write. As soon as the thought occurred to me, I gasped and leaped across the short distance to stand between the two of them and the small door that opened out into the palace courtyard.

"Stellan! You tell me right this second what the two of you are doing." I hoped I was overreacting, but I couldn't risk the chance my guess was right.

Stellan squared his shoulders, drawing himself up to his newly acquired height.

"I won't let you stop us, Verene."

I narrowed my eyes at him. "I don't like the sound of that. Is that a threat, Stellan?"

"Stellan!" Elsie hissed, and this time she did grab his arm, giving him a look that was half-afraid, half-reproving.

He looked down into her face with a determined expression. "I already told you. I'm not going to let anything—or anyone— stop me." He glanced back in my direction. "Not even you, Verene. Even if I have to put you to sleep."

"Well unfortunately for you, I have every intention of stopping you. And you'll find I'm not so easy to put to sleep as that."

Elsie pulled at Stellan's arm, her eyes frantic. "I told you this was a bad idea."

But Stellan's face merely set into more obstinate lines. "This is our only chance. You know that. I'm not losing it." He sucked in a breath. "I'm not losing you."

She flushed, glancing at me and then quickly away.

"Stellan." I folded my arms across my chest. "Are you or are you not attempting to sneak into the sealing ceremony happening first thing this morning?"

He said nothing in response, not meeting my eyes.

"Mother and Father have already told you they won't consider letting you be sealed until you finish first year at least. You're about to start at the Academy—is it really so awful to wait one more year?"

I glanced at Elsie and bit my lip. "And I really, really hope that Elsie is a friend, keeping you company against her better judgment. Because if she's a commonborn, and you're planning to sneak her into the ceremony as well, then you're worse than a fool."

"You don't understand, Verene," Stellan said, a hint of desperation in his voice.

I kept my gaze steady, not giving him even a hint of softness. "I understand that if you manage to do this to yourself, you'll be in more trouble than you're ready for. I can't even imagine how Mother and Father would react. But if Elsie does it?" I shook my head. "If you care about her at all, Stellan, then you won't want to see her suffer the sort of consequences that would fall on an unknown commonborn who committed the same offense. You're a prince, Stellan, which means you'll get leniency she won't. And you should know that."

He blanched, looking down at her with a protective expression that made his face both gentle and strong at the same time. But when he looked back at me, his eyes hardened.

"This is our only chance. I'll deal with the consequences afterward."

I barely refrained from rolling my eyes. I knew I was only two years older than my brother, but had I ever been that young?

Darius's face flashed in front of my eyes, and I nearly winced. I knew what it was like to throw caution to the wind and let myself be ruled by emotion.

Certainty gripped me. "You love her," I said softly to Stellan, unable to resist another curious glance at Elsie.

The poor girl looked miserable—embarrassed and terrified at the same time. But when she saw me looking at her, she straightened.

"I told him it was a bad idea, Princess Verene. He shouldn't risk all of this for me."

"You're risking more than he is." I sighed, thinking of the risk he didn't even know he was taking. "Or at least, more than he knows he is."

Stellan's eyes snapped to mine. "What's that supposed to mean?"

I met him look for look. "How about you start by telling me your story? Since I'm not the one sneaking around in the dark."

Elsie straightened, nodding decisively. "We have to tell her, Stellan. I'm not letting you attack your own sister."

She marched over to one of the over-padded sofas and sat down. When Stellan stayed where he was, she crossed her arms.

"I'm not going another step. If you go through with this, you'll be going to that ceremony alone."

He deflated, hesitating for only a moment before crossing over to sit at her side.

I watched them both, bemused at the change in the nervous girl and the way she masterfully put a stop to my brother's fool-hardy blustering. Grabbing the closest chair, I pulled it into position between their sofa and the door, perching on the edge.

"I know you've been practicing ever since you turned sixteen last winter." I examined my brother. "But would you really have tried to use your ability to steal all my energy and leave me unconscious?"

For a moment my brother bristled at the suggestion that he

wouldn't have succeeded in such an attempt, before his shoulders slumped.

"Honestly? I don't know. I've done it before in practice, with a volunteer. But could I actually attack my own sister?" He looked at the girl beside him. "I'm not sure."

"I don't believe you would have." Elsie placed a gentle hand on his arm.

My parents had been privately training my brother since his sixteenth birthday, experimenting with his spoken energy mage powers. We had always known Stellan was an energy mage, but only since his sixteenth birthday had they discovered he possessed the unique ability to both give and take energy.

I knew my parents had been scouring the Sekali Empire since, hoping to find other young energy mages who might be interested in attending the Ardannian Academy this year, as well as an experienced instructor to work with them. Our mother was the only other spoken mage able to draw on the energy of others, but she did it using power, not directly with energy as Stellan and true energy mages did. And she had no experience with giving energy. But she had obviously managed the training well enough if Stellan had gained so much control already.

Stellan ran a hand over his face, looking weary now, as if he hadn't slept all night. Which was quite possibly the case. He had fought with my parents over the question of being sealed, but this sort of defiance wasn't like him.

"I know you would prefer to start at the Academy already able to write," I said, my voice gentle, "but is it really a matter of such concern to you that you'd risk all this?"

Sealing only blocked power, not energy, rendering the mage who worked the sealing composition and everyone in its range unable to access power. For commonborns, that block meant they were free to write without unleashing uncontrolled destruction. For power mages, it meant the end of their abilities.

It wasn't normally an issue for energy mages at all as they

were born with their ability to access power blocked. Like me. Although my similarity to any sort of regular energy mage ended there.

My brother, however, had been born with a spoken ability like my mother. And like her, any attempt to write would unleash uncontrolled destructive power. But unlike her, his spoken words controlled an energy ability, not a power ability. Which made his unsealed status an inconvenient curiosity. I could understand why he had come up with the idea of joining a group of commonborns at a sealing ceremony and being sealed beside them. But I also knew from personal experience that he might have unsuspected abilities lurking inside him.

I had told myself last summer that if he was still determined to be sealed when I returned this summer, I would find a way to warn him, even if it meant revealing my secret. And he clearly could not be more determined. But I hesitated to speak in front of a complete stranger. I needed to understand what was happening here before I could decide how much of my own story to impart.

"I wouldn't risk anything for my own sake," Stellan said after a significant pause and an encouraging look from the girl beside him. "But I would risk anything for Elsie."

I cleared my throat, uncomfortable with the adoring look Elsie was giving him. Clearly they knew each other well—or thought they did—and yet I had never met her, or even heard of her. Which didn't bode well for her identity. Why had they kept their relationship, whatever it was, such a secret?

As if hearing my thoughts, Stellan spoke again.

"Elsie is a servant here at the palace." He gave me a defiant look. "A commonborn."

I kept my face impassive although my heart sank all the way to my feet. Stellan was a mage and a prince of Ardann. I couldn't see how anything but heartbreak could come from such a situation.

"I met Elsie two years ago," Stellan continued. "After you left for Kallorway. With you and Lucien both off studying, it was so quiet around here. I started spending more time in the rest of the palace, and one day I ran into her."

Elsie shook her head. "You're being gallant again. What actually happened is that you found me crying and swooped in to rescue me." She looked at me. "I'd only just moved to the palace, and someone gave me wrong directions. I got completely lost and had despaired of ever finding my way where I needed to be. But Stellan knew all the shortcuts, and I wasn't even late." She beamed at him.

I almost grimaced. It wasn't hard to imagine why a youthful Elsie had fallen hard for the handsome prince who came to her rescue. Or why Stellan, feeling alone, might have been drawn to her in return.

"Elsie had just been accepted into the palace training program," Stellan explained to me. "She isn't a chambermaid, or anything like that. And she's brilliant, so some of the others in the program have resented her since the start. They know she's the best of them. The head of the program is obsessed with punctuality, and they knew if Elsie failed to appear, or arrived late, that he would be prejudiced against her after that."

I frowned, trying to remember the details of the training program.

Elsie ducked her head, clearly embarrassed by his praise. "Not brilliant enough to be referred to the University. But my teacher suggested this option instead, and it seemed like a wonderful opportunity. My family comes from a small town, and I'd never even been to Corrin before."

Her words sparked my memory. Ordinary commonborn schools finished when the students reached ten years old. In the past, only the very occasional student with a genius level of recall could hope to complete years of private tutoring between school and admittance to the Royal University. My Uncle Jasper had been one of them.

But since the beginning of sealing, further options had opened for the more promising students. School teachers, sealed themselves, could recommend their more intelligent and diligent students to a number of different locations. For the most academically minded, the University now ran an entire commonborn stream, accepting a full class every year. And a separate institution had been set up specially to train teachers for all the commonborn schools.

For those inclined toward finance and trade, apprenticeships with the merchant families were highly sought after. And for those with a more practical inclination, the program at the palace trained commonborns for a life of future service in positions of authority. The young people who came through the program would eventually occupy senior positions doing everything from supporting Ardann's diplomats to managing the other palace servants.

Any one of these options was considered highly desirable because these were the four streams that contributed most of the commonborns to the sealing ceremonies. If you won a position as a University student, future teacher, merchant apprentice, or palace trainee, you were almost certainly guaranteed a place at a future sealing ceremony.

"If Elsie is in the palace training program, why are you trying to sneak her into a sealing ceremony?" I asked. "How old are you, Elsie?"

"Sixteen." She bit her lip and looked like she wanted to say more but instead glanced at Stellan and remained silent.

"If you're sixteen, shouldn't you have a place at that ceremony without any subterfuge required? I thought that was the age the participants were all sealed."

"That's how it's supposed to be," Stellan said. "But there have been so few ceremonies lately that there haven't been enough places. So Elsie has had to compete for a place at the ceremony." A miserable look descended over his face. "And she would have had a place—she *should* have one—but I destroyed everything for her."

"No, don't say that," Elsie cried immediately. "Of course you haven't destroyed everything."

But his words made sudden sense of his strange behavior. Stellan had somehow been responsible for Elsie not being one of those chosen to be sealed, and his guilt was driving him to go to any lengths to fix the wrong.

"I talked her into slipping out of the palace for a whole day," Stellan said. "It was supposed to be a day off, but then the head of the program ran a surprise testing exercise. Elsie missed the whole thing and went from the top of the group to the bottom. Given how the head feels about punctuality, you can imagine how he feels about being absent altogether."

"That's unfortunate," I said, "but surely it's better for Elsie to work her way back up to the top of the group and wait for the next ceremony."

Stellan shook his head, his eyes frantic. "We can't wait. There are no second chances. All those not chosen for sealing are being sent away later today."

"Sent away? What do you mean?"

"There's a lot of competition for the places at the ceremony," Elsie said. "And I suppose they're afraid of bad blood between those who succeeded and those of us who trained for two years and are now unable to pursue any of the career options we'd hoped for and worked toward. Instead we're being sent out to positions in other towns or on mage estates—places where they can use the skills we've learned even though we're not sealed."

I nodded. It made a great deal of sense, actually, and also explained the fevered desperation driving Stellan. He had not only destroyed Elsie's chances but was about to lose her in the process.

"You're a prince, Stellan," I said without thinking. "Surely you have enough influence to help Elsie without resorting to this terrible scheme."

He gave me a significant look. "Yes, exactly, I'm a sixteen-year-old prince. How exactly do you think they're going to react if I attempt to intervene on behalf of a commonborn servant as young and beautiful as Elsie?"

I winced. He was right, of course. If Stellan so much as mentioned Elsie's name, it would ensure she was not only excluded from the ceremony but assigned to a position as far from Corrin as possible.

I opened my mouth to speak, but he cut me off.

"And don't suggest I ask Mother and Father to help. I'm not willing to risk it."

Once again I had to acknowledge his fears weren't ground-less. Our mother herself had been born a commonborn, so our parents didn't have the prejudice against them that many mages still did. But our parents loved us and wanted the best for us. And they knew firsthand the difficulties of a match between a mage prince and a commonborn girl. And that was despite the fact that in their case, Mother had proven herself a powerful and unique mage before the court was asked to accept a romance between them. Elsie had no such claim to recommend her, and my parents would foresee the same difficulty and pain in their future as I did. It was entirely possible they would side against them—judging that a heartbreak now at sixteen was preferable to what might potentially come in the future.

I looked at the sofa and saw the two of them were holding hands, their faces a tragic mix of despair and hope. Recklessness filled me. Only two years stood between us, and I knew what it was to feel so deeply. I spoke without further thought.

"I'll help Elsie in exchange for a promise from you, Stellan."

CHAPTER 2

"You'll help Elsie?" Stellan asked, a light springing into his eyes at the same moment as Elsie asked, "What promise?"

Seeing the way they both thought immediately of the other only confirmed my decision. If Stellan cared this much about this girl, then she must be special. And if our family was responsible for her change in fortunes, then I would do what I could to fix it. The fact that I would gain in the exchange was only a bonus.

"Stellan, you can't request Elsie be included in the ceremony, but I can. I'm officially an adult now, and as a royal, I'm entitled to one personal servant who has been sealed. Someone I can trust to be in my rooms and around my compositions. I don't have one yet, and if I request Elsie specifically, she'll be included in the sealing ceremony."

I looked at Elsie. "I can't imagine being a maid is your dream, but it doesn't have to be forever. Sealing, on the other hand, is. I have no possible reason to interfere with the palace's training program, so this is the only way I can get you into that ceremony."

Elsie looked at me with wide eyes. "Are you sure, Your Highness? Holding a position like that for one of the royal family is considered prestigious. No one wants to waste a sealed servant on menial tasks. It's a respected position, usually overseeing junior servants to complete the more basic work." She hesitated. "Personal servants often end up developing a relationship of trust and responsibility with the person they serve."

I grimaced slightly, thinking of Ida at the Academy who cared for my rooms. In Kallorway they seemed to have no problem using sealed servants as basic maids. Hopefully that would start to change now that Darius was in power, but how long would it take for the Kallorwegian mages to see the wasted potential among their commonborns?

Elsie must have misinterpreted my expression because she looked away, biting her lip. "I understand if you want to change your mind," she said. "Royals don't usually have personal servants who are only sixteen. Just think of Leila."

Mention of my mother's friend made me grin. Leila had been the first commonborn my mother hired after she took up her official role as the Spoken Mage, and in the decades since, the woman had become a legend around the palace, wielding more authority than many mages. If Leila was who Elsie thought of when I offered the position as my personal servant, then it was no wonder she considered the role prestigious.

"I think you might be forgetting I'm only eighteen myself," I said. "I'm still at the Academy which means there's no team of junior servants. I'm afraid even after you're sealed, there will be menial work. At least for the next two years."

"I don't mind working my way up," Elsie said quickly. "I always expected that."

I nodded. "Excellent. Then I'm sure we'll deal well together."

Stellan, who had been looking between us with growing concern in his eyes, focused his attention back on me.

"But that means you'll be taking her to Kallorway with you. She'll be leaving anyway."

I gave him a stern look. "Yes, of course it means she'll have to come to Kallorway with me. But you'll be going off to the Academy here yourself, remember. And this isn't about the next year or two, anyway. If we do this, it's about Elsie's whole future."

Stellan gulped and nodded. "Yes, of course."

I didn't feel any need to tell him that taking Elsie away was one of the elements I liked best about this plan. Stellan was about to begin at the Academy where he would be mixing in an informal environment with every other Ardannian mage his own age. If Elsie was far away and out of reach during the coming year, it would be a true test of their feelings and devotion. For all I liked what I'd seen of Elsie so far, I still couldn't help wanting a simpler future for my brother.

"But what about that promise?" Elsie's brow wrinkled as she glanced sideways at Stellan. "What do you want from Stellan?"

"I want him to promise he won't get sealed for another two years at least," I said.

He started. "Two years? But that's longer than even Mother and Father said."

I shrugged. "That's the deal I'm offering. You wait at least until you're a third year, and I'll get Elsie sealed today."

Elsie relaxed and even smiled. "But that's an easy promise to make, Stellan. You shouldn't be going against your parents or limiting yourself anyway. I've been telling you that all along."

My liking for the girl increased by several points, although Stellan didn't look as satisfied with her words. Elsie looked over at me.

"I know I should never have let him talk me into it in the first place. I knew it was a bad idea. But..." She looked at him, so much emotion in her eyes that I knew she had been equally horrified at the thought of being sent away forever and never seeing him again. Had she trusted in his rank to save her from the consequences that would follow the inevitable discovery of their crime?

"How will you do it, though?" Stellan asked. "Get Elsie included, I mean. They always fill the ceremonies to capacity, and without me there to increase the energy available for the working..."

Elsie gave a soft gasp. "Oh! I didn't think of that." She gave me a stricken look. "I couldn't bear for anyone else to lose their place so that I could be included."

"Not even if it was one of the other trainee servants who treated you badly?" I asked, curious. "Don't you deserve the spot more than them?"

She shook her head. "They aren't truly bad people. It's not their fault we were all set up in competition with each other. And none of them were responsible for me missing that final test."

Stellan growled something too low for me to catch, giving me the impression he didn't feel as forgiving as she did. But I could see why my warm-hearted brother had fallen in love with her.

"So you were planning to give the sealing mage some extra energy?" I asked Stellan. "To cover there being two extra people in the ceremony."

He nodded while I fished around in one of my pockets.

"Thankfully, I have a solution for that." I pulled out a parchment triumphantly. "I have a written energy composition from Bree—a fortunate thing since we don't want to involve you in this at all. I'll offer it to whoever is organizing the ceremony in exchange for including Elsie. I imagine they'll jump at the offer since this has to be enough to cover more than just her. I'm sure they have a long list of people who've missed out."

Sealing ceremonies were so few that the entire idea wouldn't have been sustainable without the reappearance of energy mages. We didn't have many in Ardann, but we always managed to acquire some extra energy for any mages completing a sealing. In the Empire, where they had access to both more energy mages and more power mages willing to be sealed, the arrival of the energy mages had been what allowed them to continue sealing their entire commonborn population, despite its growing size.

By now the sky outside had lightened considerably, dawn breaking. I glanced out the window and stood.

"So do I have your promise, Stellan? Not until third year?"

I didn't just want the two years so he could have time to discover any potential other powers for himself. I would be finished at the Academy at that point, forced to make decisions about my own future. One way or another, I would have to be more honest with my family by then. I trusted that once Stellan knew the truth of my abilities, he would see for himself why it would be so foolish to bind himself.

Reluctantly Stellan nodded, still gripping Elsie's hand.

"You have my word, Verene."

I nodded once. "Then we need to move fast. Elsie, you had better come with me. Do either of you know who is overseeing the ceremony?"

Stellan named a pair of palace officials who often worked together—one a sealed commonborn and one a mage. I nodded again before turning to Elsie.

"Do I look respectable?"

"Your...Highness?" she faltered.

"If I'm going to start throwing my rank around, I'd rather not look like I just spent the night sleeping in an armchair." I smiled at her. "You said that personal servant is a position of trust, so here's your first big test. Can you tell me the truth?"

"Oh." She looked like she wasn't sure whether or not she was allowed to giggle.

Stellan just rolled his eyes. "You look fine, Verene."

"I didn't ask you, Stellan. You may be my brother, but I do not trust you in this particular matter. I'm not sure you'd even notice if I looked disheveled."

"He's right, though," Elsie said decisively. "No one would guess you hadn't made it to bed last night."

She darted forward and poked at a strand of my hair, pushing it back into place before stepping back and regarding me critically. When she gave a decisive nod, I grinned.

"Let's go then. We don't have any time to waste."

Elsie clearly knew her way around the palace because she led me straight to the right office without hesitation. I was afraid the officials might have already left for the ceremony location, but they were still there.

They both scrambled to their feet when I barged into the room, bowing low and addressing me respectfully.

"I'm so sorry to cause trouble at the last minute," I said. "But I have chosen a personal servant from the palace training program, and I have just learned that she wasn't selected for the ceremony today. The oversight is due to a misunderstanding, of course, and I must insist she be included."

The two officials gaped at Elsie, who lingered uncomfortably in the doorway, before throwing each other worried looks.

"I'm sure you've put a great deal of effort into the various tests to measure exactly how many commonborns will be able to be sealed today," I continued, "and you have no doubt planned for a full ceremony. Obviously I would not want to disrupt your plans, and so I would like to donate this."

I handed the parchment I still held to the closest official, who looked down at it with a frown. As soon as she read the words, her brow cleared, however. She passed it along to her companion while smiling broadly at me.

"Naturally we would be only too happy to accommodate your request, Princess Verene. And we apologize for the oversight that saw your chosen servant excluded in the first place. I don't know how that happened."

I shrugged. "It's no one's fault. I hadn't made my choice known yet as there seemed no need. She was top of her group."

"I will admit," the second one said, looking up from the parchment, "I was surprised not to see your name on the list, Elsie."

"As I said, it was all due to a misunderstanding," I said. "And I apologize that since I didn't write that composition myself, I can't tell you exactly how much energy it contains. But I'm sure it will be enough for more than just Elsie."

"Don't give it another thought, Your Highness," said the first one. "That's our job, and you can safely leave it to us."

I could tell from the buzz of suppressed energy that now emanated from both of them that they were anxious for me to be gone. I had just thrown their morning into disarray, and they would be eager to ensure they could make full use of this new gift of energy.

"Where should Elsie…" I glanced back at the girl, my voice trailing off as one of the officials leaped in.

"You may leave her with us, Your Highness. We will give her the necessary instructions. Naturally you cannot be at the sealing yourself, but we will ensure that she comes straight to you once it is complete."

Elsie nodded vigorous agreement, so I thanked them again and swept out of the room. I would only get in their way by lingering, and they were right that no one would want me anywhere near the large shielded hall used for the ceremonies, despite my perceived lack of ability.

When I reached my suite, thoughts of my bed called to me. But I found Stellan waiting for me in my sitting room. He was pacing up and down but stopped mid-stride as I appeared through the door.

I hid a sigh. Apparently my pillow would have to wait a little longer.

"Well?" he asked.

"It's all arranged," I said. "Now there's nothing for us to do but wait for Elsie to reappear with the mark of the sealed around her wrists."

Stellan drew a deep breath. "Thank you, Verene."

I shrugged. "You're my brother, Stellan, and you were about to do something unutterably foolish. Of course I had to help rescue you from yourself."

He grinned. "Could you sound more like an older sister?"

"Just be glad you have an older sister," I told him, tartly. "Or you'd be left to clean up the mess you'd made all on your own."

"Are you going to get in trouble?" he asked. "I thought even royals weren't allowed to take any personal guards or servants with them to the Academy. Is it different in Kallorway?"

"Not usually." I collapsed onto a sofa and yawned. "But Mother and Father already weaseled Captain Layna into the Academy to be my personal guard. Not that she undertakes that role while I'm inside Academy grounds, but she's still there, ready for if I leave. Plus we now have a king-elect attending which seems to have thrown all the rules into chaos. He's to have an entire squad of personal guards. What's one little servant in the midst of all that?"

"What if they refuse and send her away?" Stellan asked, concern all over his face.

I yawned even harder, my jaw cracking. "Then she'll ride back to Corrin in my carriage where she will have no trouble finding a new position given she will be sealed. Stop worrying, Stellan."

"Sorry," he said swiftly. "I should let you get some sleep."

"Yes, please."

He chuckled and came over to give me a brief hug.

"I'm lucky to have you, Verene."

"I know," I told him with a twinkle. "Now go away."

He crossed over to the door, but my next words made him pause.

"Don't forget your promise."

He looked back at me with serious eyes. "I never forget my

promises. I don't know what's going on with you, Verene—although I'm sure there's something—but I'll wait."

When he slipped out the door, I stumbled to my bed, grimacing to myself. If Stellan could tell I was hiding something, then probably the rest of my family could too. How long before one of them demanded answers?

CHAPTER 3

I was once again startled awake—this time by a slender girl who catapulted onto my bed.

"What are you doing in bed at this hour, Verene? And who is that servant girl in your sitting room who tried to bar me from your bedchamber?"

I gurgled something unintelligible as I forced my eyes to focus.

"Bree? Where did you come from? How late in the afternoon is it?"

"Shockingly late," she assured me.

I groaned and threw an arm across my eyes. "In that case, I assume the girl in my rooms is Elsie—Stellan's commonborn love and my new personal servant."

"What?!?" Bree's shriek made me come fully awake, sitting up abruptly.

"I probably shouldn't have said that. You can't tell anyone about Stellan, Bree."

"Have I ever told anyone *your* secrets?" She looked at me reprovingly. "But you have to tell me everything immediately."

I told the strange tale as concisely as I could, although Bryony had a great many questions which meant it took some time.

"And so now, I assume, she's out in my sitting room," I said. "And we'll have to take her to the Academy with us."

"Well if Stellan has fallen in love with her—a palace servant!— then I'm sure she must be easy to like," Bryony said, as loyal to the family as ever.

"So far she seems even more kind-hearted than him, and she must be intelligent. I'm just hoping that a year apart will help them both gain a little distance."

Bryony's mouth twisted. "It's hopelessly romantic, but you're right, of course. I can't imagine what your aunt will say if Stellan wants to marry her when he graduates."

My mind flew to Duke Francis and Zora, as it had many times since first discovering Stellan and Elsie attempting to slip out of the palace. But since I hadn't told Bryony about their secret marriage—between a mage and a commonborn servant, just like this case—I couldn't mention them now. And I had to admit it wasn't a true comparison.

The duke had already chosen to eschew court, and he lived in such a remote location that he could keep knowledge of his marriage from almost everyone. They had advantages Stellan didn't have—the two of them ruled unequivocally over their own small domain—and yet still they felt the need to keep their relationship a secret.

I didn't know how long they had been married, but I assumed it was a love that had come to them later in life. I doubted the duke had been assigned to such a senior position as a young man. There certainly didn't seem to be any children involved. But Stellan was young and not only royal but from a unique bloodline, with a unique ability.

While my parents had quietly struck down the law that required royalty to marry only other royalty or a mage from one of the great families, the expectation of strength still remained.

No one of power or influence in Ardann would want to see one of the children of the Spoken Mage marry a commonborn, ensuring their children were born with weak abilities. It was an unpleasant fact of life, but a fact nonetheless.

I shooed Bryony out of my room so I could get dressed and emerged into my sitting room to find her already charming Elsie.

"Your Highness." Elsie dropped into a deep curtsy. "I'm so sorry, but—"

I held up my hand to stop her. "Please don't apologize for Bryony. You'll soon learn that she's a force of nature and doesn't believe in lounging in bed. She's also my closest friend and basically my cousin, so you needn't try to keep her out."

Elsie's look of relief made me chuckle.

"Let's see your wrists then," I said, and she held them out proudly.

The intricate pattern that ringed them looked elegant, and she was clearly delighted to show it off. I much preferred Ardann's approach of marking the wrists of those sealed over Kallorway's system of putting a similar pattern around their necks. Perhaps I could suggest to Darius that in the future people could be offered a choice between the two options.

"I cannot thank you enough, Your Highness," Elsie said, and I broke in before she could become any more effusive.

"Given you're now to be my personal servant, I think I will rapidly get tired of hearing *Your Highness*. How about if we stick to Princess Verene, or even just Princess?"

She bobbed a shallower curtsy. "Certainly, if that is your wish, Princess."

"And maybe dispense with the curtsying as well," Bryony suggested. "It makes me tired just watching you."

"Ha! Nothing makes you tired as I know all too well." I looked across at Elsie. "You will soon discover that Bryony likes to spend her time practicing in the training yards or running up and down stairs—and she'll involve anyone else she can in the exhausting business. But in this instance, I agree. The curtsying isn't necessary."

"Very well, Princess Verene. I'll do my best to remember."

"Excellent. For now, your duties will consist of keeping my rooms clean and assisting me with such things as ensuring my wardrobe is kept in good condition. I trust I can leave you to sort out the details."

She nodded enthusiastically.

"If I think of other tasks, I'll be sure to let you know. But in the meantime, given our imminent departure, you must feel free to take whatever time you need to get your personal affairs in order. We leave within days."

"Only days," Bryony moaned. "And I haven't even visited a single shop yet."

I eyed her with some alarm. "Why do I have the feeling that oversight is going to be remedied, and I'm going to be dragged to every shop in Corrin in the next few days?"

She grinned at me. "Because you know me too well?"

The sound of a stifled laugh made me look across at Elsie.

"You'll get used to Bree," I promised. "Everyone does eventually."

My fears proved entirely founded. I scarcely had the chance to draw breath between Bryony's arrival and our departure from Corrin. Sinking into the carriage seat at last, the journey ahead felt almost like a break.

One good aspect of the business was that my parents had little chance to question me on my sudden desire to claim a personal servant. Since I had turned eighteen in the past year, they knew it was my right to do so, but they were a little concerned how the Kallorwegian Academy might feel about the arrangement.

My breezy assurance that all would be well only made them

exchange concerned glances which filled me with guilt. My parents knew I was the crown's chosen representative to Darius, but they didn't realize just how closely I was involved in his recent seizure of power or know of my connection with the Academy's head servant.

My older brother, Lucien, who had graduated earlier in the summer, had already hired a personal servant and two more officials. But no one was surprised at that. Now that he was officially qualified as a mage, he would take on the full role of crown prince.

His absence over the summer reminded me of how busy Darius had been at the end of second year after he was named king-elect. How was he going to balance his new responsibilities with two more years of study? But, like Lucien, he couldn't step into his full role until he had been officially qualified.

Thoughts of the prince made me touch one particular pocket in my white trainee robe. Unlike my other pockets, it held no compositions but rather a single sheet of worn parchment containing a letter.

It was a letter I had read a hundred times, and yet I was no closer to deciphering its true meaning than when I had read it the first time. Although I did at least now have the assurance that it had truly been written by Jareth, thanks to a composition I had cajoled out of Lucien. Darius's brother was the last person I wanted to be thinking about, and yet his letter had haunted my summer break. I could easily call it up before my mind's eye without pulling it free from its pocket.

Verene—

I hope this note finds its way to you. Something terrible is wrong, although I cannot understand what it is. I need your help, but not for my own sake. I need your help to save Darius. It's the only reason I dare ask since I know I deserve no such assistance for myself. But for Darius and Kallorway, I implore you. Please help me. Please return next year and find out what is happening here.

    Jareth

After two years, I had finally proven to Darius the depths of his brother's treachery, and yet instead of victory, I had been left with nothing but grief and fresh questions. Every time I thought of Jareth, I inevitably thought of Darius, and the way he had responded to his brother's perfidy. Cut deeply by the one family member he thought he could trust, he had attempted to drive me away too, isolating himself completely. Sometimes it felt as if Jareth had been the true victor.

My aunt had been greatly interested to learn of Jareth's treachery, and even more to find that even as the summer wore on, no hint of it reached her ears from any source but me. It seemed incredible that not a whisper of the truth had reached the ears of any of her intelligencers.

As much as I had enjoyed the time with my family, I had been anxious for some weeks to return to the Academy so I could ask Darius what was going on. I would have liked to forget all about Jareth, but his letter burned a constant hole in my pocket. And I had come to the reluctant conclusion that I would have to find a way to speak to him.

Assuming he was still alive.

Despite his attempts to kill me, the thought that he might not be alive made me queasy. I still wasn't sure if Darius was going to survive his brother's betrayal—I was almost certain he wouldn't survive executing him. Or at least, his inner self wouldn't.

All summer I had held on to the brief glimpse of Darius's true self that he had shown between his seizure of power and Jareth's attack. He had been commanding yet personable, smiling at the other trainees and full of hope. That was the king he was meant to be, and I was resolved it was the king he would still have the chance to become.

I had finished second year determined my new abilities would allow me to protect those I loved. But over the summer I had realized that keeping them safe—even securing Darius's throne— wasn't enough. I had to find a way to free Darius of his family's evil influence. Which meant I couldn't completely let go of Jareth yet.

Thoughts of my new ability made me glance at Elsie who had dozed off in one corner of the carriage. My need to practice my ability was one aspect I hadn't considered when so rashly agreeing to take her on as my personal servant. It might prove inconvenient to have a servant always in my suite.

Bryony had been full of questions about my promised attempts to practice over the summer, but I had little of interest to report. While I had rejected my fear of my new ability, I hadn't lost my fear of being discovered. It had been bad enough when I could wrest control of any composition, no matter how power- ful. Now it appeared I could also connect to any other mage, no matter how strong or skilled, using their abilities and energy as if they were my own. Before I had been a valuable prize for either crown, now I was doubly so.

In the palace at Corrin, I was surrounded by other mages, but I was also closely observed. I had connected with the energy of several other mages, but I had hesitated to actually draw on their ability and complete a composition. Not only because of the risk they would feel the drain to their energy, but also because of the evidence it would create.

Bryony also glanced at the sleeping Elsie before giving me a concerned look.

"You were worried about being closely observed over the summer," she whispered, her mind obviously on a similar track to mine. "But what about now with Elsie?"

I grimaced. "I'll just have to find a way to make it work."

"You're not going to use it as an excuse not to practice, are you?" She gave me a stern look.

I shook my head. "No. This year I'm not holding back. I'm determined to master this new ability, and I'm not letting Darius freeze me out any longer, either."

She raised both eyebrows. "Good for you."

Her slightly skeptical expression put a defensive note in my next whisper. "He admitted he cares about me. When he tried to push me away, it was for my own safety. But I'm not as vulnerable as he thinks."

"I got the impression it was Jareth's vulnerability that was weighing on his mind. And who knows—maybe he has a point." Bryony looked worried in a way I wasn't used to seeing.

"Don't tell me you're worried about me, too!"

She bit her lip. "I don't know what to think, to be honest. Darius always said Jareth was above suspicion."

"He was wrong." My flat voice came out louder than I had intended, and I glanced quickly at Elsie to check she was still asleep.

"Yes, he was," Bryony agreed, "and yet..."

She didn't need to fill in the details. I understood her confusion. While I hadn't had the chance to show her Jareth's letter last year, I had let her read it after her arrival in Corrin. She had no more idea what to make of it than I did, although she had seemed less inclined to allow Jareth any sort of doubt. Until now.

"So you think he might be innocent?" I asked.

"Innocent?" She looked at me in surprise. "No, of course not. He tried to kill you. He tried to kill his own brother!"

"And yet...?" I quirked an eyebrow at her, and she wrinkled her nose.

"And yet while he might not be innocent, maybe there's more to the story. Maybe there really is something at play in the Kallorwegian court that can twist and destroy anyone." She looked at me, the earlier worry in her eyes. "Darius lost his brother; I don't want to lose my best friend."

I shook my head. "No one else is being lost. I won't allow it."

"When you say it like that, I almost believe you can do it, too." Her usual smile flitted across her face.

"I'm going to ask to see him," I said.

"Who? Darius? Do you think he'll still be trying to avoid you? Surely there's no need of that now he's king-elect."

I shook my head. "No, Jareth."

"Jareth?" Bryony almost choked on the name, both of us casting glances at Elsie who continued to sleep, her mouth slightly slack and her breathing regular. "How are you going to see him? Darius sent him back to the capital."

"Yes, and as you just pointed out, Darius is king-elect now. He'll either have to bring him to the Academy or let me go to the capital. Because I don't see any other way to get to the meaning behind this note."

She frowned. "So you're going to show it to Darius?"

My eyes slid away from her to gaze unseeing out the window. It was a hard question to answer when I still hadn't decided on the best course of action. Most likely, it would all come down to Darius's current state. I couldn't wait to see him again after what felt like an endless separation.

When we had parted, he had struck me as brittle—as if the layer of ice he had always worn had sunk all the way through, and a single misplaced blow might shatter him apart. And yet he was also the strongest person I knew. I desperately wanted to believe I would find him recovered. But if he wasn't, I didn't want to be the person to strike that blow.

"I don't know," I whispered at last. "But I'll tell him that Jareth tried to kill me too, and that I have to confront him for my own sake. For closure."

"Well that's true enough," Bryony said wryly. "Although I'm not sure your need for closure with Jareth has anything to do with him trying to kill you. With all your time taken up worrying about Darius, I'm not sure you've had any left for thinking about his offenses against you."

I flushed slightly. It was true that Darius had taken up a disproportionate amount of my headspace over the weeks of the summer break.

Bryony shook her head at my reaction, although there was a grin lingering in her eyes. "I suppose I'll just have to settle for being glad that you're willing to use your power over Darius. If he cares about you as much as he says, then he'll have to let you see Jareth with an argument like that."

For a moment I shrank from the idea that I was manipulating Darius's feelings for me to achieve my own ends. But then I straightened my spine, pushing the thoughts aside.

"I'll use every kind of power I have to make sure that everyone I love stays safe. Starting with telling Darius the minute we see him that I need to speak to him privately. There's no point putting it off."

"I'd applaud the sentiment if I wasn't feeling a little queasy at the idea that you think we're not safe from Jareth yet," Bryony said.

"Call it an overabundance of caution," I said. "The consequence of being raised royal."

Bryony sighed. "Well, for once I hope you're entirely wrong, and this whole business is completely behind us."

"You and me both," I said with feeling.

"And in the meantime," she added, "I'll complete my best friend duties and help you herd Darius away from any crowds and into a secluded spot."

I suppressed a giggle. "You make it sound like I want to murder him."

"He has Captain Vincent as his personal guard now, so he's the one you have to convince of your innocent intentions, not me." She smirked. "You'll just have to avoid getting too close to

Darius's royal person. You wouldn't want the situation to be misconstrued."

I swatted at her, but my heart wasn't in it. I could force Darius not to shut me out again, but that was as far as I could go. I might love him, but there were still too many barriers between us for either of us to act on our feelings.

Still, I couldn't keep my heart from starting to beat faster as we pulled through the Academy gates and climbed down into the courtyard. Last year I had run into Darius in the entranceway. I could be seeing him at any moment.

Elsie had finally woken and looked at everything around us with wide eyes. I tried to imagine seeing it from her perspective. The large building looked forbidding, its gray stone lacking ornamentation and its imposing size seeming to loom above us. When had I stopped noticing any of that?

"You'll get used to it," I murmured to my new servant.

"I hope so," she said in a voice that was almost a squeak.

A servant arrived to start unloading the carriage, and Elsie turned to him with disapproving eyes. The task of overseeing my luggage appeared to give her back some of the confidence that had leaked away at sight of our surroundings. I smiled and followed Bryony who had already bounded up the steps and into the building.

I reminded myself it was unlikely Darius would happen to be crossing the entranceway, but I couldn't stop myself looking for him. I saw several white robes before my eyes latched on to one in particular.

I gasped, my mouth falling open.

"Jareth?"

CHAPTER 4

*F*or a moment everything seemed to freeze, and then my head started to pound. This was impossible. How could Jareth be here?

I had arrived at the Academy intending to demand that Darius allow me to see him—I had never imagined he would be here, wandering around freely.

"Ah, Verene," Bryony said, in a low voice. "Am I seeing things, or is that…?"

I nodded. "It's Jareth. How can it be Jareth?"

The younger prince looked up and saw me, a light springing into his eyes. He hurried across the entranceway in our direction. My hand dove for my pockets, pulling out a shield and activating it before he had covered half the distance.

A couple of other trainees looked in my direction, their attention caught by the sudden rush of power. Their curious gazes passed from Bryony and me, standing tensely just inside the door, to the approaching prince.

Jareth slowed, a shadow passing across his face. He looked miserable and weary now, but I refused to feel any hint of pity for him.

I let my eyes rest briefly on the other trainees. I recognized their faces, although none were from our own year. They looked interested, but their focus was more on Bryony and me than on Jareth. Nothing in their manner suggested they felt any concern at the prince's presence. Was it really possible that word of his attempt to assassinate Darius had never become known in Kallorway?

But how was he free? And why was he *here*?

Bryony drew closer to me, her hand reaching for her sword hilt. I gripped her arm, shaking my head slightly.

"I've worked a shield for us both. Although I don't think he means to attack us. Look around, no one else even seems to know anything is wrong."

Bryony frowned around the large entrance hall, her gaze stopping on several passing servants who were attempting to look uninterested in our obvious tension. Slowly she let her hand drop back to her side.

"What is going on?" she whispered.

"I don't know." My voice hardened. "But I intend to find out."

I stepped forward, refusing to cower by the door waiting for Jareth to reach me. Lifting my chin, I stared him down. Shame washed over his face, and his eyes slid away from mine.

Conscious of our audience, I kept my voice low.

"What are you doing here, Jareth?"

"I'm a trainee, and classes start tomorrow." His words were brazen, but he winced as he said them.

"Where's Darius?" I asked, suddenly gripped with fear that something had happened to him.

"He's here," Jareth said quickly. "And he's fine."

"Don't you say that like you care," I hissed.

He winced again. "I understand why you don't believe it, Verene, but I do care. I care more than anything. I..."

I waited, the curiosity that had been burning all summer forcing me to give him a chance at an explanation. But his aban-

33

doned words never restarted. After an extended moment of silence, he skipped the topic altogether.

"He's here, and he's close. He's always close." He glanced around the entrance, his eyes stopping on two uniformed guards, lingering near an open side door. "He must be talking to someone in the dining hall."

I gave the two men a cursory glance. They were dressed like royal guards, and I didn't recognize either of their faces. Presumably they were part of the new team Captain Vincent had assembled in the capital. Both of them watched us, but neither appeared disconcerted at Jareth's presence.

"I'm glad you came back," he said in a rush. "I was afraid you might not, after…"

I stiffened. "I still have two more years to complete. And neither you nor anyone else is going to drive me away."

A ghost of Jareth's old easy smile crossed his face. "I'm glad to hear it. Because Darius needs you." He hesitated. "I think I might need you, too."

"I don't care what you need," I said in my coldest voice.

He shook his head, grimacing. "All I want is to protect Darius. I wouldn't ask for your help with anything else."

"That's what you said in your letter. But you're the one Darius needs protecting from."

"I…" He ran a hand through his hair. "I can't deny it. But I'm also terribly afraid it isn't true."

I sighed. I had spent the whole break puzzling over the riddles in his letter, and now apparently it was only going to be more riddles. Before I could challenge him, however, someone strode through the open doors to the dining hall.

Immediately Jareth faded from my awareness as my eyes drank Darius in. His sandy hair was ordered and adorned with the gold circlet I had seen him wear before. The light color contrasted with the darkness of his eyes. They looked as black as I had ever seen them, but his expression was calm and controlled, his movements confident and commanding. He looked like a king.

He saw me across the entranceway, and for the briefest moment everything faltered. Something bright sparked in his eyes, and an intense expression crossed his face, gone before I had a chance to read it. Even his forward progress hitched slightly.

But then he regained his stride, moving to join Bryony, Jareth, and me. Now that I could see him closely, my initial perception shifted slightly. He looked tired beneath it all.

"You came back," he said.

I nodded, not taking my eyes off his face. "Like I said I would."

Something almost like a smile flitted across his face. "Which means I should never have doubted." His expression closed again. "But I still wish you'd stayed at home."

"Where I would be safe," I finished for him.

He didn't reply, but his eyes agreed before he turned to Jareth, his face now carefully impassive.

"You are not allowed to speak to Verene. I thought I made that clear."

I raised an eyebrow, looking between the brothers before glancing around the entranceway again.

"We need to talk," I said to Darius. "But not here."

He nodded once. "Might I suggest we adjourn to your sitting room?"

"By all means." I started toward the stairs, Darius keeping pace beside me. Neither of us spoke.

We climbed past the offices and library, turning right at the familiar level that held the suites for the royal trainees. I pushed inside my old suite without stopping to attach this year's protections for the door. After using the security compositions on my door last year as bait for Jareth, I had once again had to ask Captain Layna for new, adjusted ones. And her eyes had been a little too knowing when she acquiesced without question. Darius had said he wanted to leave Bryony and me out of the situation with Jareth, but I suspected he had told Captain Vincent the truth. Did my own captain know as well?

When I stepped into the familiar green sitting room, I turned immediately to Darius, but the words dropped from my lips. It wasn't only Bryony who had followed us in.

"Why is he with us?" I snapped out, glaring openly at Jareth now I was freed from the watchful eyes in the entrance hall. Jareth had tried—and nearly succeeded—to kill Darius. And he had tried to kill me as well. He had no place at the Academy, let alone in my sitting room.

Jareth laughed without mirth. "Everything is different this year. I'm always near, Princess."

One of the guards shut the door behind us, presumably remaining on guard in the corridor outside. For a moment I was distracted by the moving ball of energy that represented the second guard entering Darius's suite. A moment later he stopped outside the door behind the tapestry, and I realized they were taking up sentry duty outside the two entrances to my suite.

I turned back to Darius. "What is going on here? Why is Jareth at the Academy? I thought you had him securely locked up back in Kallmon?"

Darius shifted slightly, and for a strange moment I thought he actually looked uncomfortable. My eyes narrowed.

"He was locked up for weeks," Darius said, not meeting my eyes. "And during that time, I developed a composition."

"A composition?" I looked at Jareth. Power clung to him, but I hadn't even noticed it earlier. Being surrounded by power was a normal trait for a royal.

"It binds him," Darius said. "He can't access his power unless I allow it." Bryony snorted, and he glanced at her. "Which I will only do for lessons. And he cannot stray far from me. Duke Francis has agreed that, in the circumstances, I be permitted personal guards while at the Academy. He doesn't need to know they're guarding Jareth, not me. So you don't need to fear. He is always watched, always guarded."

"As I said." Jareth gave us both a pained smile. "I'm always near."

"But...why?" Bryony asked the question echoing through my head.

"So he can complete third year without posing a danger to anyone," Darius said calmly, as if it was a normal and acceptable answer.

"Darius," I said slowly, trying to keep my voice calm, "why does he need to complete third year? He's a traitor who attempted to assassinate the king."

"King-elect," Darius murmured, but I fixed him with a stern look, and he sighed.

"Yes, he is a traitor." The hard, bitter note in Darius's voice immediately belied my fear that he might have been inveigled into forgiving Jareth's crimes. "But he's also my brother. And everyone knows how close we are. I asked the Mage Council to give me Kallorway on the promise that I meant to cease the feuds and divisions, heal the fractures, and bring our people together."

"You're worried about what they'll think if your first move as ruler is to remove your only competition." I frowned as understanding blossomed. "Especially if that competition is your previously beloved younger brother. You're worried you'll look even more ruthless than your father and make everyone start doubting their choice."

"But you have good reason!" Bryony exclaimed. "He committed treason! He tried to kill you!"

"Yes, and many will believe me if I say that," Darius said.

"But others won't." I sighed and massaged the side of my head. "Some will look at the years of devotion between you and think it was a highly convenient time for such an attack to occur. An attack from which you emerged unscathed."

Darius nodded.

"But neither can you afford to appear weak," I said. "If word eventually gets out that Jareth attempted to assassinate you, and you did nothing…"

Darius shifted again but didn't respond. I bit my lip. His reasons made sense, but there was more to it than that. Darius couldn't bring himself to execute Jareth, as he would have to do if his crimes were made public. But neither could the younger brother and current heir of the king-elect merely disappear without comment. A few weeks' absence could be explained away, but not his failing to appear for third year.

"Keep your enemies close…" I murmured.

"But it's outrageous!" Bryony cried. "He can't just be allowed to continue at the Academy with access to both of you."

"He is bound and watched at all times," Darius said. "And he knows he is not permitted to speak to Verene. I will make sure he doesn't forget it again."

I shivered at the threat in his words. But at the same time, I worried for him. I understood his underlying exhaustion now. How much energy was he expending to keep Jareth bound?

As if reading my mind, Bryony spoke.

"If he truly has to be here, then I want to help guard him."

Darius cleared his throat. "I appreciate the sentiment, but I have a whole squad of royal guards on shift. I suspect guarding is better left to the experts."

Bryony rolled her eyes. "I'm not saying I want to follow him around everywhere." She gave Jareth a disgusted look. "That's the last thing I want. I'm saying that someone must be supplying these constant binding compositions." She gave Darius a knowing look. "And I suspect that someone is you. I can help with that. I can keep you supplied with extra energy."

An irrepressible look of relief crossed his face before he tamped it down. My worry increased. The effort must be taking more from him than he was letting anyone see.

"I can't let you do that," he said, but Bryony waved his words away.

"Of course you can. You're the king-elect. You have a lot more duties than just guarding your brother, and you can't afford to let yourself be exhausted by that one task."

"And you're a third year trainee," he countered. "You'll be expected to produce energy compositions as part of your studies."

She shrugged. "Allow me to be the judge of how much I can handle, if you please. And if you're concerned for me, then make it a priority to recruit an energy mage to your royal staff."

He raised an eyebrow at her.

"Not that I would ever presume to tell you how to govern," she said with a cheeky grin. "But I'm sure no one would consider such an effort to be remarkable. We're in high demand, and you have a throne now."

"You're right, of course." His expression lightened, and for the first time since I'd arrived, he looked like his true self. "I believe some of my advisors have even started making inquiries. I'll tell them to make it a higher priority."

Bryony nodded, apparently satisfied, before turning back to Jareth, her expression turning sour again.

"So how close exactly does he have to be? Can he wait through there with his guard escort?" She pointed at the tapestry. "Or are we forced to endure his constant presence?"

"No, he can go that far." Darius nodded a dismissal at Jareth without meeting his eyes.

For a moment, Jareth looked as if he meant to protest, his eyes moving from his brother to me. He appeared to be desperately trying to communicate something to me, but I had no idea what it could be and didn't intend to ask.

After the briefest hesitation, he sighed, and slipped from the room through the hidden door. A sound from the other side of the room made me turn to see Bryony had likewise slipped away, leaving Darius and me alone. I would have smiled at her maneuvering if I wasn't so concerned for Darius.

Despite myself, I moved toward him, my hand lifting toward his cheek. He stepped quickly away, however, his expression wooden.

Sighing, I let my hand fall. I could push him for answers and inclusion, but I couldn't push this.

"I'm sorry, Verene," he said, misery in his eyes. "I wanted to keep you away from the evil of my court, and instead I've brought the heart of it right to you. I told you last year, and I'll tell you again—I want you to be safer than you can ever be here in Kallorway."

"And I told you I don't intend to run away. That is still true." I hesitated. "And are you sure Jareth is the heart of the evil? Last year you seemed sure someone or something had corrupted him."

"I said what I wanted to be true. But Captain Vincent and I questioned him extensively over the period of his incarceration, and he could provide no satisfactory answers."

I frowned. It was one thing for Jareth to talk in riddles to me, but to Darius?

"But how is that possible? Surely you used truth compositions and the like to compel him to speak. How could he not explain himself?"

"Because there is no explanation?" Darius shrugged. "He claims to love me as his brother but to also desire my throne. And we both saw which of his emotions is stronger."

"Surely that can't be everything," I said. "After all you've been through together…"

Darius laughed, the sound harsh. "This argument feels familiar, but we seem to have reversed roles. Since when did you soften toward Jareth?"

"Since never," I said quickly.

Jareth's letter appeared in my mind, but I hesitated, afraid of how Darius would respond to reading it and learning Jareth had written me. Darius appeared to have found some sort of equilibrium in this impossible situation, and I didn't want to be the one to destroy it.

"So no one knows what he did?" I asked.

"Only Captain Vincent and his trusted squad."

My lips twisted. "So if something happens to you and the captain, he becomes king, none the wiser?"

"I've taken steps to ensure that can never happen."

Darius's dark voice stopped me from inquiring exactly what those steps were. I just hoped Jareth knew the threat he was under. Hopefully it would be enough to keep Darius safe. Because whatever either prince said, I couldn't be comfortable having Jareth here with us at the Academy.

CHAPTER 5

*W*hen a knock sounded on my outer door, Darius disappeared through the tapestry door and Bryony reappeared from my bedchamber. Our visitor turned out to be Elsie, and the rest of the day was consumed in the various arrangements of the start of the year.

I shielded my doors, giving both Elsie and Bryony access, oversaw the unpacking of my luggage, and called for Ida, the servant who had cared for my room in first and second years. When she appeared, I introduced Elsie and explained that she would be taking over Ida's duties.

"I know after two years of such exemplary work, I can put my trust in you to show her around and explain how things are done here," I said. "Now that I am eighteen, it is customary in Ardann for me to take a personal servant."

I left out that in ordinary circumstances I would have waited until after graduation and was rewarded for my tact by the disappearance of the confusion and hurt on her face. I didn't want Ida thinking my hiring Elsie had anything to do with her.

"Of course, Your Highness. I can assist Elsie and ensure there is no disruption to your care."

"Thank you," Elsie said with a bright smile. "That's an enormous relief. I'm sure I wouldn't be able to get on at all without your help. I was new to the role in Ardann, let alone here in an unfamiliar place. But obviously you're greatly experienced if you were given care of Princess Verene in the past."

I smiled as Ida's expression grew warm and sympathetic. Elsie had struck exactly the right note, sounding genuine rather than falsely ingratiating. She might be young, but she was clearly adroit at handling people. I still knew so little about her, and it was good to see she could put aside her pride when needed.

As she was leaving, Ida hesitated, however, looking at me. "It isn't the usual way of things here. I don't know if—"

"I'll talk to Zora," I said quickly. "In fact, I'll go and do it now."

I found the head servant in her office and was greeted with warmth. As with Ida, I made it clear that Elsie's presence had nothing to do with any deficiency in the Academy staff. And I carefully let enough hints fall regarding my having personal reasons behind the appointment that I knew she would pick up on them. Just like I knew she was far too canny to press a foreign princess as to what those reasons might be.

Before I even finished my speech, I could read the acceptance in her eyes. Not even royals were supposed to bring personal servants to the Academy, but then they hadn't had an Ardannian royal before. Or a king-elect. And the list went on.

"Captain Vincent informs me we're to host your personal guard again this year as well." A hint of humor colored her words.

"Certainly not." I let myself grin back. "Only the king-elect is permitted a personal guard within Academy grounds. I wouldn't dream of offending Duke Francis or Captain Vincent by bringing my own."

"If you say so," Zora said with a shake of her head. "I suppose in that case it's convenient that our good captain has need of an Ardannian perspective on his various ongoing investigations."

Her voice was dry, and I wondered just how much she actually knew. I kept my face impassive, however.

"Fortunate indeed. Especially if I want to leave the Academy and need a personal guard for the purpose."

She chuckled. "If you're worried about Francis protesting, you needn't be. He understands that change has come, and he's not going to worry about something like an extra servant in the Academy."

"No, that's your job," I said.

She grinned. "Aye, he knows he can safely leave such matters to me."

I bit my lip, curious, but also wary of prying. "Do you ever wish things could be different?" I asked.

She regarded me with an indulgent expression. "We've all wished that. It's why we supported the young prince."

"But about you and the duke, I mean. Do you ever wish you could be more open?"

Her shrewd eyes weighed me. "In truth? No, I don't."

"Never?" I tried to keep the surprise out of my voice.

"Mayhap it's because I'm not young and romantic, but I never had a hankering to have people bowing and scraping. My authority over my own domain is absolute, and that's enough for me. The rest would bring too much unpleasantness to be worth it. We have a happy life here in our own little world, and neither Francis nor I have ever wished for more."

I sighed softly. It was what I was afraid of. There would be no such quiet, secluded life for Stellan and Elsie.

"I'm glad you've found happiness," I said.

"I know it, Princess," she said. "It's why I was willing to take the risk of telling you in the first place. You aren't like other royals."

I smiled. "How could I be when my own mother is a commonborn?"

Zora snorted. "Calling the Spoken Mage a commonborn seems a bit of a stretch."

I shrugged. "And yet she was born as one. And my favorite aunt is her commonborn sister. Aunt Clemmy doesn't have a shred of ability of any sort, but everyone loves her. You can't help it."

"Not everyone, I'm betting," Zora said, a darker note in her voice.

"No," I said, feeling suddenly weary. "I suppose not everyone. But everyone who truly knows her."

"Yes, that's it precisely," Zora said. "I'm quite content here where everyone knows us. I have no desire to open our business to the rest of the world."

"Perhaps…" I hesitated. "Perhaps, if you ever have a spare moment, you might be willing to talk with Elsie. Take her under your wing, even. I don't want to ask too much, but she's not just an ordinary maid. In Ardann, royals are permitted a sealed private servant which is a much more responsible role than just keeping my rooms neat. One day, after I graduate, she will be more like a secretary or assistant. She's still young and has herself only just graduated from our palace's initial training program. I would love it if she could use our two years here to her advantage —and it just so happens that when it comes to learning from the best, she couldn't be better placed than this Academy."

Once again, her eyes seemed to weigh me.

"I will meet this Elsie of yours, and see what can be done," she said. "But I make no promises."

"I wouldn't ask anything more," I said. "And indeed, I'm grateful for that."

I left her office after that, confident I had done everything I could to establish Elsie at the Academy. She would have to manage the rest herself. From what little I'd seen of her so far, I was increasingly confident she would excel.

In the dining hall, we had once again moved up a table, now occupying the place reserved for the third years. My eyes rested for a moment on the table furthest to the left. The fourth years. How distant fourth year had seemed when I first stepped into this hall. And yet now it seemed to barrel toward me at a pace too fast for me to grasp. When I graduated the Academy, I would have to find my place in life, and I was still far from knowing what that should be.

"Ready to be ruling the Academy?" asked a voice beside me, snapping me out of my daze.

I looked at Tyron with a blank expression, and he nodded at the fourth year table with a grin.

"Oh! No, just remembering first year actually." I glanced over my shoulder at the table that held the first years. "It seems a long time ago."

"How young and innocent we were, hey?" His voice held a laugh.

"Well, I don't know about that." I returned his smile until my eyes alighted on Jareth, sitting further down the table, and my smile fell away.

Tyron followed my gaze, giving me a quizzical look when he saw the direction of my attention, but I just shrugged.

"I, for one, was never innocent," Bryony announced, taking a place across from us. "Or at least, that's what my mother tells me."

"That I can well imagine," Tyron said.

"Don't listen to a word she says," I told him. "Both her parents dote on her."

"My father dotes on me," she corrected, already shoveling food into her mouth. "My mother alternates between pride and despair. She has yet to decide which one will win."

I rolled my eyes and filled my own plate. As I was doing so, Isabelle walked past on the other side of the table, and Bryony made a welcoming gesture for her to join us. She didn't pause, however, continuing on without acknowledging the invitation.

Bryony frowned after her.

"I don't think she even saw you," I said. "She's always kept herself a little apart, but she looks particularly abstracted. Maybe she had a bad summer."

"Or a good one, and she doesn't want to be back here," Tyron suggested.

I watched the other girl choose a seat away from anyone else and slowly begin to serve herself food. It made me sad to see her sitting alone, but we could hardly force her to join us.

I shook myself and turned my attention back to my own table mates. "What are you both planning to do after graduation? Have you decided yet?"

"Graduation? That's two years away!" Bryony gave me an exasperated look. "Let me guess, you're already stressing that it's getting close and you don't have an answer to that question."

Tyron raised an eyebrow. "Do princesses get choices?"

I grimaced. "Not many. But what about you? Do you already know? The two of you are the opposite of me—you're overflowing with choices. I'm sure anybody in Kallorway would be eager to have you."

"Ah, but we still have families," Tyron said. "We might not be royal, but that doesn't mean we're always free to make all our own choices."

Bryony winced. "Are yours exacting? I suppose they want you to go home to the Empire."

Tyron hesitated. "Not the Empire necessarily. But they certainly have high expectations."

"I suppose it's a good thing we still have two years, then, as Bryony just reminded us," I said. "Hopefully you can find something you want to do that will meet with their stamp of approval."

"Perhaps." He looked more wistful than usual.

"You said your family lives among one of the sealed clans," Bryony said. "I suppose they provide energy compositions for the sealing ceremonies. I've heard it pays well. And I can imagine it provides its own sort of satisfaction."

I glanced at her, wondering if she was thinking of the composition of hers that I had used to have Elsie sealed.

"Ardann pays well for the same service," I said, although I felt compelled to add, "although we don't have nearly as many ceremonies as the Empire, of course."

"Perhaps I need to take a tour of all three lands and determine which home will be the most lucrative," Tyron said with a smile. "That's what I'm hearing the two of you saying, anyway."

Bryony wrinkled her nose. "If wealth is your only consideration. Personally, I intend to choose the most appealing location." She glanced toward one of the windows. "And I can tell you now it won't be anywhere as remote as this. They couldn't convince me to stay on at the Academy for anything."

"Do you think they might try?" I asked.

She shrugged. "They could do worse. Amalia has a lot of knowledge—well she's bound to, given she's basically an expert on everything—that's how she got to be in charge of discipline studies. But they would do well to have an actual energy mage on staff who could rotate around the classes."

"It would certainly be a more reliable strategy than waiting for trainees like us to turn up," Tyron said.

"Maybe you should start by asking Amalia how much they'd be willing to pay you," I suggested with a straight face. "You could get your first point of reference in your search for the most lucrative career."

"Ha! I'm not some innocent first year, dear Princess, to be so easily fooled. As if I would ask Amalia such a question. Can you even imagine?"

We all fell silent for a moment while we did exactly that.

"She might find it a little presumptuous," I admitted, struggling to keep the laugh from my voice.

"To say the least," he muttered. "I don't know where all her bitterness comes from, but I wouldn't fancy a lifetime working under her."

Bryony shuddered. "Oh goodness, no. Only imagine being stuck out here in the middle of nowhere and working with Amalia every day for the rest of your life."

I remembered both of their words when we sat down in class for our first discipline lesson later the next day. When I first arrived in Kallorway, I had thought Amalia hated me in particular, and assumed my lack of ability was the issue. But it was true her caustic manner seemed to extend to most people. Had she always been that way?

She greeted us with her usual lack of enthusiasm and explained that we would once again spend our year progressing through the other classes. But this time we would spend a full month with each one. Last year I had greeted this news with enthusiasm, seeing it as an opportunity to practice my own ability on a range of unsuspecting mages. Would I do the same thing this year?

With the discipline instructors at my disposal, I could conceivably craft almost any composition I wanted. But I would have to be careful in choosing them. If I started composing whirlwinds or growing gardens, it would be hard to keep my ability hidden.

But now I was back at the Academy, some of my caution from the summer fell away. I itched to try my new ability again and remember the sensation of power and mastery that came from composing with the strength and control of an expert. Just as long as I didn't allow myself to become lost in that feeling of power like I had during second year. But already I felt a much greater caution than I had then. Any composition I crafted would be done with the energy of someone else. And since I didn't intend to ask their permission, it would be stolen energy. I couldn't take that lightly.

CHAPTER 6

*I*t was hard to focus on the idea of training when everywhere I turned, I was confronted by Darius, with Jareth his constant shadow. Seeing the two of them side by side always sent my pulse racing, my mind and emotions a tangled mess of fear and desire and confusion. I had told myself I would force Darius to keep me closer this year, but how could I do that when he always had Jareth with him? Jareth even slept in his sitting room, now, ensuring the door behind the tapestry had lost its temptation for me.

Darius had only come through the door once, keeping a wary distance from me that set my heart aching. He wanted to check I had extended my security protections to the door behind the tapestry now that Jareth shared his suite. I assured him I had, although I also told him I had left his access in place. Unfortunately he didn't seem inclined to use it.

"How was the summer?" I asked him. "I worried about you—especially when I didn't hear anything public about Jareth."

Darius's face twisted at the mention of his brother. "Dealing with Jareth took more of my time than I had to give. Just when I could have most used his support, he was making my role harder."

"I'm sorry," I whispered, only just holding back from closing the distance between us. I wanted to ask him about matters of state, and what demands had been made on his time, but reminded myself I was the princess of another kingdom. I couldn't ask such questions.

We existed in a strange place, especially now our shared purpose of winning him his throne had succeeded. What was my role as Ardann's representative now? And what about just as me, Verene? The emotions that stretched between us were even more precarious, pulling us in too many directions at once.

But so far he hadn't tried to freeze me out—even his comments about Jareth were more open than he was likely being with anyone else. I didn't want to risk damaging that by pushing too far, so I held my tongue.

In public, he no longer showed me a cold face either, smiling when he saw me and greeting me with more warmth than he did the rest of our year mates. Or so it seemed to me. I responded in kind, despite the jolt I felt every time I saw Jareth at his back.

The other third years seemed to accept the two brothers' new closeness without question. They probably thought Jareth had become Darius's number one advisor in his new role as king-elect.

Or perhaps they didn't think about it at all. Frida and Ashlyn both seemed subdued, spending even more of their time together, their heads often bent close in quiet conversation. The change in their manner was disconcerting, but I had little available headspace to put much thought into it. Especially since they belonged to the faction that had most strongly supported Darius.

Royce had withdrawn even further from the rest of the year. After I twice saw him coming down the stairs from a higher level, I asked Bryony if he no longer resided on my floor with the royals. We were in my suite with Elsie at the time, and she answered first.

"He requested the move himself, apparently. That's what the servants are saying, anyway. He has a regular room on the third year floor now."

Bryony raised her eyebrows. "I have seen him up there, but it doesn't seem like him to ask for such a thing. He's always been insufferably proud. How did he even end up with a royal suite to begin with? He's only a second cousin to the princes."

"I always assumed they wanted more trainees on this level because of me," I said. "And as for him moving now..." I wrinkled my brow, considering it. "He's part of the king's faction. It makes sense since his father was always Cassius's closest friend. But the rest of the king's faction supported the crown, more than Cassius himself. They were remaining loyal in anticipation of a stronger king. I suppose, now the new king has arrived, Royce's family must be feeling vulnerable. If they're still close to Cassius, they likely know how Darius feels about his father. Maybe Royce wants to stay out of Darius's way and avoid drawing attention to himself?"

"I suppose that makes sense," Bryony said. "He's certainly gone quiet in most classes."

"It's Wardell, Armand, and Dellion who interest me most," I said.

"Because their families support the general?" Elsie asked, surprising me.

She was proving to be such a non-obtrusive presence in my suite that I sometimes forgot she was even there. And I had to admit, I was growing used to the extra comfort provided by having someone always on hand to assist—ensuring everything from the fire to my hot water was prepared as needed.

The more I saw of Elsie, the more I understood why Stellan had been drawn to her. She was hard-working, intelligent, and kind-hearted—not to mention beautiful. And the more I experienced that side of her, the harder it was to know what manner I should adopt in our interactions. I wasn't used to feeling such social unease—but then I had never had a servant who my brother seemed determined to make my future sister-in-law.

With the whirl of activity of traveling to the Academy behind us, I had undertaken to teach her to read and write. The others sealed in the same ceremony would all have begun lessons through the various programs that selected them. Sometime during the preparations and packing in Corrin it had occurred to me that as the one who put Elsie into the ceremony, it fell on me to ensure she received the necessary tutoring. But we hadn't had the opportunity until the quiet evenings in my suite at the Academy.

It was no surprise she learned quickly, given her sharp mind. And I soon realized her presence in Kallorway had an added benefit that hadn't occurred to me when I made my rash suggestion to Stellan—Elsie could provide a level of access to the opinions of the servants that had been denied me before. I could talk much more freely with her than the guarded questions I put to Ida or Zora.

"Do they gossip in the servants' quarters about court and politics?" I asked her. "What do they say?"

"They say the general was taken by surprise, and that now he's biding his time," she said. "They seem rather proud about it all."

"Proud of Darius taking General Haddon by surprise?" Bryony frowned in confusion.

"They're all passionately loyal to Duke Francis," Elsie explained. "And he was the one to call the emergency meeting of the Mage Council, so they feel a sort of ownership of the incident by extension."

Bryony snorted. "A loose sort of ownership."

"But more than they've probably ever felt before in the affairs of the court and Mage Council," I said. "And that's a good thing. I assume it only cements their support of Darius."

It wasn't a question, but I gave Elsie an inquiring look, and she nodded.

"I've never heard anyone with a bad word to say about the prince."

"Well, that's reassuring, at least," I said. "I just wish I knew what the general's faction are thinking."

"For that you need Dellion," Bryony said cheerfully.

I narrowed my eyes at her. "That doesn't seem such a happy prospect to me."

She grinned. "That's because you're the one who has to talk to her. It has nothing to do with me."

When Elsie giggled, I bent a disapproving look on her. She tried to suppress her smile but didn't entirely succeed. I could only assume that two years of close association with my brother had reduced her formality around royalty because she didn't act like most other servants. Either that, or she was spending too much time around Bryony.

"Now, unlike the prince, Dellion has managed to earn a few detractors among the servants," Elsie said. "Mostly the ones who've had to do room duty for her suite."

Bryony leaned forward, her eyes eager. "Ooh, don't tell me the high and mighty Dellion is a mess inside her room. She never has a hair out of place."

"The same can't be said of her room, apparently," Elsie confirmed. "There the servants say everything's a mess. And she complains if anything isn't done to her complete satisfaction."

I sighed. "If my getting close to Dellion is the only way to find out General Haddon's opinion, then I'm afraid that information is going to remain closed to us."

"Come now, Verene! You should have more faith in yourself than that." Bryony's eyes laughed at me. "And surely even Dellion is better than Wardell. He would probably get the wrong idea and decide you're madly in love with him."

Elsie choked on a laugh, and I glared at them both indiscriminately.

"Which means Armand is my only hope." I sighed. "We're all doomed."

But to my surprise, not long later, I found myself facing Dellion in combat class. Our year had once again been relegated to the training yard without any hint so far of the arena, and I suspected I wasn't the only reason this time. Darius might still be a trainee, but he was also king-elect. Would attacking him in the arena have a traitorous aura to it?

And then there was Jareth to consider. Darius was allowing him access to his power for composition class, but the melee of battle in the arena was another situation entirely. Had Darius intervened with Duke Francis to ensure he wasn't required to set his brother loose in the arena?

Bouts in the training yards were well and truly familiar after more than two years, and in that time, I had never crossed swords with Dellion. She didn't acknowledge my look of surprise, however, acting as if it was perfectly normal for us to practice together outside of the arena.

She was a fluid, elegant fighter, and I had to work hard to beat her. But my skills had already been strong when I arrived at the Academy, and sparring with Bryony for two years had only improved them.

"Good bout," Dellion surprised me by saying when I finally defeated her. "We should have done this before now."

I said nothing, not wanting to interrupt this unexpected connection by pointing out that I had never been unwilling. I expected her to walk away immediately, but she lingered.

"I can never beat Darius, of course. And this year he fights with a new ferocity. He defeats me too quickly—I can't get a proper practice in."

I kept my face impassive, although my eyes flew to Darius who was in the middle of a bout with Jareth. Ferocious was a good word for how he appeared. Dellion seemed bemused enough about the change in Darius to confirm she didn't know the truth about Jareth.

"And as for Jareth..." She frowned, her eyes still on the fight between the princes. "He's lost his edge." She glanced sideways at me. "Does he seem different to you?"

"Jareth? Different?" I stalled, trying to think of an acceptable answer.

"It's a subtle thing." She sounded like she was already regretting starting the conversation. "Maybe you have to know him well to see it. But he's lost his fire. And it hasn't done anything for his skills with a sword."

I bit my lip. "I suppose he does seem a little...different."

"So here I am, forced to seek out you and Bryony if I want to keep my skills sharp," Dellion said.

"You're always welcome to have a match with me, but I don't think you'll have much more luck with Bryony than with Darius."

"Is that right?" A gleam leaped into Dellion's eyes as she watched Bryony easily defeating Tyron not far from us.

I had clearly sparked her competitive instinct, and she prowled away, our conversation apparently forgotten. I watched her go with a slight shake of my head before my attention was irresistibly drawn back to Darius and Jareth's duel.

It was a strange thing, but I *had* noticed a difference in Jareth. But not the difference Dellion referred to. I already understood the loss of his *fire* as she called it, but what I couldn't as readily explain was my loss of uneasiness around him.

I still hated him, and my body sometimes reacted in instinctive fear when I caught a glimpse of him at a specific angle that recalled how he had looked with his knife raised the night of the attack. But the old reaction had disappeared. For two years I hadn't been able to spend time with Jareth without a disquieting feeling of unease—a certainty that he was hiding something, and that he couldn't be trusted. Although I had never been able to explain it rationally—at least not to Darius's satisfaction—it had been a strong enough sensation that it had overridden my trust in Darius's assessment of his brother.

And now Jareth had proven himself untrustworthy, and yet the feeling was gone. Or was it gone because his duplicity was no longer shrouded in mystery?

The change only added to the many mysteries that hung about the younger prince.

But Darius had done his job well, and Jareth didn't attempt to approach me again as he had done in the entranceway. He had claimed to be pleased to see me, and to want me to take some sort of action to protect Darius. And yet no threat had made itself apparent, and Jareth made no effort to give me further information.

Which meant I needed to take the initiative myself. When I had thought Jareth still imprisoned, I had been willing to push until Darius allowed me to confront him. Surely I could find a way to talk to him when we fought and studied beside each other every day?

I watched the two princes all through lunch, composition class, and then the evening meal, but could come up with no way to get Jareth alone. My plan to tell Darius I needed to see his brother for closure fell apart given he remained at the Academy studying alongside us. And I could well imagine how Darius would react to my asking him to leave me alone with Jareth. I could confront Jareth in Darius's presence—but would he be honest with me, in that case?

I was still considering the issue in combat practice the next morning, causing Bryony to throw up her hands and abandon me in disgust.

"I don't know what has you so distracted this morning, but you're a hopeless opponent. I'm going to see if Dellion wants a bout." She waved away my hurried apologies, strolling off in search of her chosen new sparring partner.

When I turned around ready to find someone new to fight myself, I almost jumped.

"Jareth! Where did you come from?"

He held up his sword with an inquiring look. "Would you like a bout?"

I cast a quick glance at Darius. He was occupied in an intense bout with Instructor Mitchell—the only one who could match him on a close enough level to actually absorb his attention.

I wanted to repudiate Jareth, but I couldn't turn away the opportunity he was providing. Silently I raised my blade, and he smiled, dropping into a preparatory crouch.

If I had been distracted with Bryony, I was on full alert now. Every nerve thrummed. I didn't think Jareth would try to do me any actual harm in the middle of class, but I wasn't willing to bet my life on that assurance.

He had initiated the bout, and so I expected him to go on the attack first. He hung back, however, keeping his moves defensive. At first I moved slowly as well, wary given what I knew of his skills. But as I drove him across the yard, I remembered Dellion's assessment. Jareth fought differently now. He lacked fire.

I moved to a higher intensity, driving my next attack with more force. Jareth gave way before me, and I easily scored a hit, causing him to yield. My final momentum had driven me close to him, and he speared me with his eyes, talking rapidly in a low voice.

"We need to talk. If I come through the tapestry door after Darius falls asleep tonight, will you refrain from launching an attack the second you see it's me?"

I didn't have time to hesitate or to think his request through.

"I'll be waiting."

He drew back and gave me a shallow bow.

"Thank you for the bout, Princess."

"Jareth." Darius's furious voice made us both turn to face him, hopefully looking less guilty than I felt. "I told you to stay away from Verene."

"It was just a practice bout," he said. "You were occupied with Mitchell, and Verene was available. I didn't so much as scratch her."

Darius regarded him with narrowed eyes for a moment before turning to me.

"I'm fine," I said. "Truly."

His eyes ran over me, as if needing to see the truth of my words for himself. But I detected something else in his face before he nodded and pulled his brother to the other side of the yard. Longing.

It made me shiver, my heart racing faster than during the fight with Jareth. If Jareth didn't always stand between us—the worst sort of chaperone—would we be able to keep to our separate resolutions to maintain distance?

I glanced around, looking for a new sparring partner—anything to distract me from Darius and everything we couldn't be. My eyes fell on Isabelle, and I stepped toward her.

By the time I'd reached her side, however, any thought of suggesting a bout had died. She stood alone, shoulders slumped, her mind clearly far from combat. But just before I reached her, she looked up, her eyes latching on to Darius, and a strange expression filled them. I couldn't tell if she was afraid or angry or merely defeated.

Isabelle's family had chosen to keep themselves away from court and politics. I had always thought of her as standing separate from either faction. But did she have some reason I didn't know to resent Darius and his new status as king-elect?

"Is something wrong, Isabelle?" I asked softly.

She started and stared at me as if she hadn't seen or heard me coming. She was lost in her own thoughts a lot these days.

"What do you mean?" she asked.

I shrugged. "You just don't seem like yourself this year."

She flushed slightly. "I'm sorry if I've walked straight past you at some point or something. I keep resolving to be more present, but I can't help…"

"Can't help…?"

She sighed. "I can't help thinking of home all the time. And every time I see Darius, it just brings it all back."

"Darius?" I looked across the yard at where Darius was now sparring with Jareth. "What does he have to do with your home?"

"I know it's all foolishness," she hurried to assure me, as if afraid I might take offense. "It just reminds me, is all."

I stared at her. "I'm sorry, but I really don't know what you're talking about. What is foolishness?"

"Oh! Sorry. I guess…" She forced herself to laugh. "I guess it's easy to forget I'm not back home where everyone is so focused on…"

Something was clearly distressing her, so I held back my irritation at her constant half-sentences.

"What are they focused on in the north-west?" I asked. "Something different from here at the Academy?"

Isabelle glanced across the yard to where Ashlyn and Frida were crossing blades. A loud clang rang out as Ashlyn defended herself from Frida's attack.

"Some in the Academy are very aware, but I suppose not all." She sighed. "It's the harvest. We lost it all to blight."

CHAPTER 7

I gasped. "Oh Isabelle, I'm so sorry. Your family's whole estate?"

I tried to remember if she'd ever said what crop the farms on their estate grew. I didn't think she'd ever mentioned it, though— merely that their estate was largely made up of farming land.

She shook her head, but her words dispelled any feeling of relief.

"Not just our estate. The whole north-west."

"The whole north-west?" That was most of Kallorway's growing land. If the harvest loss had been that widespread...

"But surely the whole region doesn't grow the same crop?" I asked. "Don't tell me there was a blight across all the crops!"

She nodded miserably.

"But...how have I not heard about this?" My eyes flew involuntarily to Darius, although much of the damage must have been done over the break, and I hadn't heard it from my aunt, either.

"Duchess Callista has instructed the growers to keep it as quiet as possible," Isabelle said, referring to the Head of the Growers. "Prince Darius doesn't want panic in the kingdom about an entire lost harvest."

"But they can't keep it quiet forever." I frowned, realizing this must be the source of Ashlyn and Frida's subdued demeanor this year as well. They were both grower trainees, and Ashlyn's mother was Head of the Wind Workers—a discipline that usually worked closely with the growers.

"Duchess Callista consulted with Duchess Ashten, and almost the entirety of both the grower and wind worker disciplines have been assigned to the north-west," Isabelle explained. "They helped all the farms that lost their crop sow a late harvest, and now they're bending all sorts of rules about interfering with the weather to ensure this second round of crops is successful."

"That sounds dangerous," I said uneasily.

She grimaced. "Not as dangerous as an entire lost harvest."

"I should have asked you what was going on sooner," I said. "I could tell something was wrong."

She shrugged. "It's none of your affair."

"Yes, but..." I bit my lip. "I know I'm from Ardann, but I've been here for more than two years now. I care about Kallorway. And we're year mates, Isabelle. I care about you."

She gave me a look of faint surprise which made me feel guilty. I had been too absorbed in my own affairs for the past two years and hadn't made enough of an effort with Isabelle.

"I just keep reminding myself that with so much power and expertise focused on the problem, this harvest *has* to be success-ful," she said. "Wouldn't you agree?"

I quickly nodded. "Absolutely."

I certainly hoped so for more than just Isabelle's sake. But another question was still tugging at my mind, and I couldn't resist asking, "But what does any of it have to do with Darius? You said seeing him reminds you of the situation. Was he in the north-west over the summer?"

"No, not personally, although he sent plenty of representa-tives, of course, as well as consulting closely with the duchesses."

"So what—"

"It's just silly superstition, like I said." She shifted uncomfortably. "I know better than to put much stock in it."

Sudden understanding hit me. "The people have been waiting so long for change. And now, just as it's come, they're hit by disaster. It must not seem like a good sign for Darius's reign."

Isabelle nodded. "Of course it can hardly be Darius's fault that the crop failed. But no one can remember such a widespread blight before. It makes people uneasy."

My heart sank even further. "But it's not just superstition, is it? There's a reason the crops don't usually fail on such a level. Everyone must be asking why the growers didn't catch it in time to stop the spread. Some people will be wondering if Darius is too young to have charge of an entire kingdom."

Isabelle shifted uncomfortably, confirming my words.

"But the growers are going to fix it," she hurried to say. "Prince Darius has shown that, as king-elect, he's willing to send whatever resources he needs to rescue the people of the northwest. That has to mean something. It does mean something."

"I hope so," I said, my voice low and my eyes on Darius. "Just as long as this crop doesn't fail too."

"Yes," Isabelle said unhappily, "as long as this crop doesn't fail."

I told Bryony and Tyron about the crop failure over lunch.

"That's awful," Bryony cried. "And now I feel terrible for not making more of an effort with Isabelle on our first day back." She looked down the table as if she meant to find the other girl and forcibly drag her to sit with us mid-meal.

"But they have a solution?" Tyron asked. "So there's some positive, at least."

"As long as nothing goes wrong this time around." I sighed. "It really is a strange and terrible thing to happen so soon after Darius became king-elect."

"You don't suspect foul play, do you?" Bryony looked at me with wide eyes. "But I thought the growers supported Darius?"

"As far as I know, they do. And I don't know what to think." I just hoped Darius hadn't missed something in the weeks he was focusing on Jareth, developing a composition that could bind him.

In composition class, I tuned out Instructor Alvin's cheerful lecture and examined my classmates instead. Wardell and Armand's uncle was Head of the Creators, and if they knew about the issues with the harvest, they didn't show any concern. And Dellion and Royce seemed similarly unbothered. Whatever else had happened, Darius had at least succeeded in preventing any sort of widespread panic across the kingdom.

As usual, Alvin had returned to basics in class for the start of the year, but he had now moved his focus to increasing my year mates' stamina through endless repetition. A mage couldn't increase their natural strength—that was determined by blood-line—but a large focus of their four years at the Academy was increasing their stamina in order to maximize the strength they did have. As they learned greater and greater control, it would increase the level of composition they could achieve without exhausting their energy.

My abilities posed many challenges, but stamina wasn't one of them. When you were stealing the energy from others, you didn't need to worry about your own. But unfortunately, Alvin's stamina exercises with the class made it difficult for me to practice. When the instructors were already pushing the other trainees close to exhaustion, I didn't feel right about dipping into their energy myself.

When Amalia told us in discipline class that we were to start working with the Royal Guard trainees the next day, I hoped that might finally give me the opportunity to start practicing. But it was hard to focus on anything else she said when my thoughts were full of the new information from Isabelle and the coming meeting with Jareth.

Could the failed harvest be what he wanted to talk to me about? Did he know something about it?

After the evening meal, I paced my sitting room. How long would it take Darius to fall asleep? He spent most composition classes deep in royal reports, and I imagined he spent his evenings in a similar fashion—if not using communication compositions to talk directly with the various discipline heads. I just hoped he didn't work until late into the night. With every hour that passed, my tension levels were rising, and I wasn't sure how much more I could take.

"Is everything all right, Princess?" Elsie finally ventured to ask.

A section of my sitting room had been closed off with wooden screens, and behind it she had a comfortable bed and chair as well as a small table and a chest for her clothes and other belongings. The arrangement reminded me of the time Bryony had spent sleeping in my room, but Elsie had more space and furniture behind her screens since she would be there the whole year. She usually spent her evenings hidden away in this space, but she must have heard my pacing because she kept emerging to regard me with concern.

"Yes, I'm fi—" I cut myself off, rethinking my words.

Was I fine? I was willingly allowing Jareth to come secretly into my suite where I intended to meet him alone.

Except I wouldn't be alone. Elsie would be here, even if she was behind her screens. I could be putting her in danger as well as myself.

"Actually," I said, "could you please run and find Bryony for me? Do you know where her room is on the third year floor?"

"I can find out easily enough." Elsie's brow cleared, apparently reassured by my sending for Bryony.

She left on the errand immediately, but now that I had made

the decision to send for my friend, it seemed an age until she finally appeared. When she did arrive, she burst into the room like a whirlwind, already talking before Elsie could get the door closed behind her.

"Verene! What's wrong? Elsie said you sent her to get me? And that you've been pacing the floor like a caged animal."

I glanced at Elsie who looked slightly guilty. "It's no more than the truth, Princess Verene. And I assumed you'd want Bryony to know since you sent for her."

"Well?" Bryony asked, ignoring this interchange. "What is it?"

I hesitated, looking again at Elsie.

"It's clear enough there's something going on this evening, Princess," she said. "Would you like me to stay, or would you like me to occupy myself in the servants' hall?"

"Elsie, you're a gem," Bryony said warmly. "Do hurry up and go so Verene will tell me what's wrong."

Elsie grinned. "If the princess is agreeable."

"Yes, thank you, Elsie. I do appreciate it."

She slipped out of the room without delay, and Bryony pounced on me.

"I'm sorry to ask you to come so abruptly," I said. "But I suddenly realized I should have told you earlier today and asked you to be here."

"Told me what? What do you need me for?" she asked.

"Did you see Jareth and me in combat class?"

She nodded. "Yes, and I wasn't the only one to see. Darius looked ready to punch his brother."

"I'm fairly certain Jareth only asked me to bout so he could have a chance to talk to me. And he said he would come to see me tonight after Darius falls asleep."

"Jareth? Coming here?" Bryony cried. "But why didn't you tell Elsie to have me bring my sword?"

I laughed. "And what would she have thought of such a request?"

"I can't believe you were going to see him without me!"

"It does seem a little foolish in retrospect," I admitted.

"A little? How many times has he tried to kill you at this point?"

I winced. "That was different. Darius has him bound now. He can't compose, and I'm sure Darius wouldn't let him get his hands on any compositions from anyone else."

"And what about these guards of his?" Bryony asked suspiciously. "How is he going to sneak away from them?"

"They guard the suite from the corridor at night, I believe," I said. "Darius sleeps in the bedchamber and Jareth in the sitting room. Like with Elsie and me."

"And what about the door behind the tapestry?" Bryony asked. "Have you been unguarded all this time?"

"I put my usual door guards on that door as well this year."

"But let me guess," Bryony said with a knowing look, "you made sure Darius has access through them just like Elsie and I do."

I ignored her jibe. "Jareth did warn me he was coming. If he had evil plans for this meeting, he probably wouldn't have done that."

Bryony looked like she was about to argue this point, but a knock made us both freeze. We turned slowly toward the tapestry in time to see it ripple and move as the door behind it was opened.

"Come in, Jareth," I said quietly, signaling to the composition on the door to let him through.

He stepped into the room tentatively, his hands held in front of him in a non-threatening manner. Bryony, however, bared her teeth and actually growled at him.

"Bree!" I hissed, but she didn't even turn to me.

Shaking my head, I stepped forward. "I invited Bryony to be here, too. If you have a problem with that, you can just turn around right now."

He hesitated for a moment before shrugging. "If you insist."

"I do."

For a moment we stared at each other before he looked away, running a hand through his hair.

"I suppose I should begin by apologizing to you, Verene."

"Which of the attempts to kill her would that apology be for?" Bryony asked hotly.

"Bree." I sighed.

I didn't like Jareth any more than she did, but I wanted answers, and I doubted constant antagonism was going to get them.

"No," Jareth said, "it's fair enough. Not that all the attempts were me. But I was involved in some of them."

"At the end of last year when I was dragged out of the entranceway," I said, unable to resist getting some answers at last. "The second man was you, wasn't it?"

He nodded. "I stashed the cloak in a bush when you were looking the other way and then pretended to have just come out of the building."

"I knew it!"

"Of course it was him," Bryony said scathingly. "And he was no doubt one of the attackers at the village as well."

He shook his head. "No, that wasn't me. That was…"

I waited with raised eyebrows, but he grimaced and threw his arms wide. "I don't know. Or I can't say. I'm not sure which one."

"What does that mean?" I asked.

He sighed. "I wish I knew."

"I agreed to this meeting because I want answers," I said. "I'm not interested in any more riddles from you."

"So you did get my letter?" he asked eagerly. "I was afraid you might not come back after everything that happened."

"Why are you so eager to have her here?" Bryony demanded.

"You helped Darius win his throne," Jareth said, his eyes on me. "I'm hoping you can help him keep it."

Bryony snorted.

"I know you have every reason not to believe me," Jareth said, his voice pained, "but I care about my brother, and I want his reign to succeed. I've always wanted that."

"Attempting to stab him in his sleep is a funny way to show your loyalty." I stared him down, my voice hard.

"I think...I think that wasn't me." He groaned. "I know that sounds crazy, but I've spent so many hours turning it over in my mind, trying to understand, and it's the only thing that makes any sense."

"Actually that makes no sense at all." Bryony's voice was flat, her eyes unforgiving. "We both saw you with our own eyes. It was you."

"I don't mean it wasn't me physically."

"Are you saying someone else was controlling your body?" I asked, skepticism in every word.

It had been months since the attack, so I couldn't remember every detail, but a composition like that would have required enormous power. If that sort of power had been clinging to him, I would have taken control of it in an instant.

"No, I don't mean that, either." He sounded almost as frustrated with himself as I felt.

"So it was you in that room, and no one was forcing you to act," Bryony said. "That doesn't sound like it was someone else at all."

Jareth sank into a chair, his whole body drooping. "I wish I could explain it better. Then maybe I could have convinced Darius."

"Don't think you're going to weasel us into trying to convince Darius to free you," Bryony said fiercely.

"I hope Jareth knows we would never do that." I let ice invade my voice and face.

"No, of course not," he said quickly. "I want you to find out what's going on. To protect Darius. I don't care about myself. How could I after what I tried to do?"

He sounded so pitiful that I had to tamp down an upwelling of pity and remind myself how non-existent his answers had been so far. Bryony was clearly ready to kick him back out of my sitting room, but something about his words and manner made me pause. His emotions, however unlikely, seemed genuine. And while it was possible the entire thing was a giant act, it was hard to believe he would pursue such a nonsensical line if he was making it all up. Bryony and I didn't have him under any kind of truth composition, so he could surely have come up with a far more convincing lie than whatever this tangled mess of words was.

I sat down as well, keeping a close eye on him, and gestured for Bryony to do the same. She hesitated a moment before giving a huff of exasperation and dropping into a chair.

"When you attacked Darius last year," I said, "you entered his suite through mine. You were trying to frame me for the assassination, weren't you?"

"Yes," he whispered, miserable.

"Why?" I asked.

"Because I knew that would sow the maximum amount of chaos and confusion. Killing Darius would have hurt Kallorway, but throwing the kingdom into conflict with Ardann at the same time would do far more damage."

Bryony made a squeak of outrage, but Jareth looked up and met my eyes, torment in his.

"But I love Kallorway, Verene. That's what doesn't make any sense. I might not like the court, but I've always loved my kingdom. I don't want to see it destroyed."

"Well, let's pretend for a moment that's exactly what you do want. I suppose that's why you tried to assassinate me as well."

He nodded.

"I knew you had to be involved," I said, "after you saw the

compositions guarding my door. But the assassin named your father."

"My father is a clever man in some ways, but he also has certain weaknesses—blind areas, I suppose. And your parents are one of those. At first, I was just trying to get you to leave the Academy. I didn't want Ardann and Kallorway forming an alliance, but I also didn't want any serious crime being traced back to me. But after Father saw the hold you had over Darius, I was able to work on him—to push him further and further away from reason and good sense. With his resources, I could increase the attacks."

"Because you didn't care if your own father got blamed for it, as long as it wasn't you," Bryony said with contempt.

Jareth shot her a fiery look. "Would you care if Cassius was your father?"

Bryony opened her mouth only to close it again because even though this was Jareth, he had a point.

"So your father provided the compositions to steal my energy," I said. "I suppose he got them from the energy mage you have in your Armed Forces."

Jareth nodded, while Bryony looked disgusted to hear that one of her own people had been involved.

Jareth must have seen her expression as well, because he quickly said, "Not that he was involved. As king, my father could ask for supplies of any type of composition without question."

"And that was one of the reasons Darius had to remove him from power sooner rather than later," I said grimly.

"I sent for my father as soon as Darius told me of the emergency Council," Jareth said. "Especially when he said you had arranged for it. Darius on the throne with Ardann as his ally was the opposite of everything I had been trying to achieve."

He grimaced. "But they sealed the room, and I couldn't intervene to delay the meeting and give my father time to undermine Darius's efforts. Darius was named king-elect and given all the power, and my father came to me and said that if I wanted to be king one day, I would have to kill Darius."

"And so you attempted to do it," I said.

"I have never wanted to be king, that was just the lie I sold my father. But I saw immediately that killing Darius and making it look like you had done it would serve my purpose even better than killing you would have done. And so I acted."

"And yet you claim to care about your brother." Bryony shook her head.

"That's what I can make no sense of," Jareth said. "I *do* care about my brother. More than I care about myself. Just like I love Kallorway. I always have. And yet, at the same time, I hated Kallorway and wanted to see it destroyed no matter what it took. Those two feelings can't coexist—they shouldn't be able to. And yet they did. I felt them both, and I couldn't see how they contradicted each other. I simply...believed them both. And one of them overrode the other sometimes—it compelled me to act. That's how it was on the night I attacked Darius. Right up until I saw him dying on the floor beside me. That sight broke through whatever strange barrier kept my two feelings separate. My love for him overwhelmed the other and completely wiped it out. Suddenly I couldn't understand how I had come to do such a thing."

"You keep talking in the past tense," I said. "You don't have these competing feelings now?"

"If he ever did," Bryony muttered.

"No, they're gone," Jareth said. "I can remember the thinking, but I can't connect with it. It seems as horrifying and foreign to me as it should always have felt."

"So you think someone did this to you...somehow," I said, trying to wrap my mind around the idea.

"Even power has limits," Bryony said. "Haven't you been listening to our instructors? You can't change someone's *thoughts*."

"I know it sounds impossible. That's exactly what Darius said. I just know it's what happened." He glanced at me. "And sometimes impossible things do happen. Just look at Verene."

"Don't tell me you were foolish enough to say something like that to Darius during his interrogation," Bryony said. "You must have known how he would react to you dragging Verene into it. You might convince me you couldn't possibly be a criminal mastermind, after all."

Jareth winced. "I never meant to suggest Verene had done it. That would make no sense. But as soon as I mentioned her, Darius exploded and would listen to no more."

"As you should have foreseen," Bryony muttered.

"Never mind that," I said, not willing to let my thinking be derailed by talk of Darius. "If we're willing—for the sake of this conversation—to assume Jareth is telling the truth, we can take it a step further and assume—for the moment—that somehow someone found a way to put a thought into his mind. It seems to me the relevant question in all of this is not so much *how* but *who*. Because whoever it is has revealed their aim—and apparently it's not to assassinate me, or even Darius. Their aim is to destroy Kallorway—and they don't mind dragging Ardann into the chaos."

Silence fell between us as Bryony looked at me with wide eyes, her hatred of Jareth momentarily forgotten. Jareth was the one to break the heavy silence.

"Exactly. And I am bound and restricted on every side with no one even believing my warnings. That's why I need you, Verene. You have to save Darius and Kallorway."

CHAPTER 8

"*B*ut even if you choose to believe every word of his story, it makes no sense he can't tell us who was responsible," Bryony said, for the tenth time.

We had already been debating the conversation with Jareth for days.

"Yes, there was definitely another attacker involved—beyond his father's assassin," I agreed. "So he wasn't doing it alone."

"And he said the attack in the village wasn't him or Cassius. But he must know who it was. Because those attackers had the energy stealing compositions from his father."

"Is it really any stranger than the rest, though?" I asked.

"So you agree we should discount the whole thing, then?" Bryony's voice said she didn't believe I thought any such thing.

"I didn't say that," I protested.

"No, I know you didn't." She sighed. "You seem determined to believe him."

I bit my lip. "I just keep thinking…What if he's telling the truth? Can we afford not to believe him? It's not as if he's asked us to set him free or anything."

"I suppose that's true," Bryony said, every syllable begrudging.

"But what he said about the perpetrator of this fairy tale of his still makes no sense."

When pressed, Jareth had claimed he didn't know who he had been collaborating with. But then he had corrected himself to say he couldn't say. Only to change his mind, with a confused look, to say he didn't know. Eventually he had given up—and his face suggested he was just as exasperated by his confusing utterances as we were.

When I reminded him that he had told us his thoughts were his own again now, he had only been able to shrug and say that as far as the other thoughts were concerned, they were. But for some reason, if he knew the identity of the mastermind behind it all, he couldn't communicate their name.

We didn't see him in the Royal Guard class, which I should have expected. Darius had organized for Jareth to be transferred to the law enforcement class with him. His entire plan revolved around Jareth remaining near him at all times, and I could only imagine the toll such a situation must be taking on Darius.

Amalia had said we would stay with each discipline for a full month, but we had only been with the Royal Guard trainees for a few days when she announced an unexpected change.

The law enforcement instructor had been called away from the Academy unexpectedly, and Amalia was needed to take over his class. So we were swapping early.

Darius didn't even look up when we first entered his classroom, his head bent over a stack of parchments that looked like his usual collection of reports. Given his distraction, I gave myself a moment to properly examine him.

Bryony's extra energy must have been helping because he felt less drained than before. But his face and eyes still held a lurking weariness I didn't like. Now that I knew about the failed harvests, I knew he was under even more pressure than I had realized. And he was carrying it all alone with his betrayer shackled to his side.

For the moment all I could do was slip into a desk at the back of the class which gave me a view of the side of his face. But determination to help him filled me. I might be Ardannian, but Darius trusted me, and that would have to be enough. I couldn't leave him to shoulder these burdens alone.

"Prince Darius." The sharp tone jerked my attention back to the front of the class.

I could still see Darius's profile in my peripheral vision, however. He looked as lost as I was.

"I'm sorry, what was the question?" he asked in a level tone.

Amalia's cold eyes remained steady on his face. "I can't speak for your regular instructor, but in my classes, I expect *all* my trainees to be paying attention to the lesson."

The softest rustle from the room expressed the class's shock at hearing Darius being spoken to in such a manner. I gripped my desk to force down a protest. Darius was already far more advanced in law enforcement than any lesson Amalia might be teaching, and he was also responsible for running the kingdom. Reading reports in lesson was a far better use of his time than listening to her lectures.

"If you repeat the question, I'm sure I can give a satisfactory answer," Darius said, his own voice and eyes cold.

Heads whipped back and forth between the king-elect and the senior instructor. Amalia's eyes narrowed, but she backed down, repeating the question in a begrudging tone.

"For what crimes may the victim request that suspects be questioned under a truth composition?"

"That depends," Darius said, his voice still holding a dangerous edge. "If the victim supplies the truth composition themselves, they may request it for any crime. However, whether the suspect is thus constrained—and on a voluntary or compulsory basis—is left to the judgment of law enforcement officials. For a commonborn, or a mage unable to supply their own compositions, they may request it only in cases where death or significant injury has occurred. And the final decision still remains with law enforcement."

Amalia continued to regard him with a sour expression but could apparently find no fault with his reply. After a moment, her eyes flickered back to the rest of the class. Before she could continue quizzing them, however, Darius spoke again.

"It is a law I intend to change."

Amalia's head whipped back to him, along with most of the class.

"The law should be impartial," he said, although no one had requested an explanation. "And no one should be above it. The current law clearly favors some over others."

"A noble view," Amalia said, although her tone didn't match her words. "And one that has been espoused before by some—the rebels back in the war days particularly. But it's not as simple as saying it should be so. Where are these extra compositions to come from?"

Darius let his eyes wander over the crowded room. Since he had chosen law enforcement in our first year, the number of trainees studying the discipline had risen sharply.

However, he said only, "I didn't say that all crimes and all accusations would warrant the use of a truth composition. Merely that a more impartial system must be established. Naturally I would not bring any changes to the Mage Council for ratification without extensive consultation with Duke Gilbert and his discipline."

Amalia gave a sound between a snort and a humph, but once again must not have been able to find fault with his words. She turned, as if to pose her next question to the other trainees, but Darius spoke again.

"I may not have been alive in the years of the war, but I am aware of the damage done to Kallorway by my grandfather's policies during that time. Many of the current fractures in our society can be traced back to then. Unlike Ardann," he nodded in my direction, "we did not require equal battle service from all. Some were able to excuse their families from bearing any of the risk, with others required to undertake greater risk to compensate. I believe that we cannot allow such systems to continue to fester in our kingdom—even in matters of less moment than full war. I intend to rule in a different way."

"Once again those are noble sentiments," Amalia said. "But I think you will find that some resist your changes, while for others it will be too little, too late. It is always the privilege of youth to think that the scars and wounds of decades can be healed by good intentions."

"By good intentions, no," Darius said. "But by real change and sacrifice, yes. But you're right that healing cannot be achieved unless everyone is willing to forgive and work together for the future."

Amalia gave a soft sound, like a snort, but didn't actually protest. I wondered who she thought would be the barrier to Darius's efforts.

After watching her for a moment, Darius turned back to his reports. I wanted to cheer for him. He might be a third year trainee still, but he had reminded Amalia—and the class—that he was also king-elect. And that he intended to be a new kind of king.

My expression must have shown my feelings a bit too clearly because Amalia's eyes narrowed again when they passed over me. Back in first year she used to try to catch me out in the same way with questions, but I had been too interested in the class to be caught not paying attention.

I listened now with only half an ear, occupied by thoughts of how I could use class to practice my own ability. Last year, when I had been focused on taking control of someone else's composition, classes had been the ideal opportunity. But now that I wanted to actually connect with someone and use their ability, a classroom seemed much too public. I couldn't start writing a composition where anyone could see me. How would I possibly explain it?

Unless I could think of an excuse as to why I might want to write out the words of a composition. Could I claim I was just taking notes—memorizing compositions in case they came up in exams? As long as I waited to test them out back in the privacy of my suite, it might work.

I would have to keep the compositions small, of course. I didn't want to drain enough energy that someone might notice— or that their studies might suffer. But not all the years were being pushed as close to exhaustion as the third years.

My eyes landed on Amalia before moving away. I couldn't blame my reluctance to connect with her on fear that she would somehow sense my interference in her energy—not when the Head of Law Enforcement hadn't noticed when I connected with him. In truth it was a more simple reluctance based on my dislike of her. Connecting with her might not give me the ability to read her thoughts, but I had no desire to immerse myself in any part of my unpleasant instructor.

Eventually I settled on a fourth year trainee I recognized from when we had worked with the law enforcement class in second year. Simone had struck me then as quiet but skilled and seemed an appealing candidate now.

I took a moment to concentrate on the energy I could sense in every person in the room. It didn't take me long to focus in on Simone. I hesitated, though. The familiar part of my ability— taking control of a composition that was in the process of being worked—was second nature now. But I had very little experience with this new ability.

I knew from my experiments with Bryony that I didn't need the other mage to be in the process of working a composition for me to connect with their energy and access their ability. But then her energy was familiar to me. When I had first connected with Duke Gilbert, I had done it after taking control of one of his shields. Touching his working had given me a feel for his ability and energy that had paved the way for me to then connect with him directly. Did I need that now?

I bit my lip. If I hadn't needed that step with Bryony, then it wasn't an essential part of the process. Likely it had happened that way with Duke Gilbert merely because it was the first time I had ever accessed my second ability to connect with another person. I had been following an instinct without even realizing I was capable of such a thing. Surely now that I was acting with purpose, I wouldn't need to get that inside feel for her energy and ability before making the connection?

I concentrated on the sense of Simone's energy again. It took me a moment to pick it out from among the many people in the room, but once I had the sense of her in my mind, I could feel a faint tug. I had felt it before on the few occasions I had used my new ability, and I had to admit I had been suppressing it all summer—especially around the familiarity of my family's energy.

I let go of that block now, letting myself follow the pull.

"Connect," I whispered, and my awareness submerged itself in her energy.

Immediately I knew I had been right about Simone's skill level. I wasn't overwhelmed in the way I had been when I connected with the duke's vast ability, but I felt immediate confidence that if I borrowed her ability, I wouldn't end up with an error in my composition as I might with a first year.

It was a strange feeling to be inside the ability of another, and I couldn't help but be glad I hadn't tried it with Amalia. I could now sense Simone's energy as easily as my own and access all the parts of her knowledge that were linked to the crafting of compositions—everything I needed to compose in her place.

My mind grasped it all far too swiftly for normal comprehension—as evidenced by how quickly it would fade once I disconnected. But although I could see into even the back recesses of her ability, her mind influenced the way the compositions appeared to me. Duke Gilbert's ability had felt like whirling chaos, vast enough that I struggled to focus within it, but Simone's was much more limited. And my consciousness was drawn toward a clear composition.

I recognized it as the truth composition Amalia was lecturing the class about. But I could understand the complexity and nuances of it far better than I had a few moments before when I had nothing but my own mind and ability to draw on.

I couldn't read Simone's thoughts to know what she was thinking about the composition, I could tell only that she had currently focused her ability on it. And I was too lost in my own working to retain normal awareness of what was going on in the room around me. It was possible Simone was actually in the middle of composing the truth composition, or merely that she was preparing to do so. Either way, her focus drew me in, and I felt the pull to compose it myself.

But unlike during the Council meeting when Duke Gilbert had been focused on a specific composition, I understood what was happening this time, and I resisted. The truth composition was a complex one, even for a fourth year, and Simone still lacked full proficiency with it. On top of that, it was unsuitable for my purposes in every way.

I wanted a composition that would take little of her energy as well as one that I could easily test alone in my suite. But could I break past Simone's own focus to access the rest of her ability for myself? I thought I could, but I had never actually tried before.

I pushed deeper into the wealth of knowledge and experience she had gained in more than three years at the Academy. Topics, most of them related to law enforcement, sprang into my mind. When I concentrated on one, knowledge of compositions that should have been unfamiliar filled my thoughts. I let my awareness skim over them, looking for one that would work for me.

My mind caught on a working used when examining the scene of a crime. The primary composition could return all the objects in an entire room to the positions they had previously occupied. But with my access to Simone's understanding of the working, I could easily see how it might be modified to work on a single object—say a cushion. With such an adjustment, the composition would require little power and would therefore drain a negligible amount of Simone's substantial energy.

Only peripherally aware of my physical body, I drew a parchment toward me and began to write. Since I was making substantial changes to the established composition, I took my time, writing more words and limitations than Simone needed to use. When I finished by writing the words, *End binding*, I immediately whispered, "End," cutting my connection with Simone.

For a moment I stared down at the composition written in my own handwriting before remembering I sat in a classroom full of people. I looked up, scanning the trainees around me, but no one appeared to be paying me any heed. Even Bryony didn't sit with me when we visited other classes—her presence always required at the front of the room.

Just as the tension in my shoulders relaxed, however, Amalia began to move between the desks, coming in my direction. I tensed again. In my focus on finding a simple, weak composition, I had forgotten my cover story. If Amalia saw what I had been writing, she was unlikely to believe it was exam preparation.

I whipped another parchment off the pile on my desk, placing it over the completed composition and frantically filling it with a few scrawled notes on truth compositions. When I sensed Amalia's looming presence, I forced myself to look up and nod at her calmly.

She looked down at the parchment in front of me with a skeptical expression but made no effort to take it or expose the one below. After a moment that seemed to last forever, she continued on without speaking, reaching the back of the room and turning to start down the next row of desks.

I let out a slow breath.

As soon as my hands stopped trembling and Amalia had moved far enough forward I could only see her back, I whipped the composition from under the top parchment and stuffed it away into one of my pockets. I looked up from doing so, feeling the weight of eyes on me.

My gaze locked with Darius's. Apparently he wasn't quite as absorbed in his reports as he had appeared. He gave the slightest upward lift to one eyebrow, but I just shrugged. He was too far away to have seen anything written on my parchment, and he couldn't possibly guess my secret merely by knowing I had written something I didn't want Amalia to read.

What would he say if I told him the truth? I longed to do it, tearing down the barriers between us. But as always, fear held me back. Darius wasn't just a year mate I had fallen in love with. He was now king-elect of an entire kingdom—a kingdom that was traditionally enemies of my own. What would happen to me when Kallorway had need of my ability and his duty outweighed his love?

But my heart didn't agree with my head, crying out that I could trust Darius. He had tried to send me away because he wanted to protect me from his court. He would always protect me. And if he knew of my capacity to protect myself, maybe he wouldn't fear for me so much.

But still I hesitated.

When class finished, I could barely sit through the evening meal, the composition in my pocket seeming far heavier than the negligible weight of the parchment. I ate as fast as I could, wishing Bryony and Tyron goodnight as soon as I finished the last mouthful.

In the safety of my suite, I called for Elsie but got no response. I checked my bedchamber and even peeked around the screens into her section of the room. My servant was nowhere to be seen and must be in the servants' dining hall, eating her own meal.

Satisfied I was alone, I pulled out the parchment and looked at it. Reading through the words, written in my own clear hand, felt surreal. Surely this was just another parchment like any other, and when I ripped it, nothing would happen. And yet, I remembered the feel of the power building as I wrote the binding words and then holding, shaping itself through my words as it poured into my working.

I had specifically designated a cushion in the composition, instructing the power to return it to the position it had been in five minutes before. So I needed to choose one and move it before I could test out my working.

Somehow all the cushions but one had ended up on one of the two sofas, so I focused my attention on the lone one that occupied the other. I had put as little power into the composition as I possibly could, so I didn't want to ruin the experiment by trying to do anything too complicated with the chosen cushion. Eventually I just dumped it on the floor, a few feet away from the sofa.

With that taken care of, I drew a deep breath and ripped the parchment clean through. I had only begun the motion when I heard the door latch lift, but it was already too late to stop.

My eyes flew to the doorway, and I knew that for once my court mask had failed me. I must look as guilty as I felt.

In my peripheral vision, the power unleashed by my composition scooped the cushion from the floor, sending it flying through the air back to its original position on the sofa. My fingers twitched, and the scraps of the completed composition drifted to the floor.

Elsie closed the door behind her, a faint crease in her brow.

"I'm sorry, Princess, I didn't expect you back from the meal so soon, or I would have made an effort to be back earlier myself."

Regaining control of myself, I shook my head. "Nonsense. There's no reason you need to be here every moment I am."

Her slight frown didn't lift. "Are you concerned with the state of your rooms? If there's a particular way you prefer things to be kept, I hope you would let me know."

"Oh...no," I said, realizing how my composition must have appeared. "That was just an experiment from class. I'm not going to start sourcing compositions to do your job for you."

She relaxed, a smile finally appearing as she moved briskly into the room. "I must admit, I always imagined Academy trainees completing far more interesting studies. But then I always thought books were supposed to have stories as well."

Her expression darkened as she dwelt on her favorite disgruntlement. Upon learning to read, she had been bitterly disappointed to discover that most books focused on topics such as history, economics, and law rather than being the captivating stories she had always imagined.

I chuckled, and she grinned at me, the disappointment dissolving from her face. She had reached me now, and before I knew what she meant to do, she had bent down and picked up my two discarded parchment halves.

"Here, I'll clean these up for you," she said, just as I uttered a wordless protest.

Straightening back up, her eyes drifted down to the torn paper in her hands. She instantly froze, looking up at me, then at the cushion on the sofa, and then back down at the words on the two halves.

I snatched them from her hands, but the damage was already done.

"Princess Verene," she said, her voice squeaking slightly, "that's your handwriting."

CHAPTER 9

For a brief second, I thought of disputing it. But Elsie had grown too familiar with my penmanship in the countless hours I had spent teaching her to read and write.

"Do you...Are you...I thought..." She couldn't finish a single sentence, her eyes enormous as she stared at me, apparently forgetting the difference in our rank in the face of her shock. "Even Stellan seemed sure you didn't have an ability."

I sighed and sat down on top of the fateful cushion. "So was I when I left Ardann for my first year here. Why do you think I was so insistent Stellan not seal himself any time soon?"

Elsie gasped, her hand flying to her throat. "We have to warn him! You have to tell him..." Her voice trailed off, possibly because she remembered who she was talking to.

"I already made him promise to wait another two years," I said. "I'm hoping if he does have any further undiscovered abilities, they'll have shown themselves by then. If not...Well, I'll have graduated by then and will have to have made a decision myself."

"A decision about what?" Elsie asked.

I spread my arms wide. "Everything? I don't even know some

days. I have an ability—a strange one—and I don't know what to do with it. I don't know who to trust with it."

Elsie looked at me, her eyes reproving. "You can trust your brother."

I nodded. "I would trust Stellan with my life. My aunt, on the other hand..." I sighed. "I trust her to do what's best for the kingdom, which makes her an excellent queen."

"But not always an excellent aunt," Elsie said slowly.

I nodded.

"Stellan has sometimes talked about—" She cut herself off, and I didn't press her to continue. I liked that she kept my brother's confidences.

After a moment, she sat down on one of the chairs, and shook her head. "All this time, I thought..." She looked up at me. "You said you had a strange ability?" She pointed at one of the scraps of parchment. "That looks normal enough to me."

My mind raced. I couldn't avoid Elsie knowing some part of the truth now, but that didn't mean I had to tell her the whole truth. I didn't have to tell her how my ability worked.

But it galled me to take such a course. I was sick of keeping secrets, and Elsie lived in my suite. It would make my life easier if she knew the truth. As long as I could trust her.

I weighed her with my eyes, and she sat quietly, meeting my eyes steadily as if she understood she was being assessed.

I had said I trusted my brother, and I also trusted his judgment. He had known Elsie for far longer than I had and had been willing to risk everything for her. Everything I had seen in her time with me only confirmed that assessment.

But one threat did still exist. Her feelings for my brother made her loyal to our family, but they might also work against me.

"If I tell you the truth," I said, "will you tell Stellan? Can I trust you?"

I had expected her to answer quickly and vehemently, but

instead a slight crease appeared in her temple as she considered the question. Her hesitation lightened my mind, suggesting as it did that I could take her coming answer seriously.

"I love Stellan," she said after a moment, stating the emotion without self-consciousness. "I don't see how I could help it. But you have taken me on as your personal servant. You arranged for me to be sealed. I owe you my loyalty, and I would never willingly betray you. I believe Stellan would understand that. As for anyone else..."

She shook her head vehemently. "I would never tell your secrets to someone else." Her eyes strayed to the tapestry, and I flushed slightly. She had obviously discovered the door behind it and knew where it led.

"Thank you, Elsie," I said. "I appreciate your words and your service. And I hope you know that I take my responsibility to you and your future seriously."

She nodded. "How could I doubt it after the way you brought me here and then taught me to read and write yourself?"

"Well," I said, "here is the truth of my abilities. When I came to Kallorway I could do nothing but sense power. During first year, I discovered I could also sense energy."

She sat up straighter at this, her gaze keen and curious. No doubt she was thinking of Stellan. But she didn't interrupt.

"Since that point, my new abilities have grown. I appear to be an energy mage, but one with a unique ability I've never heard of before. I can use spoken words to take control of someone else's composition as it's being worked and twist its shape. And I have recently discovered that I can also use spoken words to connect with another mage's energy. While connected, I can use their ability as if it was my own, drawing on their energy to do so."

Her mouth fell open. "But that's...that's..."

I nodded. "Exactly. As far as I know, it's unprecedented and has the potential to be enormously powerful—and destructive. So you can see why I'm not rushing to spread word of it around."

I waved the papers I held. "This was a composition I wrote in class today while connected with a fourth year trainee. Just an experiment."

"In class?" Her eyebrows rose. "So you've told your instructors?"

I shook my head, a faint flush staining my cheeks. "No, I'm trying to train myself in secret. That's why I waited until I was alone to work the composition." I grimaced. "Or at least, I thought I was alone."

"I'm sorry about that," she said softly. "But I'm not sorry to know the truth. It must have been awkward for you to be creeping around your own suite trying to keep your efforts hidden."

"It was a little," I admitted.

"I'm not here to make your life harder, Princess Verene. Especially not after everything you've done for me." She hesitated. "I know it's not my place to say, but I think you should also consider telling Captain Layna."

I raised both eyebrows. "Captain Layna? I didn't realize you knew her particularly."

"I didn't when you took me on. But I suppose it's natural we would be drawn to each other somewhat since we all arrived. We're the only two Ardannians here, other than you. You said you've been training by yourself, but I think she could help."

"You work for me," I said, "but Layna doesn't. She answers to her superiors at the Royal Guard, and they're the last ones I would want to discover the truth."

Elsie's mouth twisted slightly, and she spoke slowly as if choosing her words carefully. "Of course she does officially. But she's in an unusual situation and has spent a lot of time here. I think she feels more loyalty to you than to them at this point."

I considered her words. While I remained inside the Academy grounds, Layna wasn't officially my personal guard. But if she knew I needed assistance with my training, I didn't doubt she would immediately volunteer. And it would certainly be helpful to have a power mage to openly train with. But I wasn't as convinced as Elsie that it was safe to tell her the truth.

"I'll consider it," I said at last, and Elsie nodded.

It felt significant, welcoming her into my secret like this. As if we had become a team in a way we hadn't been before. The thought led to another.

"I wonder if you might do something for me, Elsie," I said.

"Of course. Anything you like," she said promptly.

"I've recently heard some rumors about failures in the harvest. I don't know how widely talked of it is among the servants, but I was wondering if you could see what they might have to say on the topic." I hesitated. "In particular, anything they might have to say about Prince Darius."

"The king-elect?" Elsie pursed her lips thoughtfully. "If the harvests are failing, I imagine it's seen as a less than ideal start to his rule."

I nodded, as always impressed by her quickness. She nodded decisively.

"You can leave it to me, Princess. I'll find out what the mood is among the servants." She frowned slightly. "We're our own little world here, though—except for the village. Their opinions might not align with the rest of the kingdom."

I shrugged. "I would still like to know what they think."

Elsie nodded and then glanced at the pieces of parchment still clutched in my hands. "Would you like me to burn those for you?"

I started and handed them to her. "Yes, please."

She stood, taking them and beginning to move away before pausing and looking back at me.

"You have an extraordinary gift, Princess Verene. And I don't doubt you'll find the right use for it."

I smiled and thanked her, but as I watched her hurry about her task, I wished I felt half her confidence in me. I would have preferred an ability that gave me a voice of my own, not one that let me steal the voices of others.

As the days passed, I tried connecting with more and more of the other trainees. I continued to choose small compositions to practice, but I chose them more carefully than I had the first time. I had learned from my mistake.

I kept them basic—well-known and practiced workings that I might claim I wished to study—purely academically, of course. I no longer invented compositions that, if seen, would be as obviously out of place as a flying cushion.

Darius continued to watch me, as if aware something strange was happening, but he never pressed me as to what it might be. And the shadow in his eyes grew deeper and deeper. Given the news Elsie soon brought me about how blight continued to threaten the second harvest, I hardly found it surprising.

Worried, I chose a seat across from him and Jareth at the evening meal one day. Bryony faltered for only a stride before sitting smoothly beside me. Tyron, an expression of mild surprise on his face, took the seat next to Jareth. The prince gave him the barest nod, his focus on me.

"This is an unexpected pleasure, Verene," he said.

Darius turned a glare on him, and Jareth raised both hands placatingly. Had he thought I sat here for his sake? That I had some news about his claims of mysterious enemies?

I ignored him, my worried eyes on Darius.

"I've heard something troubling," I said, between mouthfuls. "About the second harvest."

Darius looked up swiftly to meet my eyes, and I read the truth in his gaze. My shoulders slumped.

"It should be the smoothest harvest in history with so many growers to oversee it."

"Yes," Darius agreed. "It *should*. And yet it is not. We are succeeding at keeping the plants alive for now, but the food is not yet safely harvested. We can't afford any complacency."

"No, certainly not," I agreed, and couldn't help adding, "but you are allowed to sleep. Have you been resting at all? You look exhausted, despite..." My eyes flicked sideways to Bryony.

"You should have said something," she said sternly to Darius. "I can help out more. And I'm sure Tyron would be happy to help as well."

Tyron looked slightly startled at being brought into the conversation, but his good humor didn't abate. "I'm sure I would be happy to do so if I had any idea what you were talking about."

"I've been providing Prince Darius with compositions," Bryony explained.

I gave her a slight glare, afraid she meant to reveal too much, but she merely said, "It's no small matter to run a kingdom while still a trainee."

Tyron nodded at Darius. "I would certainly be more than happy to help, of course. I appreciate Kallorway giving me the opportunity to train at your Academy."

"I can assure you we don't exact such heavy payment from our trainees," Darius said. "Not on top of your studies. I'll be fine, although I appreciate your willingness."

Tyron hesitated, as if he meant to argue the point, before he shrugged and returned to his meal. I wanted to glare at Darius for refusing the extra help but refrained from doing so in public.

That night I knocked on our shared door, however. Gone were the days when I might barge through without warning—not when Darius had Jareth as his constant roommate.

My knock was quickly answered, but it wasn't Darius's face that greeted me.

"Princess Verene, twice in one day. What a pleasant surprise."

"Jareth." Darius's voice whipped across the room, cold and commanding.

Jareth stepped away from me with a resigned, self-depre-cating smile, giving me a clear view into the sitting room. When Darius glared at him, he disappeared altogether into Darius's bedchamber.

"Is everything all right?" Darius crossed over to me.

He took my hands, the action seeming more reflex than conscious decision, and my fingers burned where they touched his.

"It's you I'm worried about," I said. "I can't bear to see you being worn away like this. Keeping Jareth bound is too much on top of everything else."

He frowned. "Are you suggesting I release him?"

"No, of course not! I…" I grimaced. "I suppose I don't know what I'm suggesting. I'm just concerned about you."

Darius's face softened. "It's no wonder I love you, Verene," he said softly, as if the words slipped out without his even realizing. "And I only wish my kingdom was good enough for you. If it was, I would never stop fighting for you."

My heart stuttered at his declaration, tears welling in my eyes. "I don't care how good Kallorway is, Darius. You're good enough for me, and I know you're going to make your kingdom a better place."

"I'm going to try." He sighed. "I don't seem to be succeeding too well so far, though. I can't even manage a successful harvest."

"That is not your fault," I said fiercely.

"Isn't it?" His eyes narrowed, the familiar look of hard deter-mination returning. "Because the more time that passes, the less I can believe this is a natural phenomenon. So maybe it is happening because of me."

I gulped. "What do you mean to do about it?"

"I mean to ensure a successful harvest. And then I will find whoever would dare to risk so many of my people because of some political squabble with me." From the look on his face, I wouldn't want to be that person when he found them.

"Could your grandfather be behind it?" I asked tentatively. "I can't work out what he thinks of your early rise to power."

Darius shook his head. "I'm not saying my grandfather is an ally, but he has fought for this kingdom for more decades than I've been alive. He wouldn't try to starve it just to spite me. That's the difference between him and my father. He's a canny player, and he believes no one can rule as well as him, but he does have a love for Kallorway beneath it all."

"But your father no longer has the resources for such a maneuver, surely," I said, fear tinging my voice after all I had gone through at the old king's instigation.

Darius's eyes turned hard. "No, it couldn't be my father. I'm having him watched far too closely for him to manage something of this magnitude. And in truth, I cannot say for certain there is a nefarious hand behind it. Too much power already lingers around the crops to tell if further power has been used to taint them."

I reached up to touch his cheek. "I wish I could help you shoulder your burdens, Darius. I wish you would let me." And inside, another voice, *I wish I dared let myself be honest with you.*

He allowed the tender gesture for only the briefest moment before pulling away.

"Don't tempt me, Verene," he said, his voice almost a groan. "You don't know how I long for you."

My heart beat so rapidly I feared it would leap from my chest.

"Surely it must be possible for—"

"No!" He cut me off. "My own brother is a human blight I have shackled to me day and night. It is precisely because I love you too well that I won't let you too close."

He stepped back, breaking all contact between us. "See how weak I am with even the slightest temptation? There's a reason I must keep my distance."

I wanted to plead with him, but the small voice at the back of my mind kept my mouth closed. Darius was not the only barrier to our unity.

Apparently the law enforcement instructor showed no signs of returning any time soon because Amalia decided that if we weren't free to attend other classes, they would have to come to us. Small groups from other disciplines began attending the law enforcement class which now more closely resembled an expanded energy mage class.

When Isabelle appeared with a group of wind workers a few days after my conversation with Darius, the smile on her face took me by surprise. My astonishment only grew when she spotted me in my usual place at the back of the class and came to join me.

"Don't you want to be near the front with Bryony?" I asked.

"Not today," she said. "I'm afraid I'm too distracted to concentrate, so it's best I hide myself away."

I wondered if I should warn her that sitting toward the back wasn't enough to hide anyone from Amalia's notice but was distracted by the difference between her words and demeanor.

"Have you had further bad news from home?" I asked tentatively.

"Quite the opposite." She beamed. "They were able to separate off the small number of plants bearing the new blight and have subsequently saved the crop. It will be harvest time soon."

A grin spread across my face, my eyes flying to Darius's profile.

"That is excellent news, indeed! I'm so glad to hear it."

A loud throat clearing made Isabelle jump in her seat. I carefully kept my face impassive as I looked across to see Amalia looming over us.

"I expect full attention in my class from all trainees, regardless of discipline or ability," she said, her voice awful in its softness.

Isabelle's eyes widened, and she nodded swiftly.

"My apologies, Senior Instructor," I said in a neutral tone.

Her eyes narrowed, but as usual, she struggled to find anything concrete to fault me with. A look of frustration flashed across her face, and she looked across at Darius.

"That applies to all my trainees," she said in a louder tone. "Pretty speeches about equality and all being subject to the law are all very well, but I would have you all remember that in my classroom, I make the law. And I expect all trainees to obey it without exception."

Darius abandoned his reports and turned slightly in his chair to face us.

"Is there a prob—" he started to ask, but I cut him off. Somehow Isabelle's good news had hit me as hard as any bad news might have done, and I couldn't bear to see Amalia attacking Darius again just as it looked as if he might finally get a little relief.

"Prince Darius is in this class to learn law enforcement compositions," I snapped. "And we all know that he is already far more advanced in those than any third year. He has a kingdom to run and doesn't have time to allow the overbearing pride of an Academy instructor to interfere with his duties. Or haven't you heard there's a crisis facing this kingdom? If the harvest fails, many will suffer. How can you think your lectures compare with that?"

I finished my speech to ringing silence as the entire class stared at me wide-eyed. It wasn't like me to lose control like that, but having done so, I couldn't afford to give ground or show weakness. I kept my back straight and my gaze steady as I stared Amalia down.

For a brief moment, rage transformed her features. But with a visible effort she reined it in. Turning slightly, she regarded Darius in silence before turning back to me.

"I have indeed heard about this crisis to the harvest," she said, in what I could only feel was a deceptively calm manner. "But I hadn't realized any of my trainees were so necessary for its smooth function. If the king-elect's input is so essential, I wonder that he is hiding here at the Academy so far from the fields."

I stiffened even further, and Darius's face hardened into ice. Surely as a senior instructor, Amalia knew that the Mage Council had decreed Darius must finish his four years at the Academy before being crowned.

"You know that he cannot leave the Academy," I said in a low, angry voice.

She looked contemptuous. "I know nothing of the kind. The Academy does allow field trips, after all." She turned to Darius. "I wonder you don't suggest such a thing to Duke Francis. I'm sure, like everyone else, he will be more than happy to accommodate someone as important as the king-elect."

Darius's eyes narrowed. "Duke Francis's priority is the learning of the trainees. As it should be."

"And with such momentous goings on in the kingdom, what could better promote that learning than an excursion to the north-west fields?" Amalia spread her arms wide. "I'm sure there is much I could teach there, given the sort of mixed discipline classes I have been forced into running." Her expression and tone suggested that the current unusual teaching situation was somehow Darius's fault as well—but that she was naturally capable of rising to any challenge.

Darius gave a bark of laughter. "So you're volunteering to facilitate such an excursion, are you?"

She narrowed her eyes, but what could she say to that after her previous statement?

"I serve as the Academy Head commands," she replied.

"Excellent." I jumped in. "In that case, I'm sure the duke will think it's a good idea." I turned to Darius. "Don't you think so, Darius? I'm sure we could all learn a lot from the growers and wind workers stationed at the fields."

I didn't speak the rest of my thoughts. If we were there in person, we could make completely sure no one interfered before harvest was completed. And Darius could show his people that he cared enough to come in person. Amalia might have meant to be spiteful, but we could use her opening to our advantage.

After a tense moment of silence, Darius suddenly relaxed.

"An excellent suggestion, Instructor," he said. "I will talk to the duke this evening."

"Oh please, oh please, oh please, let it be the third years going," Isabelle whispered beside me, her eyes shining at the prospect of an unexpected trip home.

CHAPTER 10

I wasn't present at Darius's meeting with Duke Francis, but Isabelle got her wish. A junior instructor was assigned to take over the law enforcement class for the period of our absence, while Amalia was instructed to supervise the trip. Since all of her own energy mage class were third years, along with the two princes, it was decided that sending a year level rather than a discipline class—which mixed trainees from across the years—would be the least disruptive.

Mitchell seemed relieved to be free of our troublesome class for a while, and even Alvin didn't protest the break in our composition training.

"As senior discipline instructor across all the disciplines, Amalia is just as capable of training you in composition as I am. I have no hesitation leaving you all in her hands. In fact, I am excited for you to gain such a wonderful opportunity to see compositions being used in the field." He winked. "Literally."

Ashlyn groaned quietly, but she had been full of enthusiasm when Duke Francis announced the trip. As grower trainees, she and Frida had the most to learn from the visit, and she claimed they were the envy of the rest of their grower class.

Isabelle hadn't waited for the duke's official permission but had immediately contacted her family, with the result that we had all been invited to stay at their estate. She buzzed with constant excitement in the lead up to the trip, eyes aglow and more than usually chatty.

"I can't wait for you all to see my home," she said at the evening meal the night before we were to leave. "It's beautiful, especially the ocean."

"I'm looking forward to it as well," I confessed. "In Ardann, the Grayback Mountains block the entire eastern coast. I'm told it's an impressive sight from the sea, with the cliffs plunging straight down into the water, but I've never seen it for myself."

"But you have been to the beach before?" Isabelle clarified.

I nodded. "I've traveled to the south of Ardann to see the ocean. But between the river delta and the southern forests, we don't have long stretches of beach the way you do along your west coast. And certainly no farming land abutting it."

"Well, you're doing better than me, at least," Tyron said. "I've never seen the ocean at all."

"Never seen the ocean?" Isabelle stared at him as if she couldn't imagine such a life. "But the Sekali Empire has beaches all along their western coastline just like we do."

"True," Bryony said, "but don't forget how big the Empire is. The emperor's lands stretch all the way from the western beaches to the eastern coast which is blocked by the Graybacks. And the Graybacks bend west to cover the entire northern border of the Empire as well. So the only accessible beaches are on the west coast—which is a long way to travel for many people."

"Your parents never took you?" Isabelle's voice was laced with sympathy, as if she thought such an oversight must indicate neglectful or uncaring parents.

Tyron shrugged. "My father isn't one to waste time and effort on such frivolous activities as visiting the beach."

Bryony clapped her hands. "Then we get to take you for your

first visit. It just goes to show your excellent wisdom in selecting to study at the Kallorwegian Academy."

Tyron gave an amused smile. "I can't say the possibility of visiting a beach factored into the decision making at all."

I chuckled. "Considering we're located nowhere near the beach, I can imagine it didn't." I looked at Isabelle. "What are the roads like between here and your home? I know we won't be able to take one of the major roads the whole way like we did when we went to the capital last year."

"They're well enough," Isabelle said. "They'll get less passable once winter hits, but for now they should be easy going for the carriages."

The next morning, we gathered in the courtyard in front of the Academy to find four carriages prepared for our departure. As well as the twelve third year trainees, we were joined by Amalia and a junior instructor I'd never met. Elsie was also traveling with us, at my insistence, and Zora herself had come out to see us off.

Or at least, so I thought, until I saw her climbing into a carriage. I grabbed at Elsie's arm, stopping her from following the head servant into the vehicle.

"Is Zora coming with us?" I asked, eyes wide.

Elsie nodded. "I only found out this morning, or I would have told you. Apparently she says it's been far too long since she left the Academy, and she has a hankering to see the ocean again."

I raised both eyebrows. If Zora was accompanying us, it wouldn't be for such a frivolous reason, I felt sure. But I let Elsie go, and she disappeared into the last carriage after Zora, the junior instructor following her.

Amalia preferred to ride, along with Captains Vincent and Layna, and the entire squad of royal guards chosen to join us on the journey were also mounted. Layna waved to me merrily, apparently pleased to be briefly returned to her role as personal guard, before turning to say something to the grim-looking

Vincent. Unlike Layna, it appeared the captain in charge of guarding the king-elect was far from pleased about his charge leaving the safety of the Academy walls. From the twinkle in Layna's eyes and the laugh on her face, it almost looked as if she was teasing the Kallorwegian captain, but she got no response from him.

"Come on, Verene! Don't hold us up." Bryony stuck her head out of one of the carriages to reprove me.

With a smile I climbed in to join her, Tyron, and Isabelle.

"Sorry, I wouldn't want to keep Tyron from his first sighting of the ocean for even a moment longer than necessary."

Tyron rolled his eyes. "Anyone would think I was some poor neglected waif, the way you all carry on. What's the big deal about the ocean anyway?"

Isabelle stared at him. "What's the big deal about the ocean? But it's—"

Bryony cut her off with a hand on her arm. "No, don't say anything. Leave it as a surprise. He'll see for himself."

The carriage lurched and rolled through the Academy gates, riders flanking us on both sides as soon as we reached the road beyond. For a short distance we would be able to travel along the main road before it curved south to head toward Kallmon. At that point, we would join a smaller branch, heading directly west through the Kallorwegian farmlands toward the ocean.

I had never seen Isabelle so animated, her chatter filling the carriage as she and Bryony kept us all laughing between them. I had always had the impression Isabelle loved her home and the coast itself, but I'd never realized just how much she missed it when she was at the Academy.

As we traveled west, the temperature changed. It was a gradual shift but enough to be noticeable, the chill of the oncoming winter replaced with an unseasonable warmth.

"I suppose we have the wind workers to thank for the weather." I peered out one of the windows at the stunning blue sky against the backdrop of green and yellow fields.

"Yes, it's been an enormous effort from the whole discipline," Isabelle said. "We've talked about it endlessly in our discipline class. The wind workers would never interfere with the normal seasons in such a way for anything less than the loss of the entire harvest. And there are some among the discipline with serious concerns about the consequences."

"What sort of consequences?" Tyron asked.

Isabelle shrugged. "It's hard to say exactly. Wind working is a difficult discipline because the forces of nature aren't always predictable—and they're so interconnected. What you do in one area can have unforeseen consequences in another. Many fear a backlash of some sort. We have watchers stationed throughout the rest of the kingdom to report the appearance of any strange weather."

I kept my eyes out the window. I knew Ardann's wind workers were doing the same—at least now that I had reported exactly what was going on to my aunt. I supposed Darius was relying on his own watchers to identify any concerns before anything untoward reached as far as Ardann, but I still wished he had informed my aunt himself. I could understand why he might not have wished to do so, but it only exacerbated my concerns. Monarchs didn't play the same games as the rest of us.

We rolled past field after field, the seemingly never-ending sight bringing into perspective Kallorway's initial loss. It was no wonder they were taking the risks to ensure a successful late harvest.

After a full day's travel, we stopped for the night at a prosperous-looking inn located where our road crossed another main road heading south toward the capital. Captain Vincent had sent guards ahead to secure the accommodation, ensuring our party had the inn to ourselves. His zealous protection of Darius ensured we were all able to have our own rooms, and I slept deeply, exhausted by the travel.

In the morning, I nearly ran into Zora in the corridor.

"Good morning, Your Highness." She gave me a small, dignified curtsy.

"Good morning. I must say I was surprised to see you join us. Delighted, of course, but surprised. Can the Academy really spare you?" I wanted to ask her what Duke Francis thought of his wife's departure but wouldn't risk doing so in an open corridor.

"They'll all get on well enough without me for a week or two." She grinned. "It's good practice for them."

"I'm sure if nothing else it will increase their appreciation for you when you get back," I said with a smile of my own.

She chuckled. "That is one advantage, yes. But it was time and past for me to step outside our isolated domain. I value the bubble we live in at the Academy, but it's never wise to forget that bubbles float in a wider pool."

"And they can burst," I said quietly.

"Aye."

I dropped my voice lower. "You and the duke put yourselves at risk when you supported Darius. He won't forget it."

"Aye, that's likely true—but neither can he help the chaos he brings with his presence. This is a pivotal time for Kallorway, and sometimes it's important to keep your fingers on the pulse."

I nodded. Elsie had reported that the servants at the Academy were loyal to Darius, but that likely only increased Zora's desire to see for herself the currents in the broader kingdom.

"I hear the harvest is going well," I said. "So I hope we will all soon be returning home after an uneventful trip."

Zora chuckled. "I'll join you in your hope—even if I lack the optimism of youth to convince me such a thing is likely."

Royce came down the corridor, and Zora curtsied again and moved away. He looked at me with narrowed eyes.

"I hear we have you to thank for being dragged into the middle of nowhere on the edge of winter."

"It doesn't feel like winter to me," I said, with a level voice.

He rolled his eyes. "Oh, I know you can do no wrong now that Darius has stolen his father's throne. We all know your *special position.*"

My eyes narrowed, and I stepped forward. "What exactly is that supposed to mean, Royce?"

He held up both hands placatingly, although his expression remained both bitter and mocking.

"Nothing at all. Just that the new king-elect has gone soft where Ardann is concerned."

I gave him my coldest look. "I wouldn't recommend testing Darius. I don't think you'll find him *soft.*"

Royce looked away, not meeting my eyes, and I nodded once before continuing down the corridor myself. Royce might bluster, but his family had thrown their full support behind a king whose days were over. He had no power anymore.

After breakfast, we loaded into the same carriages we had used the day before, Isabelle even more buoyant now we were mere hours from her home.

"I have ocean views from my bedchamber," she told us, as we passed over the final miles. "You'll have to come up and see it."

A voice hailed the carriages, and our pace slowed, the carriage creaking as it came to a halt. Bryony stuck her head out the window.

"Someone is greeting Amalia," she said. "It looks like a farmer."

"We should go see what's happening." Tyron was already opening the carriage door, and I followed close behind him. If we were going to stop, I would welcome the chance to stretch my legs.

Captain Layna immediately appeared at my side, alert but not agitated in any way. I glanced up at her.

"I just thought I would take the opportunity to escape the carriage for a moment. You're not worried?"

She shook her head. "Instructor Amalia informed us this morning that we should expect a stop along the way."

Darius's voice spoke from just behind us. "We are here because of the harvest, and she thought it worth stopping to examine some fields and talk to a farmer. It was a good suggestion."

I smiled at him, relieved to see he looked lighter than he had at the Academy—less constrained. It must have been difficult for him to be tied to one remote corner of the kingdom with such events going on.

"Let's go examine some fields, then," I said. "I'm ready for a walk."

He smiled back at me, and Jareth stepped forward to join us. As soon as he appeared, Bryony also hurried over, standing defensively at my side. Tyron wandered up in her wake, although Isabelle had walked down to the next carriage to talk to Ashlyn and Frida.

"Where are we going?" Tyron asked mildly.

"To look at some fields." Bryony sounded disgusted but also determined, so I didn't bother telling her she didn't have to come.

The five of us walked forward to join Amalia who had dismounted to continue her conversation with the farmer. After much bowing to Darius, the farmer began to talk of his fields. When he gestured for us to walk between the rows of plants, Layna also dismounted, keeping close behind us on foot with Captain Vincent in tow.

The farmer showed us his crop proudly, marveling that it was possible to grow it successfully so late in the year. He pointed out several places where a plant had been uprooted, leaving a gap in the row, explaining they had been tainted by blight.

"The growers have stuck close, thank goodness," he said. "And they monitor all the fields regularly. They warn us if any plants need uprooting before they have a chance to spread their disease."

Darius frowned, his gaze running down the rows within view, picking out the occasional empty place. "Is it normal for single plants to be infected at random in such a way?"

The farmer rubbed his chin. "Well, I don't know that I would call it normal, Your Majesty. But then nothing about this year has been what you might describe as normal. Not to my reckoning."

As he finished talking, I looked up abruptly. All around me, Darius, Jareth, Amalia, Layna, and Vincent did the same. Only the two energy mages and the commonborn farmer didn't react to the massive wave of power that suddenly roared toward us from multiple directions.

CHAPTER 11

"*A*ttack!" Vincent shouted, diving toward Darius at the same moment as Layna pushed me down between the tall rows of plants.

Both of them had shielding compositions released before I even had a chance to orient myself, pressed against the dirt. The power hit their shields and demolished them, but although every muscle in my body tensed in anticipation of being hit by the attack, nothing happened.

Instead the power rushed past me and my guard, focusing its ferocity on a single target. Darius.

Vincent was already shouting for backup, a whole stack of parchments in his hand now. I could hear pounding footsteps as guards raced toward us. But even as Vincent ripped through all of the compositions in his hand, the attacking power hit Darius. I had pushed myself into a sitting position, my mouth opening to try to intervene, but I was too late.

My eyes were locked on Darius at the moment of impact. His constant personal shields held for a moment and then died, their power dissipating.

"Darius!" I screamed.

Bryony and Tyron, both also crouched in the dirt now, spun toward Darius at my shout, but nothing visible happened. The power from Vincent's released compositions swirled around us, confusing my senses for a moment until they resolved into a series of shields that formed a large bubble around us all. Other shoots of power stretched away from us, but I ignored those.

Inside the protected bubble, there was no sign of the attacking power. I gaped at Darius.

"It took down my shields," he said in response to my expression. "But it must have used all of its power to do so and had nothing left for the actual attack."

Even as he was saying the words, a second attack struck, but this one burned itself out against the multiple shields the captain had put in place. Shields that saved me from needing to reveal my abilities in front of so many alert people.

"Thank goodness Captain Vincent is so quick," I said, "or you would have been unprotected from that second wave."

The captain glanced back at us at the mention of his name.

"Get your personal shields back up, Prince Darius. Whoever these people are, they're not lacking for power."

Darius nodded, his hand diving into a pocket and retrieving a number of compositions. Soon the familiar sensation of power enclosed him again.

I forced myself to take deep breaths, trembling all over. Darius had survived. We all had. And reinforcements were coming. Already I could see the gold robes of the extra guards racing down the row of stalks toward us.

"Where even are our attackers?" Bryony asked, crouched beside me now and looking cautiously in all directions. Her view was blocked by the greenery on all sides.

"Hiding somewhere in this field," Layna said grimly.

"In my field?" The farmer sounded shaken and terrified. "I swear I know nothing of this."

"That will be easy enough to ascertain," Layna said, her voice cold, and the man's face paled.

"Don't worry," I said. "As long as you submit to their truth composition, you have no reason to be afraid."

His wide eyes focused on me. "Of course, Your Highness! I have nothing to hide."

"We don't know how long these mages have been tracking us," I said. "They may have just seized the opportunity provided by our stopping."

I sidled away from the farmer and over toward Darius, being careful not to poke my head up where it might be spotted.

"There was a lot of power in that first attack. And they're clearly after you. Did Captain Vincent bring enough guards?"

Darius looked in my direction, his face more relaxed than I was expecting. "I'm sure he did. He'll no doubt take care of them, whoever they are."

I rocked back slightly onto my heels, unsure how to respond. I could get involved myself—perhaps try to connect with one of the attackers—but Darius didn't seem to feel it necessary to prepare any of his own compositions. Perhaps I was better off avoiding any risk of exposure and leaving it to the expertise of Captain Vincent and his guards.

"We can never be sure of that," said another voice in my other ear, startling me so much I nearly lost balance and tipped out of my awkward crouch. Layna reached out a hand to steady me. "That's one thing that's drilled into us in training. You never know how much preparation and how many mages might be involved in an attack. They could have amassed a vast amount of power."

"And you think this is one of those situations?"

"No," she said promptly. "Vincent and I are well prepared. I'm just warning you that complacence is never a good idea. And I'll let Vincent know to warn his own charge of it later as well."

"Panic isn't helpful either," I pointed out, and she dipped her head in acknowledgment.

"There are four of them," Bryony said from further down the row. "I can feel them there, there, there, and there." She pointed in four different directions.

Captain Vincent broke off talking with a newly arrived guard to glance in our direction.

"You're sure of that?"

Bryony nodded. And now that she had pointed it out, I could feel them too, although faintly. They were hanging back.

"Yes, she's right," I said. "I can feel them too." I glanced at Tyron, and he nodded his support.

"I could do with an energy mage on my team," Vincent muttered. "You've more use than one." His next words were whispered to the guard beside him, and I didn't try to catch them.

The man sprinted away, bending low to remain hidden, and I soon heard the rustle of stalks as guards spread out in multiple directions.

"I've already sent some compositions to hunt them down," Vincent said. "Now they've got my guards on their trail too. They won't be at large much longer."

"What about the rest of our group?" I asked, belatedly remembering the year mates who hadn't accompanied us into the field, as well as Elsie. I hoped she wasn't too terrified by the news we were under attack.

"They'll be sheltering in the carriages," Amalia said. "Vincent left two of the guards with instructions to watch over them. Given the focus of the attack is on us, I can't imagine they'll be in any great trouble. As long as none of them decide to play the hero."

Jareth sniggered. "Somehow I can't see Royce risking himself in some sacrificial move on anyone else's behalf."

I smiled before I remembered who had spoken and turned my

face in the other direction. A loud shout, followed by the sound of a scuffle, pulled all our eyes to the north. But the crop continued to block our view.

Before long, however, a guard called that he had one of them in hand, and we heard the sound of someone being dragged in our direction. Soon similar sounds were heard from all around us, and before long, four guards stood in front of us, four men held in their firm grips. We all stood to face them.

"They're not mages," Jareth said in a tone of surprise, and my eyes flicked between the men's necks.

Sure enough, all four of them bore the marks of sealed commonborns. I frowned. That meant not all of our attackers were here. Someone—or multiple someones—had provided those compositions.

"You're sure there's no one else anywhere near?" Vincent asked, directing his question at Bryony.

She nodded. "Completely sure. Unless they've found some way to shield their energy. And if they'd managed that, you'd think they would have shielded these men as well. They certainly don't seem to have any lack of power to throw around."

Vincent grunted and nodded. "My own compositions are also showing no further sign of anyone else. But we'll track the culprits down using this lot, don't you worry."

"Have they been checked for further compositions?" Darius asked.

"Yes, Your Highness," said one of the guards who held them. "None of them had any more. They seem to have used everything they had in those two waves."

Vincent grunted again. "A poorly managed attack—but for that we can be thankful."

"Or perhaps they just weren't prepared for the strength of our defense," Darius said.

Vincent looked skeptical but didn't dispute the words. "I will interrogate them personally and determine—"

"When we arrive at the estate," Darius cut in.

Vincent cleared his throat. "I would prefer to ascertain any relevant information immediately, Your Highness. Since we haven't apprehended the mage behind this attack, there may still be a current threat."

"I will not have our entire party kept waiting in the middle of a field for who knows how long. There will be time enough to interrogate them once we arrive at our destination. It was an ineffectual attack that has drained their resources. I don't think we have anything to fear over the remaining miles."

Captain Vincent's face was easy to read. He preferred to be the one to determine the level of threat, but he also couldn't be certain the danger was great enough to override the directions of his king-elect.

"Darius, I think we should listen to Captain Vincent", Jareth said, speaking up on the captain's behalf.

Darius narrowed his eyes at his brother. "You of all people have nothing to say on this matter."

Jareth looked mutinous but didn't actually speak again. For once I found myself in agreement with Jareth. I didn't like how the compositions had specifically targeted Darius, and I preferred to know he was safe before continuing.

"We came into this area knowing the people were under significant strain, and some of them blamed me," Darius said. "Perhaps we should have expected such an outcome. They needed to lash out, and now they have done so. There is no need to inflame tensions by conducting any more of this business out in the open."

"Darius…" I turned to him, but he held up a hand to stop me.

"We should continue with our journey. I will not have my visit to the region marred in such a manner."

Everyone began to move back toward the carriages, the guards holding the prisoners bringing up the rear.

Layna walked beside me, casting occasional unhappy glances

back at the attackers. As we neared the carriages, Vincent approached, pulling her aside to consult with her in a low voice. She kept one eye on me as she replied, and apparently they determined between them that the men were too big a risk to be allowed to travel in close quarters with their royal charges.

We were loaded into our carriages, but the prisoners were bound and thrown across the backs of horses, to be brought along at a slower pace. I got one final glimpse of them before someone shut our carriage door, unease still whirling within me.

The remaining journey was enlivened by astonished conversation about the attack. Isabelle wanted us to recount everything that had happened and was as full of shock, horror, and interest as you could wish from any audience. She seemed to feel a measure of responsibility since the attack had happened so close to her family's lands.

"I'm just glad they didn't attack all of you back at the carriages as well," I said.

"Oh no," she assured me. "There was a moment or two of chaos, and Wardell wanted to go charging off heroically to help, but Zora soon squashed that idea and had us all in the carriages." She grinned. "Much to the relief of the flustered junior instructor whose name I have yet to catch."

"What do you think they're talking about in Darius's carriage right now?" Bryony asked. "Do you think they're questioning him for not letting the captain interrogate the men immediately?"

I shifted uncomfortably while Isabelle shuddered.

"I wouldn't have the courage for it," she said, "but Dellion and Royce are in there with the princes, and Dellion might."

I could smell the salt air now, even inside the carriage, and the road had started to slope slightly uphill. We didn't go much further before Isabelle exclaimed we had arrived.

Her family's manor was a ramshackle sort of single-story house, sprawling over a considerable portion of the crown of a hill. It had no courtyard or any wall at all and gave a view over the nearby beach to the west and the farmlands to the north, south, and east. I wasn't sure I had ever stayed in such a building, but I liked it immediately.

Only a single part of the house rose to a second level—a small tower of sorts on the western side of the manor. Isabelle pointed to it, explaining that her room was in the tower.

"We're a large group," I said, suddenly struck with doubt. "And now we have four prisoners in tow as well. Is it going to be terribly inconvenient for your family to accommodate us?"

"I'll admit the number of royal visitors threw my mother into some concern," Isabelle said. "But I believe she managed to make arrangements in the end." She gave me a sideways look. "I hope they'll be suitable."

"I'm sure they will," I said quickly. "I love your house already."

A smile broke across her face. "I love it, too. I'm the oldest, so I'm going to inherit it one day, and I never intend to leave." She looked at Bryony on her other side. "I believe Mother has planned for you to share my room. I hope you don't mind. It's the nicest one in the house."

"Of course I don't mind," Bryony said promptly. "In fact, I'm sure Verene is wishing she wasn't a princess so she could join us."

She smiled broadly at me, and I made a face back at her. She was right, of course, but at least this way I could have Elsie with me. I still hadn't had a chance to check on my personal servant after the attack, since the guards had pressed us into our respective carriages, eager to leave the area as quickly as possible.

I caught sight of Elsie getting out of the final carriage, and she relieved my mind somewhat by smiling and waving at me before following Zora around the side of the house. Isabelle's parents appeared, and the usual introductions were completed, along with some extra protestations of shock and dismay when

115

Captain Vincent relayed news of the attack and insisted his guards search the entire manor for any potential threats to the king-elect.

Isabelle's parents eagerly assisted in this effort, repeating over and over that they would never have dreamed of such an incident occurring. Thankfully it didn't take the guards long to complete their task, and we were all soon inside the manor. The rooms had been decorated in a charmingly hodgepodge manner, and it made for a welcoming, homelike environment that was entirely unlike either the Academy or the palace where I had grown up.

Isabelle's twin ten-year-old brothers, clearly banished from the official greetings, found us part way into the house. Their parents' efforts to suppress their energy and enthusiasm were entirely unsuccessful, although Darius took their eager interest in him in good humor.

"They're terribly embarrassing," Isabelle muttered, but I could hear the affection in her voice.

"I'm sure they miss you when you're gone at the Academy," I said, my thoughts going to Stellan and Elsie.

If my brother hadn't been left alone by Lucien and me, he likely would never have met Elsie. But the longer I knew the girl, the less I could wish for such a thing.

I wanted the chance to talk to Darius alone, but a number of local mages and landholders from the area had gathered to discuss the harvest with him, along with several representatives of both the growers and the wind workers. So instead I accompanied Isabelle as she led the rest of us down to the beach below their house.

As we stepped outside, I looked back down the road, hoping to catch a glimpse of the approaching prisoners. But there was no sign of them yet, so I continued on with the others.

The grass around the manor gave way gradually to sand, the fine grains stretching out as far as I could see in both directions.

The crash of the waves resounded through the air as the light breeze filled our nostrils with the scent of salt. I breathed in deeply as Dellion gave a soft sigh.

I glanced across at her and was surprised when she smiled back at me.

"The ocean smells like holidays to me," she said. "And childhood. I love it." She glanced regretfully at the water, her eyes following the foaming white line where it met the sand. "It's too bad the harvest didn't need them to warm the weather enough for us to go swimming."

I shivered and eyed the waves suspiciously. "It's definitely not warm enough for that."

Dellion laughed, a low chuckle that sounded more carefree than I'd ever heard from her.

"Waves are good fun as long as you afford them the respect they deserve."

Isabelle stepped up beside us, burrowing her bare feet into the silky soft sand.

"It's much calmer in summer, and it will be much wilder in full winter. It isn't safe to go swimming then—as if anyone would want to!—but it's delightful in summer." Her eyes strayed further down the beach, and she giggled. "Have you seen Tyron?"

The Sekali boy stood stock-still on the edge of the sand, staring at the water with an expression of shock. Bryony kept trying to urge him forward—going so far as to tug his arm—but he was immovable.

"It's so...big," he said at last in a voice of slight shock. "And so loud."

"Yes, yes, it's enormous, and spectacular, and vast, and all of those things," Bryony said. "But you have to dip your feet in, at least. Otherwise you can't say that you've really been to the beach."

I laughed. "You know she'll prevail eventually."

"Fancy never having seen the ocean," Dellion said, faint traces of contempt in her voice.

"Have you seen the Sekali Empire?" Isabelle asked, surprising me with her boldness.

Dellion looked down her nose at her for a moment before shrugging. "I just can't imagine it, is all."

Isabelle's shoulders relaxed slightly, and she inhaled deeply. "No, I can't really either, to be honest. I can't remember a time when the waves weren't singing me to sleep."

I looked down the long, unbroken beach before glancing back up the hill to the waiting manor house. No wonder Isabelle preferred this life to the Academy.

Dellion transferred her attention from the ocean to me. "You were there for this attack. Was it as minor as Darius claims? The guards certainly went scurrying, and Captain Vincent seems on edge now."

I hesitated, unsure what to say. "I wouldn't call it minor," I said at last. "But Darius doesn't seem overly concerned."

"Strange that," Dellion said quietly. "I would certainly be concerned if someone was trying to kill me."

Something in her face and voice convinced me that if the general was behind any of this, then she knew nothing about it. And although I agreed with her, I also felt a surge of defensiveness for Darius. After all, who knew better than me that you could become accustomed to living quite normally with the threat of assassination hanging over you?

Elsie appeared at the top of the hill, pausing in mute admiration as she took in the vista of the ocean and the sand. After a moment, however, she continued on down toward us.

"I'm to fetch you back for the evening meal," she told us when she reached our side.

"We eat early here," Isabelle explained. "The sea air seems to make everyone hungry."

"Excellent," Dellion said, turning back toward the manor. "I'm ravenous."

Isabelle moved off down the beach, calling to the other trainees. Ashlyn, Frida, Wardell, and Armand had all pulled up their robes and were wading in the foamy shallows. Squeals could be heard over the waves as they splashed each other. They looked disappointed at Isabelle's summons, but I left her to it, turning back to the hill with Elsie.

"Are you well?" I asked her.

She gave me a surprised look. "Certainly. Why would I not be? You've only been assigned a single room, but it's a large one, and Zora has already organized for a cot to be added to it for me." She glanced at me, brow furrowed. "You don't mind having me in the room with you, do you? Zora seemed to think it a better plan than you being alone."

"I don't mind," I said. "But I meant because of the attack."

"Oh, that. I was concerned for you," she said, "but it's hard to get into a panic with Zora by your side." She grinned. "The woman is unflappable."

I chuckled. "That she is. I'm glad she was there to keep everything calm."

Elsie hesitated. "Instructor Amalia said there was a lot of power in the attack, although there was no mage on the scene. Do you think it was organized by someone disgruntled by the harvest?"

I frowned and rubbed at the side of my head. "I have no idea. I thought this second harvest was going well, though."

Elsie nodded. "That's what the servants here say. Everyone seems to be in a positive mood, although news of the attack has them worried. But it sounds as if the king-elect doesn't mean to turn against everyone else in the region."

"No, indeed! And please reassure anyone who expresses concern. He has no desire to let this incident create waves or ill will in the area."

"I suppose it must be difficult to be king," Elsie said slowly, but I could hear the uncertainty in her voice.

I said nothing. She was right, of course, and we had made it safely here just as Darius predicted. But my eyes once again sought out the road where there was no sign of the arriving prisoners. I just hoped he didn't regret his decision to delay the interrogation.

CHAPTER 12

*B*y the time we finished the meal, I was growing increasingly concerned, but Darius didn't seem particularly worried. Although perhaps that was a front he was putting on for our hosts.

Toward the end of the meal, a flustered-looking guard came in and approached Captain Vincent where he stood at attention against the wall behind Darius's chair. The man whispered to him quietly while the captain's face grew more and more furious. He responded with what was clearly a stream of orders, although he spoke too quietly for any of us to hear.

Darius continued his meal unperturbed, but I could hardly sit still until we all rose from the table, and I was able to send Layna for information. She came back looking grim and tired.

"The prisoners escaped on the road back," she said.

I gaped at her. "How is that possible? They had no compositions left."

"No, but apparently they had compatriots who did. Our guards were ambushed, and the prisoners freed."

My hand flew to my throat. "The guards?"

"They survived, thankfully. Although they might wish they hadn't when they have to front up to Vincent. They didn't even manage to get a look at the person or people who ambushed them."

I shook my head. "This is a disaster."

But when I found Darius later, he seemed surprisingly calm.

"An unfortunate development, certainly," he said. "But I take encouragement from the fact they left our guards largely unharmed. Even the attack on me didn't result in any injury."

"Because of Captain Vincent's quick and effective shielding," I said hotly.

Darius shrugged. "Perhaps. Whatever their intentions, there is nothing to be done now but await any further developments. We may hope that the harvest continues to progress well, and there are no more attacks."

I stared at him. "You can't mean Captain Vincent intends to just let them escape."

"He has a couple of guards pursuing preliminary investigations and has sent for more to shore up their numbers. He says he can't take the risk of depleting the guard around me, especially now."

"You don't seem worried," I said, brow furrowing.

"Would it help?" Darius asked, his voice light. "I will leave the matter in Vincent's hands. If he cannot locate these men, then I daresay no one could. But I'm sure he will at least uncover any more immediate threats in the area."

"No," I said slowly. "I don't suppose it would help to worry. I wish I was as adept at turning the emotion off, however."

The conversation continued to haunt me as the days went past, but no further information came my way since Vincent's guards were unable to locate the escaped prisoners or anyone who had helped them. Vincent looked thunderous whenever I saw him, but at least Darius proved correct and no more attacks were forthcoming.

Since we were ostensibly on the west coast to monitor the harvest, Amalia wouldn't let us spend all our time at the beach, despite Ashlyn and Wardell's protests. Even Tyron, apparently now a convert to the charms of the ocean, complained at being dragged through fields instead of spending time on the sand.

Although I enjoyed our time by the sea, I was also fascinated by the reports given by the growers who took us on tours through the nearby fields. My mother had always been interested in healing, and often talked about the research done by mage healers to advance their discipline's skill. The work of the growers reminded me of these stories, although they researched how to create hardier and more nutritious crops instead of how to heal human bodies.

But when one of the growers explained they had chosen their most resistant strains to plant for this second harvest—making the seeds free to the farmers with the cost borne by the royal treasury—I glanced at Darius. To my surprise, his face bore no sign of the concern I felt at the news that even these hardiest of strains were still battling with the strange blight. But perhaps he already knew the information from his reports and had processed it before we arrived.

I gave in to temptation and connected with one of the growers. I didn't attempt to complete a composition using their ability, however, merely marveling at the knowledge behind the many compositions they were using to ensure this late harvest was a success.

A couple of senior wind workers took us all behind Isabelle's house to stand on the hill and observe the sea and the fields. They explained the way the different weather systems moved in across the ocean and in grave voices spoke of the dangers of meddling on such a large scale with the natural forces.

"I don't see the good of having such power if we're too afraid to use it," Royce said, his tone contemptuous.

One of the wind workers gave him a repressive look. "We can

do much with power, and we are fortunate to have access to it, but there are forces in this world of ours that are greater still. Those who try to meddle beyond their understanding will pay the price."

"Good riddance if the price is Royce," Ashlyn muttered under her breath to Frida, who giggled. It seemed Royce and his family had been truly cast out of the faction which supported the king. I supposed it was to be expected, now that they supported the wrong king.

Duke Francis had given us permission to stay with Isabelle's family for only a week. On the second to last day, our lecture with the wind workers was canceled. I expected Amalia to take over instead, but she seemed distracted, instead leaving us to our own devices.

With nothing scheduled, I finally managed to corner Darius, if not entirely alone, then only with Jareth in attendance.

"Are there concerns for our safety?" I asked him. "Something certainly seems to be going on."

He shrugged. "I'm sure we will be informed of it if we need to be."

I eyed him with increasing concern.

"Have you spoken to Captain Vincent?"

Darius shook his head. "He knows where to find me, if he has something to report."

I bit my lip, unsure how to phrase my worries about his attitude.

"You needn't bother trying to raise his anxiety, Verene," Jareth said in a light voice. "It seems the sea air has done what I didn't think possible and caused Darius to relax."

He said the words as if it were a good thing, but when I met his eyes, I saw my own concern lurking there. I didn't like finding myself once again in agreement with Jareth.

"Are you all coming down to the beach?" Bryony asked,

poking her head into the small receiving room I had dragged Darius into. "Apparently there's quite a display."

I raised my brows at that, but she was already gone. I looked toward Darius who just shrugged.

"I suppose we may as well."

"And with that ringing endorsement," Jareth said, "let's be off."

I rolled my eyes but led the way out of the manor and down the slope toward the beach. We didn't have to go far to see what Bryony meant. Behind us was nothing but blue skies and bright sun. But when I looked toward the ocean, I gasped. For a terrified moment, I thought an enormous wave was bearing down on us, blotting out the horizon and the sky.

But a moment later I realized it was a dark wall of cloud, the occasional glimpses of white swirled in with dark gray and black. A storm was coming. No wonder the wind workers were otherwise occupied.

"It's beautiful," Dellion said when we approached the knot of our year mates on the sand. She didn't seem able to tear her eyes away from the looming clouds.

Isabelle shivered. "It doesn't look beautiful to me. Not when they haven't started harvesting the crops. They're nearly ready, and the work will begin soon, but that storm looks big enough to hit most of the fields before that happens. What plants aren't pulled up by the winds will be soaked. We could lose the whole harvest again. There aren't supposed to be any storms like this yet." She looked over her shoulder to where a huddled group of mages in wind worker blue stood on the hill beside her house.

I glanced from them to Darius. Were they hoping to find a way to suppress the storm before reporting on the possible disaster to their king-elect?

A distant fork of lightning, far out to sea, flashed through the clouds. I strained to hear the following crack of thunder, but the noise was drowned out by the sound of the waves.

"It looks like it's nearly on us," I said, "but it must be a long way off still. I suppose because it's so big..." My voice trailed away as I considered Isabelle's words and what a storm that size would do to the crops.

"Is this what the wind workers were talking about?" Armand asked, his voice grave. "Is this the natural forces of winter asserting themselves over our attempts to banish them?"

Wardell let out a sound like a scoff, but his face didn't look so certain.

"It might be." Isabelle bit her lip. "I've only been studying wind working for a couple of years. We get plenty of warnings not to meddle, but not much training on how to handle purposeful interference on this scale. All I know is that while we'll be safe enough in the manor, the crops have no such protection."

I looked at Darius who was watching the clouds as if mesmerized. "Dellion is right," he said quietly. "It really is beautiful."

"And worrying," I said in an equally quiet tone. "Kallorway can't afford to lose this harvest as well. *You* can't afford for it to be lost."

He turned to me, but his eyes didn't hold their usual fire. "I'm sure the wind workers won't let that happen."

I raised an eyebrow. "You don't want to be part of their deliberations?"

He glanced up at the group on the hill. "I'm sure I would just get in their way. I'm guessing they haven't told me yet because they're hoping to present the problem once they've already worked out a solution."

I looked past Darius toward Jareth. He was outside his brother's line of sight and wasn't even attempting to mask the worry on his face. Somehow seeing his expression turned my unease into full-blown terror.

If Darius wasn't going to act on his own behalf, then I would act for him. I turned without a word and marched up the hill. Climbing onto the manor's wide back porch, I slipped around the building, stopping near the gathered wind workers.

"We always knew this was a danger," one of them was saying.

"Yes, but we thought we could hold it off longer than this," another replied. "Long enough for the harvest."

"Saying the same thing over and over isn't going to help anything," the oldest of them said gruffly. "Where's that grower?"

He looked around for the grower they had apparently summoned. For a moment there was silence, and then a green-robed figure came hurrying up from the other side of the hill. She puffed slightly as she came to a stop in the middle of the group.

"Could the harvest be started now?" one of the wind workers asked, not wasting any time on pleasantries.

The grower grimaced. "We could start, but it would affect the quality of the grains. They're not quite ripe." She glanced toward the sea. "And besides, we could never get it done in time. Not unless you can delay that storm?"

The oldest of the wind workers shook his head, looking weary. "We already are. It would have hit by now otherwise. We sent out workings as soon as we got the first hint of what was coming. And we've probed its size, too. It's enormous. That is definitely not a natural storm."

I sucked in a shocked breath, but none of the group of mages responded to his announcement other than with a few grave nods of the head. After a moment I realized he hadn't meant to claim the storm was deliberate sabotage. They had meddled with the weather, and now we were experiencing the unnatural consequences. It was exactly what they had been afraid of from the beginning.

"It's too big and too powerful for us to dissipate," one of the younger ones explained to the grower. "Even if we pool our compositions. We would need to be able to do a working far beyond any single mage."

"Unless we had the Spoken Mage," one of them muttered, and I jerked at the sound of my mother's title.

Could we send for her? Could she get here in time? I felt sure she would be willing to help in a situation like this. But even as I thought it, I frowned. My mother might be willing to come, but would Aunt Lucienne let her?

"There are two energy mage trainees here," a younger mage commented. "Could they be of enough assistance?"

But the others shook their heads.

"I already asked Instructor Amalia," one of them said. "But we need more than the energy of two or three mages for a storm this large. Trainees don't carry enough energy compositions on their person. They get pushed too hard at the Academy. They don't have the chance to build up a full arsenal—they use them for their studies as soon as they make them."

"A pity," another said with a sigh.

My mind circled back to my mother. They had no way to seek her aid, but I could communicate with her. At least, I thought the communication compositions my aunt had given me would stretch this far. I had traveled significantly further west than the Academy, so it was possible their power wasn't sufficient for such a distance. It would be a pity to waste one if it turned out to be too far for their range, but I couldn't sit by and do nothing.

But even as I considered the matter, talk among the wind workers and the single grower continued. As their words filtered through to my brain, I realized the range of my communication compositions didn't matter anyway. There wasn't time to get my mother here. Despite the best efforts of the wind workers, they couldn't hold the storm back for long enough for anyone to travel here—let alone all the way from Ardann. This storm would hit around nightfall.

For a moment I felt paralyzed by anger and frustration. The work of so many—both mages and commonborns—would be destroyed in a single night. And then it would be the poorest of the kingdom who would feel the pinch of no harvest over winter.

But as my mind swirled round and round, like the frustrated conversation of the mages, I was reminded of my earlier shock.

One of them had said it wasn't a natural storm, and I'd been convinced they meant it was deliberate sabotage. A moment later it had been clear that wasn't on their minds, but how did they know for sure?

If someone had been working against this year's harvest from the beginning, they had shown they possessed sufficient skill to avoid detection. If sabotage was involved, then it had been done in a subtle manner, the power of their workings hidden among all the normal compositions used to ensure a smooth harvest.

I let myself believe, for a moment, that it had been sabotage from the beginning. No one would have been expecting or watching for such a thing—especially not with Kallorway at peace. Sending the blight that destroyed the regular harvest would probably have been an achievable task. But then a second harvest was planted. And whatever compositions the saboteurs had attempted were failing to bear fruit. This unseasonal crop was being watched too closely.

So what could be done to ensure the harvest failed with none the wiser? This plan was simple yet devious—send the very thing the wind workers had been living in fear of for so many weeks. They had been expecting this outcome, so it didn't occur to them to question if it might be unnatural for more reason than one. And even the most experienced among them could have little experience with this sort of mass manipulation of the weather—it was exactly what they were trained to avoid.

I frowned to myself. The combined might of the wind worker faction wasn't enough to hold this storm back. How much power did the saboteurs have to have been able to create it? Maybe my theory didn't make as much sense as I thought.

I considered stepping forward and suggesting my idea to the wind workers. Maybe they had compositions they could use to confirm or disprove the idea that this storm might be deliberately created. But something made me hesitate. They had already admitted they didn't have the capacity to stop the coming storm, so what good would it do?

Another idea had wormed into my brain and now clung obstinately despite my misgivings. If this storm was fueled by a composition, then maybe a different sort of power was needed to stop it—a power I could only work in secret.

I turned to leave the shadows of the porch and nearly collided with Elsie who had apparently been lurking behind me unnoticed.

"Can they stop the storm?" she whispered.

"No." I drew a deep breath as her face fell. "But maybe... maybe there's a chance I can."

"You, Princess Verene?" Her eyes widened, and she looked quickly around before dropping her voice even lower. "With your ability?"

"There's a chance at least. And I have to try." I bit my lip. "But I need to be somewhere private, and I don't know how long it will take."

"There you are, Verene!" Bryony hurried toward us. "I couldn't work out where you'd disappeared to. They're calling us for lunch."

Elsie looked between the two of us with wide eyes.

I grimaced. "I suppose we'd better eat first or someone else might come looking for us. But I don't want to delay it longer than that. The wind workers are saying they expect the storm to reach us by nightfall."

"Delay what?" Bryony bounced slightly, her face too excited for the seriousness of the situation, as if some of the wildness of the storm had infected her.

"Princess Verene?" Elsie gulped, her uncertain gaze fixed on me.

"It's all right," I reassured her. "Bryony knows."

"Ooh, are you going to use your ability?" Bryony asked in a

lower tone. Her eyes flashed toward the ocean. "Against the storm? But that would only work if…"

She looked at me, and when I nodded, her face flashed with anger.

"You think someone did this on purpose? Who would do such a thing?"

"The same person who would send a blight to wipe out a whole harvest. The kind of person who wants Darius's rule to fail."

Bryony's face turned hard. "But how despicable! I would believe Cassius capable of such wickedness—but not of achieving such an act. Do you really think the general would—"

I shook my head. "I'm not naming names. I don't even know for sure if there is someone behind it. For now I just want to fix it, if I possibly can."

"Of course." Her bouncing energy had changed now, her body tense and poised for action. "What do you need from us?"

"We'll join the group for lunch, but then we need somewhere quiet and undisturbed. I have no idea how hard this will be, or even if I'll be able to do it."

"Of course you will," Bryony declared. "And between Elsie and me, we'll make sure no one disturbs you. I suppose your room would be the best place. Or do you need to see the ocean?"

I bit my lip. "I'm not sure. But it might help?"

"I know the perfect spot," Elsie said. "I can show you as soon as the meal is over."

I had never sat through a longer lunch, my mind absorbed in my plan while the talk on every side was of the approaching storm and the inevitable ruin to the harvest. Wardell asked Darius straight out what he meant to do, and Darius merely replied that the wind workers said there was nothing that could be done. I caught Jareth looking at me when his brother said that, the weight of his eyes adding to the pressure I already felt—as if he knew somehow I might be able to intervene and was sternly instructing me to do so.

And then the meal was over, and Elsie was leading Bryony and me to a small room. It held a table and several chairs, and its dominating feature was a window looking out over the ocean.

"It's the sewing room," Elsie explained. "Except no one has been using it the whole time we've been here. It's a nice place to come if you want to be alone and think."

I glanced at her sideways. Was it my brother she thought of in her stolen moments alone?

"What do you need from us?" Bryony asked, pulling me back into the moment. "I assume you don't need our help with the actual working. So do we just play guard duty?"

I nodded, overcome with nerves now that I could see the ominous dark clouds before me again. How complicated were the wind worker compositions holding the storm back? What if I only succeeded in disrupting them and ensuring the storm reached us even faster?

And how powerful must the composition that had created this be? Would I be capable of controlling it?

Bryony's face appeared in front of me, blocking out the view from the window.

"You can do this, Verene," she said seriously. "You're the only one who can. I believe in you." She glanced over my shoulder. "We believe in you."

I looked back to see Elsie fervently nodding.

"And what's the worst that could happen?" Elsie added, apparently sensing my concerns. "If the wind workers can't stop the storm, it doesn't matter if it hits us now or in a couple of hours. The harvest needs much more time than that."

I nodded. They were right, of course. I wouldn't be trying this if the situation wasn't so desperate. And this was the real reason I'd included them, since I didn't really need guards now that I'd found a secluded place to work.

I took a deep breath and selected one of the chairs at the table that had a clear view out the window. Did the dark wave of the cloud look closer than it had before lunch, or was that my imagination? The waves had certainly picked up, roaring as they battered against the shoreline. It was now or never.

CHAPTER 13

*R*eaching out, I felt for the compositions working around and within the storm. Now that I was paying attention to it, I could feel the power laced throughout the vast weather system. My mind skipped along the patchwork of compositions, trying to decide where to connect. With so much concentrated focus, I could broadly sense the purpose of each working I touched. I skimmed over the ones that felt as if they were attempting to restrain and slow the storm. Without connecting with them, I couldn't tell their limitations or how they sought to achieve their purpose, but I wasn't interested in them. I was looking for a different sort of composition.

Deeper inside the looming black, my questing mind felt a different kind of working. I faltered for a moment. Could this be what I was looking for? It felt nothing like I was expecting, being far too small in scope and power. I had been looking for something vast and terrifying.

And yet, nothing in the shape of this composition spoke of restraint. It felt entirely different from the others I had encountered.

There was only one way to be sure.

"Take control," I whispered.

Within the space of a breath, I was no longer sensing the composition from the outside. Connected with the power that formed it, I could instantly grasp its every movement and purpose. Understanding filled me, and I realized that this composition wasn't working alone. Just like the patchwork of power placed on the storm by the wind workers, there was a smaller, darker mosaic at its core.

Even as my mind was far distant in the middle of the storm, I could feel my hand reaching up to massage the side of my head. I had been afraid of grasping a working of vast power that might prove too much to control, but instead I was faced with a different challenge. Would a great many smaller workings be any easier to manage?

I forced my mind to focus. I would start with this one and go from there.

This composition directed the raging storm toward shore and the fields beyond, propelling it to move faster and faster. It unleashed its power slowly, ensuring it could keep up a steady pressure. Even connected to it, I couldn't tell how long it had already been at work.

"Reverse," I murmured, forcing the power to push the storm away from shore instead.

I reached for another composition, once again speaking the words to take control of it.

I had expected another identical working, but the composition that blossomed against my awareness had an entirely different purpose. It seized the winds around it and whipped them to a new level of ferocity, sending them spiraling and swirling at faster rates. For a moment, I hesitated, taken by surprise, and then it all made sense to me.

Whoever had done this—and I now had no doubt this was

sabotage at work—hadn't needed an enormous working because they hadn't created this storm from nothing. They had merely harnessed the natural forces that were already building—shaping, directing, and hurrying them toward the fields before the crops had time to ripen and be harvested.

"Calm," I said, directing the forces of this composition to stop inciting the natural winds and instead soothe them.

I was still monitoring the change in the power's purpose when I felt the first composition I had seized sputter and die, its power exhausted. Panic filled me.

If the reversed composition had achieved any effect, it wasn't noticeable. I had thought I would be wrestling with a composition as big as the storm itself and that subduing it would subdue the storm. But all of these compositions had been directing and exacerbating natural forces. They had created a momentum that now existed beyond their power, and it would take more power to reverse it than was currently being used to encourage it.

For a moment my shoulders sagged. My efforts were worthless.

But a breath later, my spine stiffened. No. I would not accept that. If the power of one composition was negligible against the growing might of the storm, then I needed to set them all working at once—or as close to it as I could manage.

I had never attempted to control a large number of workings at once, but I didn't hesitate any longer.

"Take control," I said, seizing on the next composition my mind encountered. When I instructed it to reverse, I layered over that command the direction to hold, to wait, to do nothing for a moment.

It pulled against me. Waiting wasn't part of its original instructions, and it resisted being shaped in such a way. I ignored the pressure, reaching for another composition and gasping out, "Take control."

I did the same thing with this one, and then the same again, and again. My mind stretched and burned, overloaded and pulled in so many competing directions that I half expected a scream to come tearing from my throat.

But I had no time for such things. I reached for the next composition.

My mind now resembled the storm itself, a whirling maelstrom as I struggled to hold all the threads I had gathered. The power ripped at me, struggling to pull my mind apart and break free from my hold, returning to its original shape. I held firm and reached for the next composition.

I still sat, staring out the window at the storm, but my eyes were no longer seeing, my ears no longer hearing. My consciousness was there inside the storm with my ability.

But even as I was reaching for the next working, I could tell they were running out. There weren't enough left. It wasn't going to be enough power.

"Parchment," I croaked out. "Pen."

Distantly I heard Elsie's uncertain voice. "Was that directed at us?"

"I think so," Bryony replied. "It didn't sound like something she would say to a composition."

Someone touched my hand, prying it open and wrapping my fingers around a pen. Blindly, I put the tip against the paper I hoped they had placed on the table in front of me.

I took control of the last composition, reversing it and adding it to the collection I already held. They fought, all of them, twisting against me, but I refused to give in.

I separated off a tiny part of my mind, the only bit I could spare. Reaching back into the building around me, I sought out unfamiliar energy. There. I felt a knot of different balls of energy, none of which I recognized. Hoping for the best, I gasped out, "Connect."

The awareness that flooded me, layering over the part of my

mind that was still enmeshed deep in the storm, spoke of wind and rain and sun. I breathed a sigh of relief. A wind worker.

My hand began to move on the paper, easily latching on to the composition I wanted from the wind worker's ability. Reckless in my speed, I drew as much power into it as I dared, before finishing with the words, *End binding*.

Already I was reaching for a different mage, repeating the process. I could feel when one of the girls removed my finished composition, replacing it with a fresh sheet of parchment, but my eyes remained glued, unseeing, on the window.

"Tear them," I whispered, as I finished producing another one, and moved on to the next mage. "As quick as you can."

My ears didn't hear the sounds of the ripping paper, but I felt the rush of power that bolstered the wind workers' mosaic. Their network of workings had been unknowingly fighting all this time against the workings of their enemy, but now the two forces would work together against the storm.

My mind frayed, unable to hold so much at once, and I felt the compositions I controlled slipping.

"Go!" I yelled, releasing them all at once, my fingers ripping the final parchment in front of me. The last bit of power I had managed to harness rushed out from the composition I had written to join the power I had just unleashed inside the storm itself. I would have to hope I had gathered enough to reverse the natural forces that had been unleashed.

I blinked and slumped back in the chair, my mind ringing in the strange silence and isolation. How odd it felt to have nothing to hold inside my head but my own thoughts. How empty.

The wave of disorientation passed, to be replaced with a wave of nausea.

"Bowl," I managed to croak out, and Elsie thrust one in front of me just in time.

I heaved, losing my recently consumed lunch and everything

else my stomach was holding. When the waves of nausea finally subsided, I drew a shaky breath.

Bryony's hands appeared, holding out a glass of water and a cloth. I thanked her in a weak voice, not bothering to ask how they had known to have such supplies on hand.

Once I had wiped my face, I was finally able to take in the room around me. Little had changed despite the tumult that had been raging inside me. Only the litter of fallen pieces of torn parchment gave testimony to the battle we had fought.

I counted the pieces. Five compositions. That was five experienced wind workers I had drained as low as I dared. But I had needed to do it. I had lacked either the time or capacity to explain to them what was required, and I felt no doubt that if I had been able to make the request, they would have willingly agreed to contribute their energy and expertise to the effort.

Besides, it had actually been better this way. I had been able to combine their experience, skill, and general wind working knowledge with my specific knowledge of the dynamics of this storm and the compositions that formed it. In those desperate moments when I held on to all of the attacking compositions, I had also held the knowledge and understanding that formed them in my mind. For that brief moment, and for this specific problem, I had been far more skilled and experienced than even the longest-standing member of their discipline. And I had been able to shape each of those five compositions in exactly the same way. They had been as close to a single, enormously powerful composition as was possible for anyone but my mother to achieve.

I looked for Bryony and Elsie, but they were both staring out the window. I followed their gazes. The storm still dominated the ocean skyline, but it looked less like a looming tidal wave now, and more like a regular collection of dark clouds.

"Is it moving away?" I asked. "It almost looks like it's retreating."

"It is," Bryony whispered, awe in her voice. "Even just in the last minute I've been watching it get smaller and further away."

Elsie nodded. "It's definitely moving back out to sea."

"You did it, Verene!" Bryony threw her arms around me in a congratulatory hug. "I knew you could."

I tried to focus on the joy and excitement in her voice and ignore the small layer of awe beneath. I didn't want irrepressible Bryony of all people to be in awe of me. I could almost hear my mother and Lucien in my ear, reminding me that having an extraordinary power came with as many negatives as positives. Their words had never been comforting at the time, but I understood them now.

"I drained five senior wind workers," I said, proud at the lack of guilt in my voice. I refused to feel guilty for saving the harvest —the work those mages had all been sent here to do in the first place. "I wonder what they're all going to think."

"I don't see how they could possibly think the truth," Elsie said. "Who would?"

"That's what I'm counting on. There should be no reason for anyone to connect this back to me." I yawned and stretched. "I feel exhausted."

"Your energy doesn't feel particularly drained," Bryony said, curiosity in her voice.

"I'm not surprised. My ability uses so little of my own energy. But my mind..." I shook my head, reaching up to rub both temples. "My mind feels like it was beaten, smashed, and then ground into tiny pieces. I don't think I'm going to be able to think straight until tomorrow, at least."

"I'm getting you straight to bed." Elsie rushed over to help me out of the chair. "We'll take the back way, and hopefully we won't run into anyone."

They each took one side, supporting me as I stumbled blearily through the deserted corridors. I could hear some shouts now and the occasional sound of running feet. Had someone noticed the change in the storm? I could imagine everyone was gathering outside, exclaiming at the unexpected reprieve.

I tumbled into my bed when we finally reached my assigned chamber.

"Don't wake me until it's tomorrow," I managed to mumble before my mind finally let go and fell into blackness.

CHAPTER 14

"*Y*ou missed all the excitement yesterday," Isabelle told me as our carriage passed between the ripening fields. "It was basically one big party once the wind workers confirmed the storm had changed course and was going to miss us after all."

She smiled, the expression hardly having left her face since I had encountered her at breakfast. "I'll admit, my family have always kept away from the court and its drama. My parents used to say the court was too busy protecting its own power to care about the people. But they won't be saying that again. They've already seen that Darius is going to be a different kind of king. He sent the wind workers and the growers to help us and had the crown pay for the seed. And then he came all this way himself in our hour of need. It was a true celebration, and I'm sorry you missed it. But then you must have needed the sleep if you were able to keep resting through such a hubbub."

"Yes, I think I must have needed it," I said. "Although I'm sorry not to have been there."

"With all that running up and down stairs Bryony makes you

do, I wouldn't have thought walking through some fields would exhaust you so much," Tyron said.

"It's the sea air," Bryony interjected. "Especially when you aren't used to it. The tiredness can catch you by surprise."

"I knew there had to be a downside to the ocean," Tyron said with an easy grin. "I was starting to wonder why anyone would ever live anywhere else."

"There's also the rot," Isabelle said. "The sea air is terrible for buildings—especially anything made of wood. My parents are forever having to do maintenance."

The conversation in the carriage flowed on, and I let myself take a moment to just look out the window at the waving fields of grain, still standing proud and tall. My mind couldn't entirely fathom the idea that I had been the one to achieve that. My ability had done something utterly and undeniably useful. It hadn't stolen from others, it had taken what they had to offer and refined it for the common good—even when the intentions hadn't been good at all, like in the case of the compositions driving and directing the storm.

Bryony kept up a flow of chatter, and I flashed her a grateful smile. As always, she knew when I needed the reprieve.

But my mind wasn't entirely clear. Two concerns hovered, ready to sap away my joy. Someone—some unseen enemy—had just attempted to sabotage the harvest. And they had most likely sent the original blight as well. I couldn't keep that information to myself. I had to tell Darius. But how would I explain the certainty of my information? Especially when Darius himself was the other cause of my concern.

But there was nothing I could do about either worry for now. I had woken only in time to eat and be ushered into a carriage. I would have to wait until we got back to the Academy before I could take action.

The only thing that gave me peace in the meantime was knowing that the saboteur's other efforts against this second harvest had already failed. I might not know who it was, but the compositions that had fueled that storm had all come from the same person. And for one person, they had put an enormous amount of power and effort into the attempt. It seemed unlikely they would be able to pivot and find another way to destroy the harvest in the limited time they had left.

A small clump of people caught my attention. They stood by the side of the road, cheering our passage and waving their hats in the air. I had been seeing such sights ever since we left the manor, and they lifted my heart every time. They didn't know they were cheering for my actions, but I preferred it that way.

Whatever whispers and concerns the locals had harbored about Darius's reign had been entirely reversed. If the cheering farmers were any indication, the story of the storm was already spreading fast, and the commonborn population felt the same way as Isabelle's mage parents. As far as the people were concerned, their second harvest had been on the verge of destruction at the hands of a history-making storm until the king-elect came in person to drive it back.

I wished I could ask Zora what she had made of her excursion, and what she thought of these crowds now. Was she pleased to see the people out supporting their new king, just as her own staff did back at the Academy?

I didn't resent Darius receiving the credit. It was exactly what our trip had hoped to achieve, and I was delighted for him. But I did wonder what he thought had happened. From Isabelle's chatter, it sounded like even the mages had decided that he must have been the source of the change in the storm. The consensus seemed to be that he hadn't said anything beforehand in case he didn't succeed.

So far he didn't seem to have disputed the claims, which was a relief. But what was he thinking underneath?

This time we stopped for the night when the road we were on joined the main road that would take us to the Academy. The prosperous inn had rooms to accommodate us all and served a satisfying and hearty meal.

After the evening meal, I stepped outside to breathe some night air after the stuffiness of the carriage all day. I had thought I would need to wait until we were back in our own suites to talk to Darius, but I spotted a familiar dark shape standing gazing up at the stars a short distance from the inn.

Captain Vincent and another gold-robed mage guard stood nearby, politely positioned just out of earshot, although Darius stood alone. More importantly, for once, there was no sign of Jareth. I walked slowly over toward him, Layna joining Vincent and the other guard when she saw where I was headed.

"Darius," I said quietly, and he jerked as if he had been lost in thought and unaware of my approach.

But when he turned to me, it was with a smile, and the stars seemed to have transferred to his eyes, making it hard to remember they had ever appeared black.

"Verene." The warmth of his voice made me shiver. "It's a beautiful night, isn't it?"

The look in his eyes said the night wasn't the only thing he found beautiful, and I could feel my flush against the cool of the air.

"I'm pleased to find you in such good spirits," I said cautiously.

"I feel as if I was on the edge of a precipice and have been granted an unexpected reprieve." He shook his head. "I can admit to you, at least, that I have no idea why that storm moved away. But I am beyond grateful that it did." He gave a soft sigh. "I just wish I had the satisfaction of having found a solution myself, instead of just claiming the credit for one that materialized on its own."

His lips twisted slightly. "I'll admit I don't like taking credit for something I didn't do."

"But the harvest failure was never your fault, and yet they blamed you for it," I said quickly. "There can be no harm in letting them think this success can be laid at your door as well." The last thing I wanted was for him to be gripped by a qualm of conscience and start telling people it hadn't been him who turned the storm around.

He sighed. "I will do whatever I have to do for the good of the people, of course. And this is an easier ask than many."

I bit my lip, his words a stark reminder of why I was so hesitant to tell him the truth of what had happened. And my usual concerns were only exacerbated by his strange behavior on the trip.

"Why didn't you care?" I blurted out, desperate for a reasonable explanation. "Back in the farmlands. Why didn't you care about the storm, or about the escape of those men who attacked you?"

He frowned. "Of course I cared. That's why I pushed the duke to allow the trip in the first place."

"But you haven't been talking or acting like you cared."

"I..." He seemed at a loss for words, something I had rarely seen before. "I care, but that doesn't mean I have ultimate power over the weather. There are some things beyond me—even with the throne at my back."

I stared up at him, willing him to say something more substantial, to somehow explain the unexplainable. But instead of speaking any more about the harvest or the attack or the storm, he took a step toward me.

The moonlight clearly revealed his face, his eyes focused on me with a brightness that made my heart beat faster.

"I care about lots of things, Verene," he said. "But there's nothing I care about as much as you."

"Nothing?" I asked, my voice faltering, my heart desperate to believe his words were true.

"Nothing," he repeated, having closed the gap between us entirely.

One of his arms slid around my waist, and his gaze dropped

to my lips. "I think it must be this moonlight," he whispered, "but somehow I can't quite remember why I have to keep away from you. Can you?"

Yes, my mind screamed. *Because I'm not being open with you. Because you just said you would do anything for the good of your people. Because you've been behaving strangely for the past week.*

But nothing came out of my mouth. Instead my heart beat faster, my whole body on fire from his firm grip around my middle and the hand he plunged into my hair.

My mind might be trying to remember all that stood between us, but my heart wanted this moment too much to protest. He lowered his head slowly toward mine, and I swayed toward him.

A loud throat clearing made him freeze. I swallowed, suddenly remembering we had an audience of three guards. I tingled all over from the anticipation of his kiss, but the reminder of the outside world gave me just enough willpower to pull away.

Darius straightened, the old mask back on his face, the light gone from his eyes. It seemed he, too, had remembered why he normally kept his distance.

For a last moment he looked down into my face. "I'm sorry," he whispered, the words sounding torn from him. "I don't know what I was thinking."

He turned and strode back toward the inn, Vincent and the second guard following him, their faces carefully impassive. I watched them go, caught in the moonlight, too gripped by emotion to move.

A rustling sound from the darkness broke the moment, and I turned to see what had made the sound. Jareth stepped out of a shadow in the opposite direction to the inn.

Had he been watching us the whole time? I gave him my full glare, but his expression didn't change as he sauntered forward to join me. He stood beside me, his face turned in the same direction as mine had just been, watching the spot where Darius had disappeared back into the inn.

"He's not been himself lately, has he?" Jareth commented, as if he and I were friends who frequently met in such a manner to chat.

I wanted to turn and walk away without a word, but something made me hesitate. I glanced sideways at him.

"What exactly are you saying?" I asked.

He spread his arms wide. "I'm not even sure. And perhaps it doesn't matter, after all. The harvest was saved, and Darius seems mostly back to his old self." He looked down at me with a knowing smile. "With the small aberration of tonight. But even the strongest-willed among us have some weaknesses—and there's nothing like moonlight for bringing them to the fore."

I gave a small growl of disgust, rolling my eyes, but still not managing to make myself walk away.

"But you're concerned."

"Do you think I should be?" he countered. His eyes strayed back to the inn. "Maybe it's because I remember what it's like to not be able to explain your own thought processes. To think two things at the same time."

My eyes widened, and I turned slightly toward him. "You think whatever has been going on with Darius has something to do with what happened to you?"

He shrugged. "Maybe. Maybe not." He looked down at me. "But tell me, do you notice anything different about me?"

He stepped back slightly, moving his arms away from his body, his palms out, as if putting himself on display. I frowned at him while he watched me with a patient, half-amused expression.

It took me a moment, but when I realized what he meant, I gasped, drawing back instinctively. Layna, still poised and watchful, just out of earshot, stiffened, her weight shifting as if she was preparing to intervene.

"There's no power around you," I whispered. "You're not bound. Darius let you free?"

"As far as I can tell," Jareth said, his voice still light, "Darius forgot to renew my bonds the first night we arrived at the coast. I expect he'll remember at some point—likely when we return to the familiar environment of the Academy. I'm sure you can understand why I haven't reminded him."

"But...that means..."

"That I've been free for a week? Yes, it does. I wanted to point it out to you on what is likely my last night of freedom. I know you're still skeptical of me, and I understand why, of course. But if it counts for anything, I've made no attempt to escape, or to do anything I'm forbidden to do, such as compose. You can sense energy. Has mine been low at all this week?"

"Not that I've noticed," I said cautiously.

He nodded. "Then you know I haven't been crafting some new arsenal of compositions. In fact, I haven't composed a single one since we've spent the week on theory lessons and observing the harvest."

"Are you looking for congratulations?" I asked, wondering why I didn't feel more nervous about standing next to an unbound Jareth.

"No," he said quietly, and this time his voice sounded wistful. "I just want answers. And all I'm getting is more questions."

"Yes." I sighed. "Me too."

CHAPTER 15

$\mathscr{B}$ack at the Academy, I kept a lookout for Jareth in the dining hall. Sure enough, the bubble of power that usually surrounded him had returned. Now that he had called my attention to it, I didn't understand how I could have missed the change before. I certainly didn't understand how Darius could have—and for a whole week.

The renewal of Jareth's bindings suggested he was right, and Darius was returning to his old self, but the thought brought me little comfort. Sometime during our absence, the law enforcement instructor had returned, so I no longer shared discipline class with the two princes.

Instead, Bryony, Tyron, and I had returned to our interrupted time with the Royal Guard trainees. My success over the storm had given me increased confidence with all aspects of my ability, and I had no hesitation in connecting with the abilities of the others in the class. I rarely actually worked compositions, however. I couldn't help but feel I'd had enough practice at that to last me awhile, and I didn't want to court any additional risks.

Every day I considered knocking on the door behind the tapestry and telling Darius the truth about the storm. But Jareth's words ate at my mind. What if Darius wasn't back to his normal self yet? And what had made him change in the first place?

I hated my doubt, and I hated even more the idea that Jareth might have stoked my concerns for exactly this purpose. But no matter how many times I told myself I couldn't trust anything Jareth said, I didn't quite believe it. Because I had seen the change in Darius with my own eyes. And everything about Jareth had seemed sincere, in a way it hadn't done in our first two years.

And only at night, when I lay alone in the dark and remembered Darius's arm around me, did I acknowledge the other reason for avoiding knocking on the door. In our sitting rooms, we wouldn't have an audience, and we had shown we were both at risk of giving in to our emotions. Deep inside, I knew that we both had a tipping point that would push us too far, and I was afraid of finding out where it might be. I was still concerned by the consequences of giving in to our feelings.

When I received word that after a week of straight sunshine the harvest had begun, I breathed a little easier. And with every day that brought a report of another successful day's work, the burden lifted further. I hadn't made a terrible error in judgment by not talking to Darius—whoever the saboteur was, the storm had been their final big effort.

Of course, I still needed to find a way to tell Darius about their existence so he could uncover their identity, but it did remove some of the time pressure. Perhaps I could find a way to let him know without telling him everything?

Captain Vincent visited the Royal Guard class as a guest lecturer, and to my surprise Captain Layna appeared as well.

"Don't worry," she told me afterward, "I'm not revealing any Ardannian secrets. But I like to earn my keep here if I can."

She seemed at home with the class, and I gathered it wasn't her first time working with them. Seeing her in that setting reminded me of Elsie's words. I had found ways to practice without the captain's help, but she had the potential to be a valuable ally.

Would she stay in Kallorway with you, if you decide to stay? a voice whispered in the back of my mind, but I shut it down. Darius hadn't asked me to stay—quite the opposite—and I couldn't even consider doing so unless I was ready to tell him the truth.

To my further surprise, Dellion often sat beside me in class while Bryony was otherwise occupied. Did she feel alone now that Jareth had moved to law enforcement, and she was the only third year?

"Why did you choose the Royal Guard?" I asked her one day, emboldened by her once again choosing to join me at my double desk. "Do you have a particular role in mind?"

She tossed her head. "Of course. I am going to be the personal guard of the queen with a whole team under me. I'm the perfect choice because I won't have to hang back at royal functions, I can shadow her at all times."

I blinked. "Doesn't your aunt already have a personal guard?"

Dellion rolled her eyes. "Not my aunt. I mean the new queen."

"What new queen?" I asked, thrown off guard.

She gave an exasperated sigh. "Darius's future wife, of course. In a year and a half, he'll be crowned king. I'm sure given the state of the kingdom, he won't delay too long in marrying. That should give me sufficient time to work my way up the ranks of the Guard—at least far enough that no one will protest when I'm selected for such a senior role."

"And if the new queen already has another guard in mind?" I asked, unable to resist the question, although I hid the smile that went with it. Dellion's confidence wasn't exactly a surprise.

"Another choice?" She sounded like she hadn't even considered the possibility. "You do remember I'm Darius's cousin, don't you? And I dare anyone to call my competence into question."

But then her brow furrowed slightly as she looked at the front of the class where the instructor was welcoming Layna. When she glanced back at me, the uncertainty had disappeared, however.

"Darius will need to produce an heir, and I would be equally willing to take charge of the young crown prince or princess." She gave a satisfied nod as if she had solved the sudden potential wrinkle in her future plans. "That might even be more ideal since it will give me additional time to train within the discipline before being called on to take up the position."

She gave me a warm smile as if I had been the one to make the suggestion. "You know, you're not half as bad as I thought you were going to be, Princess. I was horrified when I heard you would be attending our Academy, and then when they asked me to show you around..." She shook her head. "But I think I'm starting to understand what my cousins see in you."

"Cousins?" I asked, emphasizing the plural.

"Certainly." She sounded mildly surprised at my question. "Darius may blow hot and cold, but I can assure you he's only ever been ice for anyone else before you. And Jareth has never had anything but good things to say about you. Especially this year. Anyone would think you had come to the Academy to save Kallorway." She rolled her eyes.

Layna started speaking, and Dellion transferred her attention to the front of the room. But I still stared at her profile. Jareth praised me when I wasn't around?

I felt as if I should be burning at the brazen effrontery of it—praising me while sneaking around in the night to kill me. But I couldn't see what he had to gain by such an approach. I had been the only one to ever suspect him, and he hadn't been making the compliments to my face. Unless he hoped reports of his words would get back to me and allay my suspicions?

I couldn't focus on Layna's words, my thoughts swept up once again in worrying about Jareth and Darius and what exactly had been going on at this Academy for the last two and a half years.

When Layna assigned the trainees a composition to attempt, I tried to force myself away from the unhelpful swirl of thoughts. I should take the opportunity to practice as well. I looked around the class, trying to remember who I hadn't connected with yet. Bryony caught my eye, smiling and waving, and her attention made Tyron look back as well, also smiling in my direction when he saw me at the back of the class.

I realized that in all this time, I had never connected with him. My focus had always been on the trainees studying the different disciplines we visited. But it would be interesting to connect with an energy mage other than Bryony. Would his ability feel different because I knew hers so well, or would it still be familiar?

"Connect," I whispered as quietly as I could, to keep the word from reaching Dellion beside me.

As always, the effect was instantaneous. My awareness flooded and filled as I plunged into his energy and with it, his ability. I had been expecting the sensation to feel similar to connecting with Bryony, except with a Tyron flavor. And I had been ready to examine the differences.

Instead I was taken utterly off guard. For a moment I couldn't make sense of anything despite the ordered nature of everything that unfolded inside my senses. Then it all snapped into startling clarity.

Before I could think further, or even move, Tyron stirred. He looked up from the composition he was writing—a standard working to give energy, the details of which I could clearly sense through our connection—and frowned. He looked first toward the front of the room where Layna conversed quietly with the instructor, and then his eyes began to sweep the class. Almost as if something had disturbed him from his working, and he was looking for the source. Almost as if he could feel my intrusion.

I gave a soft gasp and choked out, "End."

Dellion, who had just written the final binding words of her composition, gave me an odd look. I desperately forced a smile and leaned toward her, looking down at her page.

"I'm afraid I wasn't listening too closely to the instructions. What's the composition Layna has you working on?"

I fixed my eyes on Dellion as she explained in a bored voice. Calling up every ounce of my royal training, I kept my face neutral and my gaze on her as Tyron's eyes passed over us. Was he pausing? I forced myself not to look.

I kept up the conversation with Dellion, speaking half at random for another couple of minutes before I dared look back toward the front of the class. Tyron had returned to his composition.

Just looking at the back of his head, I could feel my pulse pounding in my ears. And it took all of my attention not to let my breathing hitch or speed up. Dellion frowned at me, so I forced myself to take several long, steadying breaths. I needed to be calmer before the end of class, or I might risk giving myself away.

My mind kept wanting to chase after the information I had just learned, but I ruthlessly forced the thoughts away. Calm, I needed to be calm. I ran through several breathing exercises which helped. The bell made me jump, but I resisted the urge to leap to my feet and run toward Bryony, instead taking my usual time to gather my various belongings.

I let Bryony and Tyron move out the door ahead of me while I walked out beside Dellion, calling a farewell to Layna as I went. In the corridor, our class mingled with the rest of the trainees streaming from the other discipline classes, and it took me a moment to locate Bryony in the mass.

When I found her, she was only a short way ahead, still with Tyron. Even as I caught sight of her, she looked back and spotted me as well, waving for me to join them. I wished Dellion farewell in a steady voice that made me proud and hurried forward to join Bryony.

I slipped my arm through my friend's and began to tug her

gently away.

"I have to show you something in my suite," I told her. "I promise you'll like it more than the evening meal, even."

Bryony narrowed her eyes suspiciously. "Does that mean you're going to make me miss the meal?"

I wanted to scream with impatience, but I forced myself to chuckle instead.

"Would I dare do such a thing?" I glanced across at Tyron and smiled, suppressing my thoughts and fears, and letting myself fall into the ease of more than two years of close association. "Sorry, Tyron, girl business."

He grinned. "Isn't it always? Don't worry about me. Wardell will no doubt relish the opportunity to try to convince me to join him and Armand on one of their rest day hikes."

Bryony giggled. "Now you're just trying to make us feel sorry for you."

"But who wouldn't want to go hiking with Wardell and Armand?" he said, with a straight face.

A trickle of sweat ran down my back. I couldn't keep this mask in place much longer. I needed space to process what I had just learned.

I gave Bryony's arm another tug, and we both waved goodbye to Tyron, breaking off from the main group of trainees to ascend the stairs. Only a small trickle of white robes joined us in heading for their rooms rather than going directly to the dining hall, and all of them continued up past the floor that held the royal suites. Once we turned off the stairs and started down the corridor to my room, we were alone.

I started to tremble, letting out a gasping breath. Bryony frowned.

"Whatever is going on, Verene? Is something wrong?"

"Yes," I managed to gasp out. "Something is very, very wrong."

Her eyes widened, and now she was the one tugging me along.

"Don't say anything more," she ordered me. "Wait until we're in your suite."

I nodded, which was about all I could manage as my body swayed slightly. Wearing a mask had never taken such a toll on me before. But I had never been in a situation like this before, either.

Bryony bustled me through the door of my suite, closing it firmly behind us. The noise brought Elsie out from behind her screens, and Bryony paused, her eyes on the younger girl.

"Verene?" she asked. "Do you want—"

I shook my head, having regained some control of myself. "No, Elsie can stay. She's one of us now."

A smile broke across Elsie's face at my words, but the expression quickly disappeared as she took in my state and Bryony's concerned eyes.

"Has something happened?" she asked.

"Verene is about to tell us," Bryony said. "From my perspective, we just had a perfectly ordinary discipline class, but Verene seems about to faint."

I straightened, putting strength into my voice. "I'm not about to faint. The shock just got to me for a moment." I drew a deep breath. "I know what happened to Jareth and Darius. I know who's behind everything."

"What?" Bryony cried. "You just discovered that in discipline class?"

"You mean other than King Cassius?" Elsie asked. "We already know he's been behind some of it at least."

"Yes. I mean, no." I began to pace up and down. "Do we?"

Bryony's eyes looked as if they were going to bulge out of her head. "Stop that dreadful pacing and sit down and tell us what's going on. *Who's behind it?*"

I stopped as requested but couldn't bring myself to sit.

"It's Tyron. It's quite possibly all been Tyron from the beginning."

CHAPTER 16

"*T*yron?" Bryony gaped at me. "Impossible! How could it be? How could he manage such a thing? *And...and why?* He's not even from Kallorway."

"Yes," I said grimly. "That might be the most disturbing part. Because I can't tell you why. I can't read minds, remember. Only abilities."

"But we know Tyron's ability," Bryony said. "It's giving energy, remember. What could that possibly tell you?"

"Like I said, I can't read minds," I said, purposely taking my time to answer her question because I suspected once she heard the answer, she wouldn't hear anything said afterward. "But I can tell more than just someone's ability. I can tell quite a lot about their knowledge and experience, and even personality—as long as it relates to their ability. Connecting with the energy of a first year feels vastly different from connecting with the energy of a skilled and experienced mage. And the one time I connected with a discipline head it was...overwhelming."

"Yes, yes, but what does that have to do with Tyron?" Bryony asked. "He's a third year energy mage trainee, so you must be familiar with how his ability works and how developed it is." She gave me a significant look.

"Exactly," I said. "That's exactly what I was expecting—familiar. But it wasn't like that at all. To start with, there's no way he's eighteen like us."

"What do you mean?" Bryony asked. "He has to be eighteen. Or nineteen at the most if he's already had his birthday." She frowned. "Can you remember when it is?"

"I've never connected with Darius," I said. "But if I did, I can guarantee you that his ability wouldn't feel like any of the other third years. He not only has incredible natural strength, but he had two years of intensive private training when his start at the Academy was delayed. We know he's nothing like a third year since he can do complicated, advanced investigative compositions."

"So you're saying Tyron's ability seemed too advanced? Like Darius rather than us." Bryony grimaced. "Are you sure I'm not just a poor comparison?"

Normally I would have expected her to say something defiant and humorous, calling me to account for throwing her ability into question. The fact she wasn't doing so told me just how concerned she was by the conversation.

I shook my head. "I do think it's partially because I'm so used to your ability that it was so obvious," I said. "But not because you're weak. You're skilled and have studied hard, so I think you're a good benchmark for a third year, and Tyron's ability was...something else again. The precision and control, and the depth of the skill...I didn't have time to delve into anything in detail, but the overwhelming impression was clear. I would say he has to be at least as old as Darius. And he didn't just start late, he must have received high-level training in the time between turning sixteen and coming to the Academy."

"But how is that possible?" Elsie asked. "I thought all mages had to start at the Academy the year after they turn sixteen?"

"They do," I agreed, "in Ardann and Kallorway. But Tyron isn't from either southern kingdom. He didn't grow up here. When he said he was sixteen, who could deny it? Why would anyone even think to do so?" I looked at Bryony. "Does it work differently in the Empire?"

She frowned. "We have different schools, not just a single Academy, but the basic principle is the same. We start at sixteen. But his family lives among one of the sealed clans. I know less about how they manage things. Perhaps he was under no pressure to go away to a school since he couldn't join theirs?"

"Maybe," I said. "But I also doubt everything he's ever told us. What do we really know about him for sure? He's the only trainee here who no one knew before his arrival."

"Do you think if you connected with him again, you could learn more?" Elsie asked. "You said you didn't have much time."

I shook my head frantically. "On no account can I connect with Tyron again."

"What do you mean?" Bryony stared at me. "Why do you sound scared?"

"Because I am scared. Bree…he sensed me connecting with him and accessing his ability."

Bryony's mouth fell open. "But that's impossible! You've connected with a discipline head, and he didn't feel you. I don't care how much early training Tyron might have received, he can't be more skilled than a discipline head."

"But you're forgetting that Duke Gilbert is a power mage, and Tyron is an energy mage," I said. "You're the only energy mage I've ever connected with. And you're also the only one who's ever given any indication you felt me using your ability to do a composition. For all we know, with more training, you might become sensitive enough to feel me just connect with you. I use energy to make the connection, after all."

"You mean Tyron knows about your ability?" Elsie asked, with a gasp.

I shook my head. "I don't see how he could. He must know from Jareth that I can take control of energy workings and direct the energy toward myself. But that's all Jareth ever knew I could do—at the time, I hadn't worked out what was really going on, so my attempts at training weren't very successful. I certainly couldn't connect with another mage like I did with Tyron today."

"But you're saying Tyron was the one helping Jareth with all those attacks," Bryony said slowly. "Does that mean he was one of the attackers the night they dragged you out of the entranceway and were testing your ability?"

I winced. "I suppose he probably was. So he might at least guess I can control power workings as well. But that might actually work to my advantage in this case since it obscures the fact that my ability is essentially an energy one. And even I never guessed about the second aspect of my ability, not even when I had spent considerable time training with my first one. He can't know I'm able to connect with other mages. And he seemed to be looking around the room as if searching for the culprit, so I don't think he could tell it was me. He can't even know it was someone in the room."

Elsie relaxed, some of the tension leaving her face. "That's a relief at least."

"So what ability does he have?" Bryony asked, finally pushing the question I had been avoiding answering while we discussed the other aspects of the situation. "Because that's the bit I don't understand. We know he gives energy. I've seen him work the compositions a hundred times."

I nodded. "Yes, he can give energy. But as we know, on rare occasions, energy mages can have two abilities." I caught myself just before I added, *Like you*, remembering Elsie was in the room.

"Like me," I said instead.

Elsie's mouth fell open. "Tyron has a second ability? I thought that was just because you're the daughter of the Spoken Mage."

I shrugged, meeting Bryony's eyes. When she chose not to speak and reveal her secret, I hurried on.

"I suppose he must have inherited something different from his mother and his father. However it came about, the second ability was there, clear as anything, when I connected with his energy. The ability to give energy was on top, since he was using it at the time, but the one beneath was just as clearly defined and controlled. He's obviously just as adept at using it, maybe more so. I can't remember all the details of how it works, of course—that faded as soon as I severed the connection. But the basic concept is branded on my brain."

I paused, and Bryony leaned forward, her eyes both eager and fearful.

"Well? Don't keep us in suspense."

"I'm starting to suspect that for every energy mage ability, there's a second, more serious, more permanent version. A much rarer version. In my case I have both—my initial ability to take control of someone else's working and my second one which allows me to take control of their entire ability."

I paused and met Bryony's eyes again. They reflected understanding of what I wouldn't say aloud. Bryony's secret ability was the extension of the ability to give energy—a permanent sacrifice that could also perform miraculous healings.

"We know that some energy mages can take energy," I continued. "But if they don't drain the person completely—causing the stolen energy to dissipate—then after a short time, it pulls free to return to its proper owner."

Elsie stared at me. "I've heard of mages who can take energy, but I never knew it would spring back like that."

"We learned about it in first year," I said.

"And then we got to experience it for ourselves in second," Bryony added dryly. "It's a highly unpleasant experience." She turned to me. "But are you saying Tyron has some permanent version of that? He can permanently steal a portion of someone's energy?"

I shook my head. "It wasn't as simple as that. He can steal some of a person's energy and use it to bind them to him. That portion of energy is connected to both of them, and he can use it to...control them in a way. Or at least partially. He can implant thoughts and impel them to act on them."

Bryony sat down on the closest chair with a thump. "Tyron can control people's thoughts." She looked up at me with panic in her eyes. "Is he controlling my thoughts? I don't think I'm thinking anything new or different or—"

I held up a hand to cut off her flow of words. "I don't think Tyron is controlling you. Or ever has. Why would he? And I can promise you that you've always been extremely Bree-like."

She smiled weakly, but there was real relief in her eyes.

"It's not an easy thing to do, and it's certainly not an easy thing to maintain. He has to renew it constantly if he wants to keep it going because there's still that pull for the energy to break free from him and return completely to its rightful owner."

"And so he has to focus his attention on the people of greatest influence," Elsie said slowly.

"And we just so happen to have two such people here at the Academy," Bryony finished for her. "Two people who—unlike me —have been acting entirely unlike themselves."

"Unlike themselves...So you believe Jareth finally? You think his true self would never attack Darius?"

Bryony shrugged. "I have to believe it in the face of this. It explains everything. Darius's insistence Jareth would never betray him. Jareth's own apparent horror at what he did, and his inability to explain it afterward. He claimed all his normal thoughts were intact in his mind, but he had a second, false opinion operating alongside them, propelling him to act. His description of what he experienced is a perfect match for how you just described Tyron's power."

I nodded slowly. "And seeing Darius bleeding out broke the barrier Tyron had put in place to keep the second—false—thought process separate in Jareth's mind. He started to question it and everything it had driven him to do. And then Darius took him immediately out of Tyron's reach. By the time they came back to the Academy, Jareth was shielded. Tyron couldn't renew his control."

"So then he turned to controlling Darius," Bryony said.

"But why not control Darius from the beginning?" Elsie asked, doubt in her voice. "He was the crown prince. Surely he would be the more valuable target."

"Because Darius is always shielded," I said, realizing neither Bryony nor Elsie would be able to sense that for themselves. "Always. I bet Tyron was bitterly disappointed when he realized he couldn't reach him. So he settled on the second best option."

"So you don't think Darius's strange behavior on our trip was Tyron then?" Bryony asked, sounding almost disappointed.

I frowned, trying to work out how it could all fit together.

"The attack!" I cried, making both of the others jump. "The attack that focused all its power on Darius. We thought the first wave was just too weak to do more than burn out his shields, and that Vincent's quick actions protected him from the second wave. But what if they always knew the guards would have shields up, and the second wave was just to hide the true purpose of the first wave? What if the intention of the attack was always just to remove his shields? And then Tyron was there, ready in the brief moment that the king-elect was unprotected. Only Bryony and I would have even had a chance of feeling his energy composition at work. I certainly didn't feel anything in the chaos of the moment. I assume you didn't either, Bree?"

She shook her head. "No, but I was hardly on the lookout for such a thing."

"It was immediately after that when he started to act strangely," I said. "It was like he became detached, like he didn't care about the things he would usually care about. But the impact eventually faded—presumably because with his shields back up, Tyron couldn't renew his control. But if we hadn't intervened with the storm ourselves, his disconnection would have been long enough to allow the harvest to be destroyed without any leadership from Darius."

I felt a spike of pain as I thought of my interaction with Darius outside the inn. Jareth had seemed to think it a residual effect from what had ailed his brother the week before, and maybe he was right. For a brief moment, Darius had no longer cared about the duties of the crown and the state of his kingdom —the things keeping us separated. But he likely wouldn't forget again.

"But how did Tyron of all people organize sealed common-borns to launch an attack with power compositions?" Bryony asked. "He's here with us at the Academy all the time. And even with this extra ability, he's not a power mage." She looked at me sharply. "Is he?"

I shook my head. "I don't think there's ever been someone who was both a power mage and an energy mage. Even my mother, who can take energy, does it using power compositions."

"And now you can do power compositions using energy," Elsie said. "You're like her opposite."

I nodded, not quite meeting her eyes. She was right—I was like my mother's opposite—and that was what had always scared me. I refused to be used as a weapon against her strength.

"He's been using other people and power compositions in his attacks from the beginning," I said, steering the conversation back to Tyron. "At first he would have been able to get composi- tions and resources from Jareth—as well as from the king through Jareth's manipulation of his father. I don't know how he's getting them now, though."

"I suppose he must be controlling someone else now he's lost Jareth," Bryony said. "Or maybe multiple other people in short bursts like with Darius."

"That is a very unsettling thought." Elsie shivered.

"There's an even worse one, though." I finally sat down, collapsing onto one of the sofas. "Connecting with his ability told me nothing about his motives. He appears to be doing everything he can to undermine Kallorway—upsetting the balance between the factions, stoking conflict with Ardann, undermining their new ruler, destroying the harvest. But *why* is he doing any of it?"

"And who is he doing it for?" Bryony gulped. "You don't think he's working for the Sekali Emperor, do you?"

I bit my lip. "It's hard not to think of it as a possibility."

"Surely the most likely possibility." Elsie looked almost gray. "Even if he's twenty, like you say, he didn't just wake up one morning and decide to use his rare power to take down a neighboring kingdom. Why would he?"

Her eyes suddenly widened. "His ability is rare, isn't it?" She looked around as if she suddenly suspected herself of being surrounded by unseen, mind-tampering renegades.

"It must be," Bryony said. "I've never heard a hint of such a thing in the energy mage community. If it was common, there would be whispers of it, at least."

"I'm amazed there aren't, to be honest," Elsie said. "There are always whispers."

Neither Bryony nor I said anything, but our eyes met. We both knew it was possible to have an ability and keep it secret— as long as the circle of knowledge was small enough.

"Speaking of rumors," I said, "I did hear about some trouble in the north as far back as the start of last year. But not necessarily from the emperor himself."

"Some rebel faction?" Bryony asked, sounding relieved. I could understand her desire to believe it was rebels given she was from the Empire herself.

"Honestly, I have no idea. It seems I should have put more time into studying the politics of the Empire. Does it sound likely to you, Bree?"

She frowned. "It's always possible. But the Empire isn't riven with factions like the Kallorwegian court. The clans are always maneuvering for increased honor and position, but their loyalty to the Empire itself always seemed absolute. At least to me. It's the bedrock of their entire culture. How else would they manage to keep two entire mage clans dedicated to the task of sealing all the commonborns? They don't think individualistically in the way southerners do."

"All for the good of the Empire," Elsie murmured, and Bryony nodded.

"But they did start to have trouble when my parents were young," I pointed out. "With the whole sealing issue and the growth in their population."

"Yes, but our arrival solved that problem," Bryony said. "My father told me about it. I've never heard any such talk in my own lifetime."

"Which leads us back to the emperor," Elsie said with a gulp.

"Maybe." I frowned. "Now is definitely not the moment to be rushing to conclusions. Especially not against the most powerful of all the monarchs."

"What *are* we going to do?" Bryony met my eyes. "I don't see how you can avoid telling Darius this time."

"No." I winced. "I can't possibly keep this from him. It changes everything." And there was no way I could tell him without revealing my own ability. I had no plausible way of having so much information otherwise.

"And Queen Lucienne?" Elsie asked.

I bit my lip. My aunt was both more and less complicated than Darius.

"At least I won't have to tell her how I found out," I said. "She'll assume the information comes from Darius. But I'd rather not go to her at all until I have a little more information."

Bryony's eyebrows rose. "What sort of information?"

I took a deep breath. "I don't want to tell her until I've told Darius—and I daren't bring it up with him until I'm sure Tyron no longer has any tie to his energy."

CHAPTER 17

*L*ater that night, as I lay in bed, I asked myself if I was just delaying the moment when I would have to tell Darius the truth. But even in the midnight hours, the plan seemed sensible. I couldn't take even the smallest risk that Darius might be tricked into revealing my ability and our knowledge to Tyron.

The idea of connecting with Tyron again scared me, but Bryony had pointed out there was another way. I could do something I'd never done and connect with Darius instead.

"We were the only two who seemed to dislike and mistrust Jareth," she pointed out. "I've been thinking about it this whole time, and I think we both sensed there was something wrong with his energy. We sensed it was divided and at war with itself. I think if you'd known about your full abilities then and had connected with him, you would have been able to see the connection with Tyron."

It was certainly more appealing to connect with Darius than with Tyron again. But I still felt a reluctance—one I hadn't admitted to Bryony or Elsie. I had spent so long putting up walls between myself and Darius, and now I was going to connect my

169

energy to his. I didn't know what I would find when I did so, or how the strange intimacy of it might affect my emotional barriers, and the thought scared me a little. But not enough to make me turn to Tyron instead. Especially not when underlying the fear was a second layer of curiosity. What would Darius's ability feel and look and taste like? Would it be instantly recognizable as him in the way Bryony's was as her?

I woke in the morning far from rested but knowing I couldn't put off what needed to be done. All through combat class, I cast surreptitious glances at Darius. Somehow I didn't like the idea of trying to connect with him in a class, surrounded by other people.

When Darius began to duel with Mitchell, Jareth once again appeared in front of me. I had been about to start a bout with Bryony, but she raised a single eyebrow and left to partner with Dellion instead. We had both already completed one match each with Tyron, using all of our acting ability to appear normal.

"Have you been thinking about what I said?" he asked, fighting just as weakly and defensively as he had in our previous bout.

There were so many possible answers to that. I didn't know where to start.

He chuckled. "You're not quite as subtle as you might wish to be. I've seen you watching Darius all morning."

I flushed and launched a sharp attack he only just managed to counter.

"Yes, I have been," I said, panting slightly as I drove him across the yard. "I'm just steeling myself to do something unpleasant."

"Something unpleasant involving Darius? Now that is truly intriguing. As a good brother—if you can suspend disbelief long enough to imagine me one—should I be joining you or taking up his defense?"

My blade flashed under his guard, the tip coming to rest gently against his neck.

"Yield," he said calmly.

I kept my sword in place and leaned forward, dropping my voice low.

"Actually, I find no suspension of disbelief is necessary. I suddenly feel inclined to believe you've always been a most loyal brother."

His eyes widened, the playful smile dropping from his face. I recognized it now as the jovial mask Darius had described—as much a true part of Jareth as Darius's reserve was of him, although it wasn't the whole of him. I had thought it the cause of my unease with the younger prince, but I could see now that feeling had come from a different source.

Jareth leaned forward as well, ignoring the way his movement made my blade prick his skin. A drop of blood welled up, and I snatched my arm back.

"You believe me?" Jareth's words were quiet but intense, his eyes piercing me.

"More than that," I said. "I know what happened to you."

Jareth stepped forward again, looming over me, although I could tell it wasn't his intent. He hardly even seemed aware of what he was doing.

"You have answers? How do you have answers?"

"That is a long story. And not one for the combat yard."

"When then?" His eyes conveyed his desperation. No one could be more emotionally invested in my discovery—the reason I had felt compelled to speak when I hadn't intended to do so.

"This evening," I said, the solution to a different question flashing through my mind. "In my sitting room again."

He nodded, although I could see that waiting through the day would be torturous for him.

"Jareth." Darius's dangerous voice made us both start. He stood beside us, his hands clenched into fists, and an ugly look on his face.

Jareth pulled back, seeming to realize for the first time how close we were standing. He looked up at his brother, such a storm of emotions on his face that Darius's own expression faltered and faded. For a moment Jareth looked as if he might speak, but instead he just shook his head and headed for the far side of the yard.

I looked up at Darius, drinking in the sight of him at such close range.

"He wasn't threatening me," I said softly, aware of how it might have looked.

"I hope he wouldn't dare," Darius said, steel in his voice. "He knows I would kill him if he laid a finger on you."

I chuckled. "I'm afraid I'm the one who drew blood today." I held up my blade where a single, glistening drop of red still clung to the tip.

Darius raised an eyebrow and actually smiled, the expression warming me right down to my toes.

"You have my congratulations. But don't let Mitchell see that, or we'll all get a lecture on the limits of a practice bout."

I pulled out a cloth and wiped my sword while Darius's eyes strayed toward his brother.

"He knows he's supposed to stay away from you," he said. "But how can I blame him when I know just how tempting you are?"

"Jareth doesn't think about me that way," I said. "It's just that…" I let my voice trail off, unsure how to finish the sentence.

A flame leaped into Darius's eyes, but a moment later he tamped it down.

"Does he not? It seems impossible to think that could be true." A wave of pain crossed his face, briefly flickering until that, too, was suppressed. "But then he's done many things I once thought impossible."

It took everything in me not to speak in Jareth's defense—not for Jareth's sake but for Darius. I kept my mouth tightly closed, however. The time would come soon enough. I just needed a few more hours.

~

As always, Tyron sat with us for lunch and the evening meal, and we spent the afternoon together in both composition and discipline classes. I had thought it would be an impossible torture and had worried about Bryony's acting skills. She was an impulsive, true-hearted person, not given to deceit or hiding her emotions. But to my surprise, we both managed better than I expected.

"To be honest," she told me when we finally escaped to my suite after the evening meal, "it was easier than I was expecting. When I saw him at breakfast, it was horrifying, and I kept weighing every tiny thing he said or did, trying to see some hidden meaning. His green eyes made me think of poison, and I kept wondering what had bleached away all the color from his white-blond hair. It was ridiculous. But then as the day wore on, it was all just so..." She wrinkled her nose, apparently searching for the right word.

"Normal?" I supplied, and she nodded.

"Yes, so normal! It doesn't seem possible it could be, and yet we've sat in that dining hall and through those classes with him so many times."

"Two and a half years of it," I said. "So maybe it isn't so surprising after all. Although it's hard to believe we were friends with him for so long and never suspected a thing."

"From what you said, Princess, he trained for this," Elsie said, appearing from behind her screens. "For years—maybe for his whole life. You can't blame yourselves."

"He was protected by the same thing you are, Verene," Bryony added. "No one guesses the impossible, however well it fits the situation."

"Did you connect with Darius?" Elsie asked. "Does Tyron still have his hooks in him?"

"Not yet. I didn't want to do it in the middle of class." My reluctance might seem strange to them, but I didn't try to explain it. "I'm going to try tonight. The only problem is that two people now live through there." I pointed at the tapestry. "I'm not sure I'll be able to recognize Darius just from his energy—at least not until I've connected with him the first time."

"Is that why you asked Jareth to come?" Bryony asked.

I had expected her to be displeased with my invitation to the younger prince, but she seemed to have let go of her outrage toward him just as whole-heartedly as she had initially embraced it. In fact, she had said it seemed like he, more than anyone, had a right to know the truth.

I shrugged. "It was part of the reason. And part of it was just that I couldn't help myself. I couldn't leave him in misery now that we know none of it was his fault."

Elsie left, and I settled in with Bryony for a long wait. The last time Jareth snuck into my sitting room for a secret meeting, I had been forced to wait for hours until Darius fell asleep. So I was surprised to hear the door slide open not much later. The tapestry ruffled and bunched, the door pushing it aside as Jareth appeared in the opening.

"Sorry for not knocking," he said. "But Darius retreated to his bedchamber early, and I decided not to wait for him to fall asleep."

The impatience was visible in every part of his body, from the expression in his eyes to the tension in his muscles. I couldn't blame him for his desperation for answers, though, so I told him to come in. I couldn't even imagine how I'd feel if someone had hijacked my mind and sent me to kill Stellan or Bryony. Let alone if I had no idea what—or who—had driven me to it.

"Well?" His eyes latched on to me. "Don't keep me in suspense any longer. You promised you had answers."

"It was Tyron," Bryony blurted out, and his head swung around to her, the look on his face one of utter shock and confusion.

"Tyron? As in, energy mage, Tyron? As in, your friend, Tyron?"

"He's not our friend anymore," Bryony said indignantly. She eyed Jareth. "I hope you don't expect me to apologize for disbelieving you before. I don't see how I could have believed you."

Jareth shook his head, clearly trying and failing to process Bryony's announcement. "Of course not. But I don't understand. How could it be Tyron? And why?"

"We don't know why," Bryony said. "We still have to work that out. As for how…" She looked over at me.

"I no longer doubt your loyalty to Darius," I said directly to Jareth. "Which is why I want you to think hard about the answer to my next question. If I tell you this secret—a secret about me—can you promise to leave it to me to tell Darius? In my own time."

He met my eyes. "But you do intend to tell him?"

"I have to."

He thought for a moment before giving a swift nod. "Then you have my promise. I'm finished breaking trust—with anyone."

"In that case, I need to start with my own abilities, and from there I can explain what we've learned about Tyron."

Jareth's eyes lit up. "I knew there was more to your ability than you were sharing!"

"I'm fairly sure Darius knows it too," I murmured.

Jareth gave a wry look. "Yes, but he's far too noble—and too in love—to press you for the truth." He glanced between us both with a roguish smile. "It annoyed me no end, I'll admit."

I flushed at his mention of love, but I couldn't let myself think about Darius now. I had a story to tell.

When I reached the end of it, Jareth looked part shocked, part awed, and part angry. He paced up and down the sitting room, occasionally knocking against the furniture in his abstraction.

"But this is…this is incredible. I don't mean I don't believe you. I do, of course—you have no reason to lie—but this…" He shook his head. "What you've told me is a very grave threat to Kallorway—from multiple angles."

I bit my lip. Did he include me in that assessment?

But nothing in his manner suggested he found me either more frightening or more appealing than before. His whole focus seemed to be on Tyron.

"I agree with Bryony," he said. "This can't possibly be coming just from Tyron, there must be others behind him."

"I think that was Elsie actually," Bryony murmured, but he waved her words away.

"It doesn't matter who said it, they were right." He paused in his pacing to frown at Bryony. "Wait, who's Elsie?"

"Elsie is my personal servant," I said. "She's both loyal to me and highly intelligent. And she knows everything. She had some business this evening in the servants' hall or she would have been here."

He arched an eyebrow but didn't protest.

"I agree with you about the threat," I continued. "But don't lose all hope. We've been facing this threat without even knowing what it was for two and a half years—and we've been defeating it."

Jareth ran a hand through his hair. "Yes, I suppose that's something. Although Tyron does seem to be escalating."

I nodded. "I think it's because of his failures. He's been trying to destabilize Kallorway, but instead he just pushed Darius to take control sooner. If he doesn't achieve something significant soon, then Kallorway will be in a much stronger, more stable place than when he arrived. And that seems to be the opposite of his intention."

"I don't like that he got his claws into Darius," Jareth said in a grim voice. "How can we be sure he's completely free now?"

"That's why Verene hasn't told him yet," Bryony said. "She's going to test him."

"Test?" Jareth looked at me with a curious light in his eyes. "Tyron or Darius?"

"Darius is my preference," I said. "He shouldn't be able to sense my presence any more than other power mages can."

"So what are you waiting for?" Jareth asked.

"For you to be here so she could isolate Darius's energy." Bryony frowned slightly, her eyes losing focus. "I can sense him now—in his bedchamber, I think." She looked at me. "Can you feel his energy?"

I concentrated, reaching in the direction of the rooms next door.

"Yes, I've got him," I said.

"Do we need to do anything?" Jareth asked.

"Just stay quiet and let her work," Bryony whispered. "Not that this should be difficult for her. Not like stopping that storm."

"Stopping the storm? She did that? On her own?"

I had skimmed past that part of the story, not wanting to focus on my ability.

"Shhh!" said Bryony. "I'll tell you about that later."

They both fell silent, and I no longer had an excuse to delay.

"Connect," I said, but nothing happened.

I opened my eyes.

"Well?" Bryony asked. "Did you sense anything strange?"

"I didn't connect," I said. "That's never happened before."

"Tyron couldn't have somehow blocked your ability, could he?" Bryony asked, horrified.

I shook my head. "Tyron doesn't even know about this part of my ability. And how would he block it if he did? This is something else. Let me try again."

"Connect," I said, more forcefully. My energy reached out, and this time I noticed when it hit a barrier.

"It's his shield." I looked at Jareth in astonishment. "He must have a very broad shield if it's keeping me out."

"Darius is nothing if not thorough with such matters," Jareth said. "Especially since becoming king-elect. And we can all be grateful he is, as it turns out."

I nodded. "This might be the same one of his shields that's keeping Tyron out. It's certainly aimed at energy—and it's more than just the normal shield for preventing someone draining your energy."

"I guess that's the end of that, then," Jareth said. "You'll have to find a way to connect with Tyron."

"What? Oh, no, the shield shouldn't be a problem. Just give me a second." I sat back in the chair, concentrating on the distant layer of compositions I could feel around Darius. "I just have to find the right one."

It required some concentration, especially given the distance, but I managed to identify the one aimed at energy.

"Take control," I said.

I took a moment to feel the shape and purpose of the power that now answered to me. Darius had protected himself well, making it broad enough in scope to block any number of energy compositions, except for the ones we used in class to receive energy.

The power hummed and pulsed, but I took another minute to think. I didn't want to remove it or leave Darius without sufficient protection—especially with Tyron on the loose. I just needed to tweak it slightly, so it would allow my energy through.

"Let me in," I said, shaping the power in the way I wanted, leaving just the smallest and most individual weakness.

With such a small change, the power made no effort to resist me, settling into its new form easily. I disconnected.

"There," I said. "I shouldn't have any trouble now. Connecting with him will only take a moment."

"Verene." Jareth's voice distracted me from making the connection immediately. When I looked at him, he was staring at me with his mouth ajar.

"What?" I asked, uncomfortable. "I didn't take it down or anything. He's still protected from Tyron."

"Yes, but you could have," Jareth said. "When you told me about your full abilities, I didn't quite realize...is there anything or anyone that could stop you?"

"I...I don't know," I admitted.

"Even your mother can be blocked—as long as someone can find a way to prevent her drawing more energy," he said. "But no shield at all could stop you when you can just take control of the shield itself."

"I suppose not." I shifted on the sofa, wishing he would stop looking at me like that.

"And you could take a mage's ability and use it to compose a composition so powerful they were drained of all energy," he said. "And there's nothing they could do to stop you."

"Verene would never do that," Bryony snapped.

Jareth shook himself. "No, of course you wouldn't. My apologies." He paused. "But you could."

Bryony didn't argue this time. "Yes, there are a great many things Verene *could* do. Which is why I've struggled to get her to train with her ability at all. And why she isn't telling people about it."

"What will Ardann do, when they find out my true power?" I kept my eyes focused on Jareth, watching for the moment understanding crossed his face. "What will Kallorway do?" I didn't need to name names. Jareth of all people understood who stood behind those kingdoms and the dynamic that so frightened me.

For a long moment we just looked at each other. Then he spoke.

"Our grandfather came to Darius over the summer."

I sat up straight. Darius hadn't mentioned anything about talking to General Haddon. Had they made peace?

"He was full of advice on various matters," Jareth continued. "Darius and I both understood he was testing the waters. He wanted to see if Darius intended to accept his guidance and look to him during his reign."

"And?" Bryony asked. "How did Darius answer him?"

"My grandfather is old and wily. He has done what should have been impossible and held on to his power for decades in the teeth of the king's hatred. In truth, while we have not always been allies, he has much wisdom to offer. Darius made it clear that while he would not be dictated to, he was eager to draw on Grandfather's knowledge and experience."

"So there is peace between them?" I asked eagerly. Why hadn't Darius told me this at the start of the year?

"I would say, rather, that there is the potential for peace between them. There is one matter on which Grandfather stood firm, but Darius would not budge. Grandfather ended by calling him a young fool, too inexperienced for his position, and storming out."

"That doesn't sound like an accurate description of Darius," Bryony said. "What was the issue?"

"Grandfather says that Darius must marry as soon as he graduates and is crowned. He must marry to strengthen his position and to ensure heirs." Jareth grinned. "Apparently I'm not sufficient for the stability of the kingdom."

Bryony snorted, but my throat had closed over at the mention of Darius and marriage in the same sentence. Jareth's eyes found mine.

"Grandfather said Darius must marry someone who strengthens his position on the throne in the eyes of both factions. He said that meant he couldn't afford to marry a Kallorwegian from either side. The answer, Grandfather said, was a simple one, and he clearly expected no resistance from Darius."

Jareth's eyes pinned me to my seat. "He wants Darius to marry you, Verene. A marriage of alliance with both Ardann and the Spoken Mage directly. He says if Darius is determined to unite the southern kingdoms, then he must ensure we do not remain in a position of weakness and supplication before Ardann."

"General Haddon wants Darius to marry me?" The words came out more squeaky than I had intended, so I cleared my throat and tried again. "Even though he thinks I have no power?"

"He seems to feel that the bloodline of the Spoken Mage has shown itself to be unpredictable, and that we can still expect your children to have a chance of inheriting your parents' strength."

"He's not wrong," Bryony said, her eyes on me. "From a political point of view—at least on the Kallorwegian side—you would be an excellent choice for Darius. Far more excellent than the general even realizes."

"On the Kallorwegian side," I managed to choke out. "Ardann may not feel so warmly about the idea once they know the truth." I took a steadying breath. "And that doesn't matter anyway." My eyes found Jareth. "You said Darius refused. That he wouldn't be budged."

I forced all emotion from my face and voice, unwilling to let him see the devastation that had hit me at his words. How much rejection from Darius could I take? Why did my heart hang on to every flash of warmth in his eyes or near kiss in the moonlight in the face of such sustained dismissal?

"Darius didn't care that marrying you would be the best thing for his reign and the best thing for Kallorway," Jareth said, his face and voice not giving an inch as he drove his point home. "He didn't care that agreeing would have sealed his reconciliation with our grandfather and ensured both Kallorwegian factions fell into line behind him. All he cared about was that it wouldn't be the best thing for you. That's why Grandfather called him a fool. That's why he accused him of not being ready to rule."

I looked away, unable to meet his eyes as I drew a shaky breath. Now I knew why Darius hadn't told me of the meeting with General Haddon.

"You're worried that your power makes you a tool in royal

eyes," Jareth said. "But I think you underestimate Darius's love for you."

Bryony grasped Jareth's arm, pulling him slightly away.

"I think she needs a minute," she whispered.

I wanted to deny it, to tell them both I wasn't affected, but I couldn't form the words. I drew in one shuddering breath and then another. Darius had told me his rejection was an expression of love, but my heart had been at war with itself because it didn't feel like love. But if Jareth spoke the truth...

Surreptitiously I wiped at my eyes. It wasn't Jareth I needed to speak to but Darius. And before I could do that, I needed to be sure his mind was his own.

"Connect," I whispered.

CHAPTER 18

*I*mmediately I was plunged inside Darius's energy. The first thing that struck me was the order. The depth of his strength and knowledge didn't overwhelm me as it had once done with Duke Gilbert, but I could sense even more raw power.

I knew it was partially because I was prepared and so much more experienced myself, but it was more than that. Darius's power was focused in a way I rarely saw in other mages' abilities. He had expertise in compositions across a broad range of disciplines, and his understanding of the details and nuances allowed for a degree of control that was rare for someone so young. Darius was exactly what the royal families of all three nations worked so hard to produce—a fitting heir in power, strength, and control.

The order and control inside his ability had an added benefit. I could easily feel his energy—its capacity greater than most I had encountered. It took me only a few moments to ascertain that no part of his energy was missing or controlled. No connection snaked away from him except the one that connected us right now. I didn't know exactly what Tyron's influence would feel like, but I felt confident there was no taint of it here.

"End," I whispered, disconnecting.

Bryony caught the word, looking back at me from the conversation she was conducting in a lowered voice with Jareth.

"You did it?" she asked. "You connected with Darius?"

I nodded. "He feels clear to me. I don't think there's any lingering influence from Tyron remaining."

Jareth's shoulders sagged, and for the first time I saw how much the possibility had been weighing on him.

"Thank goodness." He looked at me. "So you'll tell him everything now?"

I hesitated.

"Yes, of course she will," Bryony said. "But not tonight. You said he was already in his bedchamber. She'll tell him tomorrow."

"Tell me what tomorrow?" asked a dark voice, and we all started, whirling to face the now open door in the tapestry.

"Darius!" Jareth sounded delighted to see his brother, but Darius didn't look equally pleased.

His eyes—almost completely black now—traveled between us all.

"How cozy," he said. "When I failed to find Jareth in my sitting room, I knew he could not have gone past the guards in the hall. But it seemed impossible to think he would dare intrude on you here, Verene. But then it looks as if it's no intrusion at all."

"Darius," I said, my voice weak with shock at being so suddenly confronted with him.

"I'll confess," Darius continued. "I don't quite know what to make of the new intimacy you seem to have with my traitorous brother."

"He's not a traitor," Bryony said, in a matter-of-fact tone. "You were right all along."

Darius raised a single eyebrow. "The events of last year would suggest otherwise."

"This is not our story to tell," Jareth said, gripping Bryony by the arm and leading her over to the door behind the tapestry. He glanced back at us just before he shut them both into Darius's sitting room. "I look forward to talking to you once you hear the truth, brother."

For a moment Darius stared at the closed door with knitted brows, as if he was considering ordering his brother back within his sight. But then he turned to look at me.

"You have something to tell me? As you can see, I am not asleep."

I stood, sat back down, and then stood again. I wasn't usually so weak and indecisive, but I had thought I would have more time to process what Jareth had told me before having to face Darius. My emotions were in turmoil, and the sight of his tall frame and sandy hair—tumbled about in a way I rarely saw in public—made it hard to think.

"I have discovered that Jareth is innocent," I blurted out.

There was no change in Darius's cold expression. "And so you formed an immediate affection for him? Perhaps it is not surprising. He has always had an easy address."

"What?" I stared at him, my eyes lingering on the way his muscles bunched, although he didn't move, and his fingers curled into fists. Sudden understanding dawned on me. Darius was jealous. Jealous of his younger, more carefree brother who had always been charming and friendly, with an easy smile.

It was unreasoning and foolish—but what about our relationship had ever been reasonable or wise? His own grandfather had upbraided him for allowing his feelings to overrule his otherwise ordered mind. It only confirmed Jareth's words. Darius loved me beyond even his life's work of gaining the throne. It seemed hard to believe and too wonderful to be real.

A sudden smile broke across my face, taking Darius by surprise. I sank back onto the sofa, more slowly this time.

"Oh, sit down," I said. "And I'll tell you everything. But it's a long story. I've only just finished telling it to Jareth because I felt he of all people had a right to know the truth of what happened to him."

Stiffly, Darius sat, casting a single glance back at the still-closed door.

"And if it needs to be said," I whispered, "Jareth means nothing to me compared to you. You should know that. But he is your brother, and he has suffered greatly."

Darius's eyes swung to me. "*He* has suffered?"

"And you have as well, of course. We have all suffered. But it was none of it at Jareth's hands. But let me start at the beginning. It will all make more sense that way."

Darius fixed his eyes on me, and I wondered why they had seemed so black earlier. They were burning now.

I thought of how he had appeared when we first met and everything I had learned of him since. I had never met someone with such selfless dedication. He had sacrificed everything for his people, and for some reason, he had now chosen to turn all that intense care on me. If I could trust anyone with my secrets, it was Darius. And it shouldn't have taken Jareth to make me realize that.

"I haven't told you the truth about my abilities," I said. "I was afraid. It seems foolish now, but that's the truth of it."

His face immediately softened. "I suspected it, of course. But I'm the last one to push you to tell me your secrets."

I shook my head. "No, I don't want secrets between us. Not anymore."

I should have realized all along what his circumspection meant. If he cared more about Kallorway than me, he would have manipulated me to tell him about my ability. It seemed so obvious now.

So I told him everything. I told him how I could take control of compositions—both energy ones and power ones—and how I could connect with another mage and use their ability as if it was my own.

He listened in astonishment—clearly his imaginings had not encompassed the reality.

I explained exactly how I had defeated Jareth and saved his life at the end of second year, and what I had done to stop the storm on the western coast.

"That was you?" His astonishment at this piece of the story was great enough to make him break his silence and interrupt. "You did it on your own? When the best of the wind working discipline couldn't manage to—"

"No." I cut him off. "I can do nothing on my own. I used to dislike and even fear my ability precisely because I can do nothing at all on my own. All those years when I dreamed of having power, I never wanted to steal it from others. But I've learned to see it differently. I didn't stop that storm on my own— I did it with the assistance of five of the strongest and most experienced of Kallorway's wind workers. It was a team effort. They couldn't do it without me, but I couldn't do it without them, either." I paused. "My dream is that one day I will be able to use my ability openly, with the permission of those whose power I borrow."

"It's a good dream," Darius said, his soft words almost like a caress. "You're incredible, Verene. I never imagined."

For a moment, our eyes met, and I forgot about my story and all the revelations still to come. But then he seemed to catch himself, shaking his head, his eyes hardening.

"It's myself I can't understand," he said. "The more time passes, the more incomprehensible it seems that I didn't try harder to stop that storm myself. I didn't even try at all, in fact. At the very least I could have contributed my strength to the wind workers' efforts."

"You can't blame yourself," I said. "That wasn't you. I thought it was strange at the time. I think everyone did. Jareth certainly did—he told me so more than once."

"Jareth? He is hardly one to talk of strange behavior," Darius said, bitterness in his voice.

"Actually," I said, "Jareth is best placed of us all to know. He recognized in you what he had lived through himself."

Darius's eyes flew to mine. "What do you mean?"

"I mean that someone was controlling Jareth for all of our first two years here. And that person briefly managed to control you during that one week of our trip. They must have arranged the attack in the field and been ready in that brief moment you were unshielded."

"But you and Bryony said there was no one else in that field but the four sealed commonborns," he said. "Are you saying the mastermind was there all along?"

I nodded. "He was right beside us, cowering inside our shields, utterly unsuspected. The person behind everything that has happened at this Academy since we started is Tyron."

Darius shot to his feet. "Tyron?"

Unlike Jareth he didn't let forth a stream of protestations and exclamations. But he did stride up and down the room, his movements feverish and his eyes bright. When he turned back to me, his face blazed with anger.

"How? How is this possible?"

I told him everything I had told the others—about how I had connected with Tyron's power completely unsuspecting, what I had found about his true ability, and the sense it had made of everything else.

"He influenced Jareth, and Jareth in turn influenced your father. It was Tyron's expert manipulation that tipped your father away from sense and caution and overset the balance in Kallorway. But he wasn't expecting or intending for you to be ready to step into the gap. He wasn't expecting my growing ability, and the way it enabled me to escape all of his attacks. He came for me himself, sent an assassin via the king, sent Jareth—even attacked with a group of his own—but he didn't manage to kill either of us."

"And so he tried a new avenue," Darius said, his voice as hard and black as obsidian. "He turned his attention to the harvest."

"I believe so. I still don't understand how he achieved it, though. He had lost Jareth at that point, and his efforts must have taken both skill and huge amounts of power."

"So did he get the compositions here, by controlling Kallorwegians? Or did he bring that power with him from wherever he was holed up over the summer?" Darius asked.

I spread my arms wide. "That I can't tell from the momentary glimpse I had into his ability. As I'm always reminding Bryony, even if I had managed more time connected to Tyron, I can't read minds. I don't know why he did any of it or what broader plot might be at play."

"And there must be a broader plot." Darius didn't say it as a question. "Someone is attempting to destroy my kingdom."

"I'm afraid it does look that way," I said sadly. "I just hope it's not the emperor. If the great Sekali Empire intends to turn against the southern kingdoms, then I fear we are only at the very beginning of the suffering to come."

Darius shook his head. "I cannot believe it was the emperor. Why would he do such a thing? The Sekalis have never shown any expansionist tendencies. And even with their recent population growth, the great expanses of their northern foothills are still only lightly settled."

"I hope you're right."

"We must find out who Tyron is controlling now, if anyone," he said. "And then we must find out who is directing Tyron."

I nodded, wincing. "You're right, of course. I'll need to connect with him again. It's the only way to find out more information about how he's using his ability now that Jareth is no longer available."

Instantly a shadow fell over Darius's face. "But you said he could feel your presence."

Reluctantly I nodded. "I'm not saying I want to do it. Just that it's the only way."

"There must be some other—"

"What? Who? You can have him arrested, of course. You're the king-elect. And I'm sure he'll tell the truth under your investigation compositions—as long as he doesn't die before you manage to get answers. He wouldn't be the first." I gave him a significant look. "We're dealing with new abilities we don't understand. It's a real risk. And it would destroy everything. We would have nowhere left to turn for answers."

He froze, his face still, although I knew his mind must be racing. "You're right," he whispered.

"But we have me," I said. "I can connect with him and find out how he's using his abilities. We can gather as much information as we can. And then, when the time comes for the investigation, I can be there, ready to intervene and seize control of any composition that comes for him."

Darius looked at me, the shadow still in his eyes. He obviously didn't like my plan at all. But neither could he put forward any other suggestions.

"It's a lot to take in," I said, wanting to turn his mind to other things. "But for all the bad news, don't forget the good. You were right about your brother all along. He has always been loyal to you. It's not his fault that Tyron infiltrated his mind. Any more than it's your fault he infiltrated yours."

Utter silence fell in the room as Darius stopped even his breaths. Was he thinking of his brother and all that had happened between them in the last year?

But when he turned his face to me, his expression was tortured rather than joyful.

"I let him inside my mind," he whispered. "And then I stood aside and let that storm nearly wreak havoc on my kingdom.

Without you, my people would have suffered, and I did nothing. *Nothing.*"

My eyes widened. I hadn't meant to remind him of his inaction in the farmlands.

"But you couldn't help it," I said. "He was controlling you. None of us knew such a thing was possible. None of us knew to guard against it."

"I should have been strong enough," he whispered. "I thought nothing could turn me away from my purpose or my people, but I just…stopped caring. How could I do that?"

I stood up, my voice fierce. "Because they weren't your thoughts. You can't blame yourself for what happened, Darius."

"But they were my actions," he said. "And it's my mind. How can I blame anyone else?"

I gave a strangled sound of frustration. "So you don't mean to forgive Jareth, then? You still hold him responsible for attacking us? Because I don't."

"No, of course I don't hold him responsible now I know," Darius said quickly. "Tyron was twisting his energy for two whole years. But he worked a single composition on me, and I turned my back on my kingdom."

I stepped up to him and tried to place my hands on his arms. He pulled away sharply.

"No," he said. "I have been right all this time. If I could betray Kallorway, I could betray you. I can't be trusted—least of all around you."

"Darius, that's not true." I stepped forward firmly and wrapped my hands around his upper arms. His muscles jumped beneath my touch. "We're going to defeat Tyron—together—and nothing like this will be able to happen again. *You* never betrayed anyone, and you never would. It's against your nature."

"And yet I just did," he whispered, before tearing himself away from me and rushing from the room.

~

I tossed and turned for most of the night. I had finally told Darius the truth and removed the barrier that stood between us, and yet still he had turned away from me. I wished there was a way for me to show him what I had seen inside Tyron's ability—to help him understand that what happened wasn't his fault.

So many times I had thought about the lack of trust that stood between us, but I had always believed we needed honesty and trust toward each other to have any hope of a relationship. But now it seemed the trust Darius lacked was toward himself.

Part of me hoped he just needed a night to process the news, and I couldn't help myself looking for him at breakfast with hope in my heart. But one look at his face dashed it. The fear that had haunted him the night before, haunted him still.

Jareth, his eyes sad, said to give his brother time. He explained that Darius had always held himself to a higher standard than anyone else, and his own disloyalty hit him harder than anyone else's could.

I didn't know exactly what had been said between them in Darius's suite after Darius returned to his own rooms, but they appeared to have fully reconciled.

At combat class the next morning, Jareth no longer had the complicated binding he had been wearing all year. Instead, he was surrounded by only a single bubble—one I recognized easily after having taken control of an identical working the evening before.

He smiled broadly when he saw us, bounding over, sword in hand.

"All is forgiven, I see," I said with a similar grin.

He nodded. "Darius says I should offer the two of you the same protection shield from Tyron if you want it."

I shook my head, lowering my voice. "I intend to go on as I always have—and trust in all of you to tell me if I start behaving strangely. I don't want to alert Tyron to the fact something has changed."

Bryony hesitated for a moment but then said she would do as I did. Only after Jareth moved back toward Darius did she turn to me with a confused look.

"Tyron can't feel power. How would he know if we suddenly started wearing shields?"

I shrugged. "Who knows what compositions he may have been given or acquired. But in all honesty, I'm just as concerned about Darius. I won't have him draining himself to provide me with a shield when I've been here two and a half years without needing one."

"If you're brave enough, I am too," Bryony declared.

"Do feel free to accept the offer," I said, "I didn't mean to constrain you. But I doubt Tyron would target us anyway."

Bryony frowned. "You can't think he's truly our friend."

"Of course not. But he knows we're both energy mages like him. Remember the way he could sense my working? If his senses are that finely tuned, then he knows it's possible for ours to be as well. He probably won't want to risk discovery by targeting us."

"What do you mean?" Bryony spoke in the same undertone I had. "I thought you said he couldn't know for sure you're an energy mage since he doesn't know how your ability works, and he saw you interfere with a power composition as well as an energy one."

"From what Jareth has said, he was definitely the second attacker that night when they dragged me out of the entrance hall. Just like we suspected. That incident alone tells us he knows I'm hiding *something*. And I don't think he made it this far undiscovered without exercising a great deal of caution. Thank goodness that even if he suspects it was me he felt in class, he doesn't know that means I now know about his second ability."

"If you're convinced he's too cautious to try to control us, that's good enough for me," Bryony said. "I don't need a shield."

"*What* did they feed Jareth for breakfast?" Dellion drawled, strolling up to us. "He can't stand still. But at least it seems to have brought the fire back to his fighting."

I followed her gaze to where Jareth and Darius had started a bout. She was right. Jareth was fighting like his old self.

"Excellent," Bryony said with delight. "More proper opponents."

"For once I find myself in agreement with you," Dellion said.

We all stood in silence for a moment, watching the princes' swords flashing before Dellion spoke again.

"You know, the more time that passes, the more I think Grandfather is right about you, Verene," she said. "But wrong about Darius. There's no point trying to bridle him. He's not near so amenable as my aunt. Grandfather would do better giving his advice and leaving Darius to find his own path to it."

I stared at her in astonishment.

"Oh, you needn't look so surprised," she said airily. "I'm a great deal more like my grandfather than I am like either my aunt or cousin. I know where my best interests lie, and the future has always rested with Darius. I just hope the rest of my family fall into line before they make fools of themselves."

With that she sauntered away as if we had only been chatting about the weather.

"I think...I think she just said she agrees with General Haddon that you'd be a good match for Darius." Bryony spoke in a voice of hushed awe.

"More importantly," I said, not wanting to think about that, "she just said she supports Darius—regardless of her family's opinion. Isabelle said her family supports him now too. I think all his work is finally paying off."

Bryony's voice turned grim. "And just in time. Because I don't think his true enemy is in Kallorway at all."

CHAPTER 19

*T*he weather had turned cold enough that combat class had become an unpleasant experience. But outside classes continued anyway, including in the arena. The Academy was experimenting with something new—sending teams of trainees from mixed year levels to compete against each other. The names of those to battle in the arena that morning were read at breakfast, and if anyone noticed that neither Jareth, Darius, nor I were ever called, they didn't comment.

I had to congratulate Duke Francis. It was a neat way of covering for the exclusion of all three of us royals from a class we should have been participating in. I could see in the eyes of both princes that they wished they could be in the middle of it, but neither protested. Officially we were all still trainees, but we wrestled with far more serious problems now, and Darius had enough drains on his strength and energy without wasting compositions in the arena.

Despite Jareth's new freedom, he never moved back to his old suite. I didn't press either of them for a reason because I was too relieved to have another line of defense between Darius and whatever forces were coming for his kingdom.

The four of us met almost nightly in either my suite or Darius's, discussing theories and plans. Between the three of us, Bryony, Jareth, and I convinced Darius that I needed to connect with Tyron again so we could learn more. No one liked the feeling that anyone around us could be under his control, but neither did we like the idea of moving to arrest him too soon and losing our only connection to whatever plot was unfolding.

"As long as Tyron doesn't realize we know, we can afford to take some time to gather information." Jareth directed a stern look at Darius. "But that means we have to be actually gathering information. And for that we're reliant on Verene."

"Not entirely," Darius said, reminding us he had also sent intelligencers to make discreet inquiries in the Empire.

But Jareth just scoffed. "I'm not exchanging a certainty right here and now for the hope of stumbling on something somewhere else. And neither would you if you were thinking straight."

He gave his brother a stern look. I loved seeing them interact, now that Jareth was restored both to his true self and his old confidence. I appreciated knowing there was someone who would stand up both to and for Darius.

"None of that matters," I said, intervening. "Because I intend to try again whatever you all think." I put my hands on my hips. "The only question is whether or not you're going to help me."

That ended the brothers' argument for good, but just started another one about how the effort could be most safely carried out. Darius insisted the most important thing was that Tyron not be given a chance to identify me as the disturbance he could feel with his energy. For me, the most important issue was that I had enough time.

"I don't know how difficult it's going to be to work out what he's using his ability for," I explained. "The more time I have the better."

In the end, much to his disgust, it was decided that Darius could have no role.

"You're too conspicuous," Bryony told him bluntly. "Always looming around looking ominous and commanding and icicle-like."

Jareth snorted and grinned, and Darius glared at him as a safer candidate for his ire than Bryony.

Bryony and Jareth were to lay the trap, allowing me to make the connection while Tyron was distracted by them and hopefully less likely to notice my intrusion.

We had chosen the chaotic moments just after the end of discipline class when trainees flooded into the halls from multiple rooms. Our small energy class had moved on to work with the healers which gave me an excellent excuse to leave class early. Despite my care since my first nearly disastrous attempt to connect with a healing composition, by now everyone in both the energy and healer disciplines knew of my squeamishness with wounds. Even Amalia was more inclined to let me leave than deal with the potential of my fainting or losing the contents of my stomach all over her classroom.

So when a wounded gardener with a long gash on his arm was brought into the class, I made several gagging noises and was sternly told to take myself off. The gardener chuckled as I left, himself watching his wound with interest. Injured people brought to the healing class were always provided with pain relief compositions first, and many of them found the entire experience fascinating.

I left the classroom but instead of heading for my suite or the dining hall, I slipped into the first empty room I passed. Bryony and I had already investigated and chosen this one as the ideal place for me to lurk. I found a comfortable seat against the wall that bordered the corridor and closed my eyes, trying to focus my mind.

All I could do now was wait for the bell. But once it sounded, there would be a rush of people outside my hiding place, meaning a mess of energy. I trusted it would be easy to find

Bryony's familiar presence, and from there, I should be able to identify Tyron.

I hoped.

Despite the fact I sat motionless, my heart pounded faster than it ever had in preparation for an arena battle. I understood why everyone had agreed I should be out of sight, but it meant I gave up the crucial advantage of being able to watch Tyron for visible reactions.

The longer I sat there, the more nervous I became until the sound of the bell made me jump and gasp. Kicking myself for being so on edge, I immediately pushed my attention out into the corridor. I heard doors opening all up and down the hall and the tramping sound of many feet.

My awareness flickered through each ball of energy searching for the familiar one I needed to find. I could picture them as clearly as if I stood outside the room. Bryony and Tyron would come out together, as they always did, although usually they had me in tow.

In the end, I heard Bryony's bright laugh before I felt her, the sound drawing me unerringly to her familiar energy.

"Bryony! Tyron!" Someone called to them to wait, and they both slowed. Bryony stopped first, the clump of energy with her coming to a halt a few beats behind. That must be Tyron, then.

I recognized both Jareth's energy and his voice as he joined them. He had timed it perfectly. They must be just through the wall. I let out a long breath.

"Connect," I whispered, forcing myself to reach for the energy I knew must be Tyron's rather than the more familiar people who surrounded him.

Instantly I was back in the ordered feel of Tyron's ability. Now that I had connected with Darius, I could feel the similarities, and it only confirmed me in the certainty that Tyron had received at least two years' intensive training before attending the Academy. His knowledge and ability weren't as deep and broad as Darius's, but they were sharply focused. As an energy mage, he might have a more limited ability than a power mage, but someone had made sure he was a master in his narrow skill set.

Much more dimly than before, I heard Jareth explaining he had been assigned by Dellion to poll the rest of our year. She wanted to ascertain who intended to remain at the Academy for Midwinter. This was actually true and had formed the basis for our plan. This year no glittering invitations had been received, and many of the Academy trainees were planning to return to their families and homes. But not everyone was going, and Dellion had decided that a Midwinter without some sort of festivities was unacceptable.

Bryony announced she was remaining and spoke for me as well, giggling when she described me as *poor Verene*, describing for Jareth my need to flee class. Once again I could picture them both clearly, seeing them turn to Tyron as they asked about his plans.

I forced my mind away from the imagined scene, however, remembering that Tyron was supposed to be the one distracted, not me. As usual, when connected with someone else, their ability and the related knowledge required to wield it sprang to my mind with sharp clarity. If only I could hold on to the details once I disconnected from Tyron.

But I knew I could not, and I had come prepared with parchment and pen. Quickly, I began to take notes in a sprawling shorthand I knew I would likely struggle to decipher later. But I couldn't take the time to write properly.

I could see now that Tyron must have put enormous energy into the composition he used on Darius, knowing he would likely only have the one chance. Usually he needed to refresh it much more frequently for it to linger more than a week. But he had also crafted it carefully, choosing to make Darius uncaring and unmotivated to act. Making someone refrain from action was a great deal easier than planting a thought process strong enough to compel them to act outside their natural inclination. He must have been refreshing Jareth's control almost daily.

Ever since my discovery, I had been watching Tyron in class, looking for some telltale leash of energy connecting him with someone else. I hadn't found one, but I hadn't known how to interpret that lack. For all I knew, it meant he had no one currently under his influence.

Now that I was inside his ability, however, I realized I had been looking for the wrong thing. There was no bright flare of energy connecting him to anyone, but something writhed inside him all the same. I doubted I would be able to notice it from the outside, but from the inside, it appeared sharp against the ordered nature of the rest of his energy.

A stolen clump of energy thrashed within him, desiring to return to its rightful owner. Sensing it through him was enough to remind me of the unpleasant sensation the one time I had drained someone of energy. My stomach roiled as being inside Tyron's energy brought back the memory. What Tyron was experiencing wasn't nearly as strong as the sensation had been on that occasion, though—the piece of energy he held was much smaller, and he seemed well practiced at holding it.

I tried to press deeper, wondering if I might recognize the energy somehow, but a voice pulled me out of myself, reminding me of the outside world.

"Jareth." Darius's voice cut through the noise, my ears catching the single word as they always caught anything Darius said.

He sounded stern, the single word a warning. Darius had reminded us triumphantly that since he and Jareth always stayed together—an effort to maintain the charade that nothing had changed—he could not be entirely excluded from our efforts.

He sounded utterly convincing—the disapproving older brother and king-elect, calling his younger brother into line for socializing outside his approved parameters. I had seen him do it a number of times. But his intervention had not been a part of our plan, and everything in me sprang to high alert. My own eyes couldn't see any warning signs from Tyron, but Darius was alerting me in their place.

"End," I whispered, cutting myself off from Tyron.

I felt bereft now, disconnected, so I strained with my ears to hear more. But my friends must have been moving again because their voices were growing indistinct. Belatedly I remembered to check for their energy and indeed found them moving away from me toward the dining hall. They moved separately now, Bryony and Tyron still together, while Darius and Jareth had drawn ahead.

I shook myself and looked down at my notes. I had learned something at least—most crucially that Tyron currently had someone under his influence. But I had lost the chance to find out who.

What had made Darius intervene? My assumption that he had meant it as a warning to me seemed safe. The distraction must have failed, and Tyron had noticed my presence. I could only hope that, whatever he'd sensed, he had no way of understanding what it might mean.

CHAPTER 20

*B*y the time Midwinter actually arrived, we had discussed every possible method for discovering the identity of the person Tyron was controlling. When pressed by Darius, I had been forced to admit I wasn't at all sure I could identify them from that one writhing piece of captured energy. That admission was enough to convince everyone the exercise wasn't worth repeating.

"We're better off waiting until the moment to arrest him comes," Darius said. "Then we'll have need of you to cut off his control and free the poor person. You should be able to use his ability to do that, shouldn't you?"

I agreed, and thus began the argument of when exactly that arrest should come. I had expected Darius to be most eager to have Tyron incarcerated, but he remained the most reluctant. In our conversations, he said he wished to wait for word from his intelligencers in case it might influence our way forward. He seemed afraid of tipping our hand to whoever stood above Tyron.

When we were alone, Bryony told me tartly that it wasn't the only thing Darius feared.

"He hates that you have to be so involved with this. He doesn't want you anywhere near Tyron when he gets backed into a corner."

I rolled my eyes at that, but Darius was king-elect. If he said to wait, we all had to wait.

"And if we have to wait," as Bryony said, "then we might as well occupy ourselves with something interesting while we do."

In Bryony's case that meant the gowns we intended to wear for Dellion's Midwinter celebration. Dellion had told us, with her most dazzling smile, that after the high formality of the last two years, she had chosen to invite only trainees to her select event.

Both Bryony and I interpreted this to mean that she intended it to be a little wild. But the dress code was still formal, and that was all that mattered to Bree. I hadn't sent home for a dress this year, consumed by guilt for still not telling my aunt what I had discovered about Tyron. I told myself I was just waiting for more information about his intentions, but deep down I knew I was avoiding the issue altogether.

Bryony, however, had merely taken it as an opportunity to provide me with a gown from the Sekali Empire. When the package arrived from her parents, she carried it reverently into my suite and solemnly peeled back the layers of cotton wrapping.

Elsie hovered nearby while she did it, nearly as excited as Bryony—which meant she was a great deal more excited than me. She had still never set foot in Darius's suite, but she had become a fixture in mine. Even the princes had grown accustomed to her presence and no longer watched their words around her.

"That silk!" Elsie exclaimed as Bryony drew out the gowns. She reached out careful fingers, running them along the material. "It's so soft. Like water."

Bryony had ordered herself a gown in deep green and had previously informed me mine was to be gold—as so many of mine were. But when she actually held mine aloft, I sat up and stared at it.

"I thought you said it was going to be gold."

"It is." She grinned at me. "A type of gold anyway."

I shook my head as I examined the dress. I had been expecting another garment in the same gold of my family's royal colors, but this dress was more of an ocher, its natural tone brightened by flashes of golden embroidery.

"It looks like your eyes," Elsie breathed.

I wasn't quite as romantically inclined as that, but I had to admit the dress would almost certainly bring out the color in my eyes—especially the occasional hints of gold.

"I thought it was time for something new," Bryony said.

I regarded her suspiciously for a moment, but she maintained her innocent expression, and I eventually turned back to the dress. It was an informal celebration among trainees. I refused to feel guilty for not wearing my family's colors.

"I wish you could come with us," I said to Elsie, once she had finished exclaiming at the two gowns.

She shook her head. "You should celebrate with your friends; I'll be celebrating with mine. And having just as much fun, I daresay. Zora is pulling out all the stops this year. Apparently since she doesn't have to organize a celebration for all of you, she's got energy enough to plan one for us."

I grinned. "I'm glad to hear it."

"And the king-elect is funding it," Elsie added. "As a gesture of Midwinter goodwill. He's in high favor among the servants at the moment."

"That's thoughtful of him," Bryony said. "It can't be a political move since the servants at the Academy were already on his side."

"I think when you rule a kingdom, everything is a political move," I murmured. "But it's also very like him. He thinks of details others miss."

"It's all that standing around glaring at everyone," Bryony said with a cheeky glance at me. "It gives lots of opportunities for noticing."

I rolled my eyes, not taking her bait, but when it came time to dress for the Midwinter celebration, I could think of nothing but Darius. He and Jareth were both to be there.

The King's Midwinter Ball was an important event in the annual calendar—thus why Cassius's machinations had caused so much consternation the year before. But this year there was both a king-regent and a king-elect which made the entire event more than a little fraught. Darius had chosen to avoid the whole situation by remaining at the Academy for the break.

"No one can blame me," he said. "Not when the Council decreed I must remain as a trainee until graduation. My father can have his pomp for now—I will be restrained to Kallmon for Midwinter often enough in the future."

"Sometimes I forget your father is still sitting on your throne, keeping it warm for you," Bryony said.

I smiled at the image but had to admit I felt the same way.

"After what he attempted through Jareth, I spent the summer ensuring he has nowhere left to turn," Darius said in a tight voice. "My father is utterly powerless, and it no longer matters how much that infuriates him."

"Grandfather is keeping an eye on him for us," Jareth added. "Whatever frustrations he might feel toward Darius are nothing to the hatred he bears our father. Now that he has the power to curb him, he won't hesitate to do so."

I slept in on Midwinter morning, enjoying the freedom. When I finally emerged into my sitting room, my breath caught in my throat. A single, vibrant purple flower had been placed on a side table beside one of the sofas. It was a flower I recognized.

My eyes moved to the tapestry. When had Darius crept in here to leave it for me? And what did he mean by it? My heart beat with hope.

I had trusted him with my secrets, tearing down the barriers that stood between us from my side. But if I loved Darius, if I saw a future for us, then that meant leaving Ardann and my family, and making Kallorway my home. Could I face such a future?

The Verene who had first arrived at the Academy could never have imagined such a thing. But I thought of the merchants I had met in Kallmon who spoke of coming change with hope in their eyes, of Duke Francis, who had secretly married a commonborn, and of Zora herself who ruled over her servants and sought no greater position. I thought of Isabelle and her family—with their love of the ocean and their dedication to the fields that fed the kingdom—and even of Dellion and her confidence that one day she would safeguard my children. No doubt she intended to eventually rise to take her grandfather's position.

But most of all, I thought of Darius—his passion and dedication for his kingdom and his people, and everything he had sacrificed. I had never imagined that someone so intelligent, so skilled, and so passionate could look at me the way he did or tell me that he loved me more than anything. If the future meant Darius, I would willingly embrace Kallorway.

That realization carried me through the day in a heady daze. The hours passed in a rush as Bryony and I prepared for the evening festivities.

Dellion had chosen one of the larger classrooms for her event, but it wasn't recognizable as such. All the desks and chairs had been cleared away, and green wreaths wound with red berries hung everywhere. Tears sprang to my eyes at the sight of the Ardannian decorations mixed in with the Kallorwegian ones. I knew they were a message for me. Dellion meant what she had said in the training yard that day. She had thrown in her lot with Darius, and she was choosing to give me the same support.

Food and drink were in abundance for the small numbers, and everyone chattered and laughed with abandon, freed by the absence of any instructors or parents. A smattering of trainees across each of the years had remained at the Academy, and it looked as if they had all received an invitation. Isabelle had gone home, as had Ashlyn, Wardell, and Royce, but Armand and Frida both remained from the third years.

Armand even asked me to dance, to my surprise. He informed me quite openly that his parents hadn't thought it worth the expense to bring him home just for the short holiday. His words reminded me that his father, at least, was sealed, and that they lived all the way down on the south coast by General Haddon's estate. I could only imagine how difficult it must be to maintain an estate of any size without access to compositions.

But while his father being sealed meant he must have supported Cassius's father during the days of the war with Ardann, he now sided with the general. So my initial surprise at Armand's openness soon faded. Dellion was the leader among the trainees from the general's faction, and she had made her feelings clear. For our year, at least, the general's faction now followed Darius, and—in some strange extension—me. And it helped that after nearly three years, Armand had finally become more comfortable with both me and the two energy mages. He remained serious, providing balance to his cousin's flippancy, but he could converse comfortably with any one of us.

I just wished thinking such a thing didn't immediately make me wonder if he had been spending too much time with Tyron. I actually connected briefly with his energy, just to be sure I could feel nothing amiss. But my concerns were groundless. Armand was neither influential nor a particularly powerful mage in his own right. He was unlikely to tempt Tyron.

After me, Armand danced with Bryony, and I had to endure an entire song with Tyron, smiling and trying to hide how often I looked toward the door.

"I needn't ask who it is you're looking for," Tyron said with a smile when our dance finished. "And I have enough experience to know it's not worth trying to hold your attention at a ball."

I grimaced. "I'm sorry, I—"

But he cut me off with a chuckle. "Didn't Dellion give you the same strict instructions as the rest of us? We're all to relax this year. And that includes you. If you want to dance all night with Prince Darius, feel entirely free."

I struggled to think of a reply, afraid of blurting out the wrong thing and somehow alerting him to my true feelings toward him. But he seemed to accept my silence as confusion over his words about Darius, merely chuckling and walking away toward the buffet.

Bryony found me after that. "Now we've both done our duty and danced with Tyron, so we're free to actually enjoy the night," she whispered.

"What does that say about poor Armand?" I asked. "Didn't you enjoy your dance with him?"

"Oh, Armand." She laughed. "He's nice enough, but far too serious for my tastes. I foisted him off onto an unsuspecting Frida. She seemed to be feeling a bit lost without Ashlyn to follow around."

I shook my head. "So now you intend to find someone sufficiently dashing, do you?"

Bryony grinned. "Of course. In fact, I've had my eye on a certain fourth year for some time now."

She pointed across the room to a tall, dark-haired boy I vaguely recognized. He possessed reasonable good looks and just the sort of rakish air designed to appeal to Bryony.

"As long as you know what you're doing," I said with a laugh of my own.

Bryony sparkled up at me. "I always do."

"That sounds ominous," said a light voice at our side. We both spun to find Jareth smiling at us. "But then I must admit, Bree, you do seem to always find your feet. Somehow."

She smiled, her look one of self-satisfaction, possibly brought on by knowing how gorgeous she looked in her chosen dress. Jareth promptly offered her his arm.

"You must dance with me immediately and tell me all your secrets."

"Oh, I couldn't do that," she protested, although she accepted his arm. "I wouldn't be half so alluring without a few secrets."

They disappeared into the crowd, and I couldn't stop myself from looking around yet again for the other, missing prince. Surely he had arrived with Jareth.

I didn't have to look long. Darius stood near the door, surrounded by a small circle of clear space. He was looking across the room at me with a thunderstruck expression. It was all I could do not to pick up my skirts and run to him.

When our eyes met, he finally began to move, striding through the crowd as if they weren't even there. The other trainees parted before him, whispering as they saw the focus of his attention. I fought down a flush. I had made my decision when I told Darius everything. I had decided to fight for him—for us—and that meant accepting the attention that would always come with him.

"Dance with me?" he asked, his voice husky and low.

I nodded, and he swept me straight into his arms. I let out a soft gasp, but he only pulled me closer. Apparently I wasn't the only one feeling reckless tonight.

For a long time, it was just the two of us and the music. We didn't talk, simply enjoying each other's presence and the unusual freedom of the evening. But eventually he spoke.

"I probably shouldn't have come tonight. I don't have a good track record when it comes to you and balls."

"Oh, but this isn't a real ball," I reminded him.

He chuckled, a rough, appealing sound. "Next you're going to tell me that isn't a real dress, and you're not a real princess. But my eyes tell me otherwise."

I flushed, realizing he had maneuvered us into a shadowy corner, and we were now barely swaying to the music.

"I came," he said, keeping his eyes glued to mine, "because I wanted to. But also because I know I owe you an apology."

"Me?"

"I've been trying to keep you out of what's been going on, away from danger. But I only have to think of what you did to that storm to realize my foolishness. You have a strength and power no one else has possessed before, and you've come into it alone in a foreign kingdom. And yet you managed to shape yourself into someone who can turn back a storm on her own."

I opened my mouth, but he shook his head.

"Close enough to on your own, anyway. Everything in me wants to protect you, and I will always strive to keep you safe. But I have to stop acting like you're weak. I never meant to do that—it was my own fear driving me."

"Thank you," I said, moved almost to tears. "And I will never stop trying to protect you—and fight for you." I drew a deep breath. "For a long time I was as guilty as you of keeping barriers between us. But all of that is over now. You know the full truth about me, except for one last thing. Here is my final truth. I intend to fight for us. The girl who can turn back a storm isn't going to let you go easily, Darius."

He tried to speak, but this time I was the one talking over him.

"If, at any point, you can look me in the eye and tell me honestly that you no longer love or desire me, then I'll turn and walk away, no matter how much it costs me. But I won't accept any other reason, Darius. You just said you're finished seeing me as weak—I hope that means you're also finished pushing me away."

I barely got the last word out when his arms tightened around me, crushing me to him, and his lips found mine. Heat burned through me at the force of his kiss and the strength of his arms. In that moment there was nothing in the world but Darius, and I forgot we still stood in a ballroom.

But when he pulled back with a despairing groan, I remembered. Looking around furtively, it appeared Darius had picked his spot well. We seemed to have escaped notice. I let out a sigh of relief before looking back at him.

The playful, loving smile fell from my lips at the sight of his expression, however.

"I hope after that kiss, you're not going to try to tell me you no longer care for me," I said.

He groaned again. "I told you I needed to avoid you and balls." He shook his head. "But I'm not going to try to tell you something so obviously false. You've already shown me that I should be full of hope that you can change Kallorway rather than fear that it might destroy you. You've even given me Jareth back."

He paused, and despite his words, dread filled my heart. And, sure enough, he continued speaking.

"I want to fight for you, too, Verene. I will fight for you. Harder than I've ever fought for anything. But first I have to be sure."

"Sure of what?" I whispered.

"Sure of myself. Sure that I'm worthy. Sure that nothing could ever make me betray you again." He hesitated. "And sure that in winning you, I'm not going to hurt you."

I shook my head. "I know you would never truly betray me. Just like you would never willingly hurt me."

But despite my earnest voice, he stepped away. "Just give me time, Verene. Can you give me that?"

Reluctantly I nodded. I had said I would fight with everything I had, but I hadn't expected the first battle to be so hard.

"I can wait as long as you need," I made myself say, my voice wavering slightly.

"As always you're too good for me," he murmured, before leaving me standing alone.

My eyes tracked him across the room to the door, and then he was gone. He had come to the dance only for me, and he had just announced that to the entire room. But inside I felt only the cold of his absence.

inter slowly started to loosen its grip while I practiced waiting. Waiting for Darius, waiting for word from his intelligencers, waiting for Tyron to make another move. Between the four of us, we watched him like hawks, Darius and Jareth setting up complicated surveillance compositions on the floor that held the third year rooms.

However, all we managed to ascertain was that Armand and Frida were sneaking out for midnight assignations in the freezing gardens.

"But why?" Bryony asked me, more fascinated with this discovery than our endless lack of progress on Tyron and his unknown conspiracy. "It's so cold!"

"I think they don't want Ashlyn or Wardell to catch them," I said.

"You know, I always thought Ashlyn and Wardell would be the two to end up together," Bryony said. "All that antagonism. Reminds me of another couple back in first year."

I rolled my eyes, refusing to enter into a discussion on Darius.

"It's not too late," I said instead. "We still have another year after this. Maybe they'll discover a secret passion next year. It would all be very neat."

But the next morning, as we all walked out to combat, we were reminded of the unlikelihood of that outcome.

"When is spring going to arrive?" Ashlyn complained to Frida, shivering dramatically. "I've had enough cold mornings to last a lifetime."

Wardell spread his arms wide with a grin. "I'll keep you warm, Ashlyn. All you have to do is ask."

She made a gagging noise and snatched at Frida's arm. "It will never be cold enough for that, Wardell. I'm lacking warmth, not standards."

As she marched away, pulling her friend along with her, Frida looked briefly back over her shoulder at Armand who walked silently beside his cousin.

Bryony giggled quietly beside me. "It's all rather dramatic, don't you think? Like watching a play about a forbidden romance."

"They'll have to decide how much they care eventually," I said. "Their relationship won't last if they can't survive stronger tests than disappointing their friends."

Bryony rolled her eyes. "You blow me away with your romantic attitude, Verene."

"I'm sorry," I said. "I guess I'm not feeling very romantic at the moment." Against my will, my eyes strayed to where Darius's tall form strode toward the training yard a short way ahead of us.

Bryony instantly gripped my arm in apology. "No, I'm sorry. I shouldn't have said anything."

I smiled at her and shook my head. Bryony was a good friend to have in the circumstances since she had all the sympathy in the world for the awful pain of waiting. She had never had much patience herself.

But none of us felt like joking when the reports finally began to filter back from Darius's intelligencers. None of them contained the sort of hard information we'd been hoping for, but none of them were encouraging.

At least the diplomats at the imperial court reported no antagonism from the emperor toward either Kallorway or Ardann. In fact, talks appeared to be proceeding between the emperor and my aunt about a potential marriage alliance between one of his granddaughters and Lucien. But the rest of their reports were unsettling.

The imperial court was tense, the emperor himself on edge—as much as the diplomats could tell such a thing. Something was going on, they reported, but none of the Sekalis were willing to talk about what. But the diplomats did seem certain it was some sort of trouble in the Empire rather than something initiated by the emperor himself.

The intelligencers told a similar story. The people of the Empire also seemed on edge, especially those in the center. Only those in the northern regions—most remote from the rest of the peninsula—seemed to possess their usual calm. But according to one lone intelligencer, even they appeared to be preparing for something.

"But what?" Darius cried, slamming the parchment down on his desk. "None of this tells us anything we didn't know at the start of the year. *There are rumors of trouble to the north.* Clearly something is going on in the Empire, and it's just as clear they don't want to tell us what it is."

"That's not surprising," Bryony said. "If there's trouble in the Empire, the emperor will see it as a matter of honor to deal with it quietly. He won't be spreading word about it unless he absolutely has to."

"But at least it doesn't sound like the emperor or his court are behind it," I said. "Which is significant. No other threat could compare to a full-scale attack from the Empire."

"And yet," Jareth murmured, "something worries the emperor who has all the might and power of the Empire at his disposal—

and more mages than we could ever hope to number. And if something worries the emperor, then it worries me."

The final report to tip Darius over the edge into action came from the intelligencer he had sent to the sealed clan. The man reported he could find no sign of Tyron or anyone who might be his family.

"Are you sure you don't sense anything strange about Captain Vincent?" Darius asked Bryony the next night.

She shook her head. "No, he feels perfectly normal. Just like he did the last three times you asked me. Verene has even connected with him. As far as any of us can tell, he's safe from Tyron."

Darius grimaced and glanced at me. "My apologies."

"We understand why you want to be cautious," I said.

"But the time for caution is past," he said grimly. "It is time for action, however little I might relish it."

He had instructed the captain to ready his squad to make an arrest but had forbidden him from telling any of them what was to come. If Vincent was surprised at such vague orders, he didn't question his king-elect.

Jareth and Bryony had both argued to be there, but Darius refused. "Far better to leave such a thing to the experts," he said. "I wouldn't have Verene there either if there was any way around it. But we need her unique gifts."

After Vincent, Darius went to Duke Francis and informed him that he wished to have some individual time with the energy mage class. If the duke was surprised at this request for special privileges, Darius didn't relay it to us. Instead we discovered his success when Amalia informed Bryony, Tyron, and me that instead of meeting with the creator trainees as we had been doing for the last few weeks, we would be back in our normal classroom the next afternoon.

Bryony expressed false surprise as we left class with Tyron, going so far as to speculate that the creator instructor had done something to anger Amalia.

"She certainly has enough anger to extend to instructors as well as trainees," Bryony said, and Tyron nodded, although he looked distracted.

Jareth had suggested just arresting him in his bed in the middle of the night, but Darius had instead come up with this plan. Again he was protecting me. He wanted an excuse for me to be present that didn't draw unnecessary attention to me.

Instead of Amalia, the classroom would be filled with Captain Vincent and his squad, ready to pounce as soon as Tyron and I entered together. Bryony had protested that with a plan like that, it only made sense for her to be there as well, but Darius had overridden her.

"Jareth can call you over on some pretext or other at the end of discipline class so you're not walking with Verene and Tyron."

Vincent and his guards were to undertake the actual task of arresting and restraining Tyron. My role was simple. As soon as the ambush was sprung, I would connect with Tyron and release the energy he was holding. I had parchment and pen ready inside my robe and didn't doubt that once I had connected with him, I would understand exactly what was required for such a composition. I certainly had no qualms using his own energy to achieve it.

I woke up restless in the morning, wondering how I would ever make it until discipline class in the late afternoon. I wished Darius could have come up with a way to arrest him in combat class first thing in the morning.

But I didn't even make it out of my rooms for breakfast before a knock sounded on the hallway door of my sitting room. Frowning—my visitors didn't usually come by that door—I went to open it.

I only just succeeded in keeping the shock from my face when Tyron greeted me from the corridor.

"I'm sorry to bother you so early, Verene," he said. "But I was hoping we could have a quick word before breakfast."

I hesitated, and he added, "It's about Bryony."

"Oh, of course," I said, not sure what else I could say.

This wasn't the plan, but then neither was my alerting him to the fact that I didn't want to be alone with him. And I certainly didn't want to be. Now that I was forced into the situation, I could think of little other than all the reasons he might suspect me of having interfered with his energy.

He stepped inside and walked confidently over to one of the sofas. As I debated whether to close the door behind him or not, a flash of movement made me glance toward Elsie's screens. She was peeping around them, her round-eyed gaze on Tyron. When she saw he had his back to her, she silently slipped across the room and out the door I still held open.

For the briefest moment she met my eyes, and I felt an up swelling of confidence. I wasn't alone.

I shut the door behind her and turned to my visitor.

"I don't think I've ever had you in here before, Tyron. Which after nearly three years seems rather remiss of me, now that I think of it."

"It's no matter," he said. "I'm here now."

"You wanted to talk about Bryony?" I prompted. "Is something wrong?"

"Well, not wrong," he said. "I just…I wanted to ask if you think there's any chance she might consider me."

I blinked. "Consider you?"

"You know." He gave a self-deprecating grimace. "Romantically."

"Oh. I…I don't know." It was true that the thought had crossed my mind on occasion in our early years at the Academy. They seemed a natural pairing as the only two energy mages. But the idea seemed so ludicrous in the face of what we had planned for the afternoon that it wiped my brain of sensible responses.

"Your blank expression is not exactly reassuring," he said, with a light laugh.

But something else sounded over his humor, and at the sound of the tearing parchment, my clarity returned. My eyes snapped to the two pieces of paper he now held in his hand.

"What was that?" I asked sharply, even as I felt something latch on to my energy and give a strange tug.

"Oh, just the love note I won't be giving her after that response," he said, still with a smile on his face.

But I had dropped all pretense. Springing to the other side of the room, I snatched up my sword. I wouldn't face him alone without a weapon in my hand.

Hurry back, Elsie, I whispered in my mind as I spun back to face him.

His own sword had appeared in his hand, his face no longer holding any hint of friendliness. The speed of his movement unsettled me. He didn't appear in the least thrown off by my response.

"So you *can* feel it," he said. "I've been dying to try."

"Of course I can feel it," I snapped back. "But you should know that since you already know I'm an energy mage, don't you?"

"I had heard that rumor."

We faced each other warily, neither making the first move. There was no way I was letting him take control of me, but neither did I want to openly reveal my own abilities.

"Just wait a moment," he said calmly, "and you'll see there's no need for us to fight each other."

"Actually," I said grimly, "I don't think that's going to happen." He might be powerful, but I had no doubts about my own capability.

His composition felt nothing like a normal drain. It didn't connect to me and start a flow of energy moving in his direction. Instead it seemed to worm inside my brain, tugging and tugging, until a piece of me broke free. It was past time for me to take control of it.

At least he wasn't a skilled swordsman. If I kept him fighting, he might not notice what I was doing to his composition—not well enough to understand it, anyway.

I lunged forward a little wildly, part of me occupied with his composition. He responded with a lightning-fast block and counter-attack that sent me scrambling back across the room.

For a moment I forgot about the composition, staring at him in shock. Nearly three years we had fought in combat class, and the entire time he had been masking his true skill level.

I felt his composition drawing the stolen part of me back to him, and nearly missed the signs of his next attack. I only just managed to block in time, skipping to the side and out of his reach behind a sofa. He vaulted over it, the smile not leaving his face.

For the first time, real fear gripped me. He fought as well as Jareth—possibly even as well as Bryony—and I didn't know if I could hold him off and reshape his composition at the same time.

Even as I thought it, I felt the stolen part of me collide with his energy. My sword arm faltered, and my blade wavered. Why was I fighting my friend?

The door into the corridor crashed open. Tyron and I both swung to face Darius, who came charging through, his sword already drawn.

"What are you doing?" I cried as he threw himself into a ferocious attack on our good friend. "Why are you fighting him?"

"Why are you?" Darius ground out as he leaped over a side table, his blade clanging against Tyron's.

I looked down at the sword in my hand in bewilderment. Why was I holding my weapon? Surely I hadn't been fighting my friend?

But then, he wasn't my friend. He was my enemy. My mind swirled, unable to reconcile the two thoughts.

"Free yourself, Verene." Darius's blade flashed almost faster than I could see as he fended off another attack from Tyron. "You can do it."

His words snapped everything into focus, and before I had time to think or second-guess myself, I gasped, "Take control."

Immediately the confusion faded away, as the energy that had wrapped itself around a portion of my mind came under my control. I could see its parameters and limits more clearly even than when I had connected with Tyron. If I hadn't already been suspicious, if I hadn't had Darius there to remind me of the truth and call my attention to the inconsistencies, I would have been just as gone as Jareth and Darius had been.

My own energy wanted to return to me, and as soon as I freed it, it sprang back to me in a dizzying rush, clearing my mind. But the energy Tyron had used in his composition—with the direction to capture and keep my energy—reached out again to seize it back.

I pressed down, holding it in place as it fought me. What could I do with it? And then a thought occurred to me.

With a few whispered words, I sent it flying back to Tyron, just as he parried an attack from Darius. He faltered, falling back, a strange look crossing his face.

Fascinated, I held on to my control over the energy of his composition, adding the single whispered word that allowed me to connect directly with Tyron as well. Now I could feel the working on both sides.

It wasn't like it had been with me. Tyron's energy was returning to its own home, so it didn't fight. Instead it seeped through the rest of his energy, tainting it with my instructions. I was fascinated to see how effective the working was when turned back against its own creator.

Without my having to speak a single command, he let go of the other energy he was keeping trapped inside. As it streamed away from him, I realized I had inadvertently lost my chance to investigate it more closely and see who it belonged to.

Tyron's face slackened slightly, and his arm dropped. Darius pulled himself up just short of another lunge, looking at me.

"Put down your sword and step back," I said.

"Your Highness, no," one of his guards called, but Darius ignored them, obeying me instead.

I didn't want Tyron faced with the same wrenching inconsistency that had helped me. He had tried to convince my mind we were friends, and the swords hadn't helped his case. Now I was convincing *him* we were allies, and I didn't intend for anyone to remind him of the truth.

Tyron looked down at his sword with a bemused look and slid it into its scabbard with a single motion. By the time he looked back up, both Darius and I had whisked our weapons out of sight.

Elsie appeared, popping around the doorway from the corridor. She must have been watching because she instantly grasped the situation. In her most commanding manner, she ushered Darius's two guards out of the room.

One of them protested, but Darius signaled for them to go, sending a single hard look in their direction that they couldn't ignore. Elsie was about to close the door on them, when a foot appeared, blocking its progress. She pulled it open again to find Vincent on the threshold.

"I hope you don't mean to banish me as well," he said, his voice neutral but his eyes threatening that he meant to be stubborn.

Darius hesitated before gesturing for him to enter. Bryony and Jareth tumbled in behind him, and Elsie finally closed the door.

Tyron looked around at us all.

"Did anyone bring any breakfast?" he asked. "I'm starving."

CHAPTER 22

*B*ryony turned astonished eyes on me, but I couldn't explain the situation with Tyron standing there in earshot.

"I'm afraid not," Elsie said smoothly when no one replied. "But I can fetch some."

"Thank you," I told her, and she once again slipped from the room.

Captain Vincent began to apologize to Darius for his guards' failure to keep up with him or to intervene, but Darius cut him off sharply.

"This wasn't a matter for guards," he said.

"I'm sure they would have intervened if they'd had another moment," Jareth murmured to the captain quietly. "It all happened extremely fast. No one else heard what Elsie said to Darius outside the dining hall, and it wasn't immediately apparent there was any sort of threat to Darius himself."

"I want to know what Tyron was doing here, instead of where he was supposed to be," Vincent said, in a stern voice.

"I came to work a composition on Verene," Tyron said in a friendly voice. "I haven't managed to work out exactly what her ability is, but I was starting to realize she was the center of everything. So when Amalia told me something was going on with our discipline class this afternoon, I knew the time had come to take the risk."

"Amalia?" I gasped. "She's the one you were controlling?"

Tyron nodded.

"I don't understand what's going on," Vincent said. "But perhaps we should all sit down."

"An excellent idea." Tyron took the closest chair.

The rest of us followed in various states of shock except for the captain who remained standing, hovering protectively behind Darius, his eyes never leaving Tyron.

"Amalia was a logical choice," Tyron said. "She's a master at almost every discipline, so she could provide me with a range of expertise as well as powerful compositions. And she doesn't seem to have any family, so she was free to accompany me this summer to visit the harvest."

"The blight," Darius said, his voice foreboding.

I threw him a look. Tyron was convinced we were friends, all wanting to help each other, as illogical as that was given what he was saying to us. We didn't want to do anything that might trigger him to throw off that illusion, as Jareth and I had managed to do.

Darius's expression smoothed out in response to my silent warning, but I could still see the danger flashing in his eyes.

"Yes, she has a lot of experience training growers," Tyron said. "She knew just how to do it so it would be out of control before their usual methods caught it." He frowned. "But then we were both stuck back at the Academy for the second harvest. We couldn't pivot once they began to watch more closely, so the blight didn't work a second time."

I leaned forward. "What did you do then?" I asked, fascinated despite myself.

"It was all Amalia's idea," he said. "She arranged to have the law enforcement instructor called away and set everything up so she would have an excuse to suggest a trip to the farmlands."

Bryony and Jareth, both sitting on one of the sofas, exchanged a look. None of us had suspected how deep the manipulation had gone.

"She was preparing for weeks in advance," Tyron continued, "amassing the compositions we would need for something as big as that storm." A shadow passed over his face. "It should have worked. I had already organized for Darius to be out of the picture. I still don't know what happened." His eyes fastened on me. "But I suspect you were somehow involved, Verene."

Captain Vincent looked at me with an interested, measuring gaze, but I said nothing.

"Should I send some guards to arrest Instructor Amalia?" Vincent asked Darius in a low voice.

I shook my head. "Tyron has released her energy. I felt it. He's not connected to anyone else now. And if there's any lingering effect, she should throw it off within hours. His normal compositions need constant renewing. We can't blame her for her actions just because we dislike her—not when we don't blame Jareth. And there would be no way to question her without revealing more than we want someone like Amalia to know at this point."

I looked at Tyron. "Amalia isn't plotting any harm right now, is she?"

"Harm?" He sounded surprised. "No, she's just been giving me information. I haven't found the perfect strategic moment to intervene again."

Darius seemed satisfied with this, signaling to the captain that he should remain with us.

"What I don't understand," Darius said, his tone deceptively light, "is why you're trying to destroy Kallorway. Where do you come from? The Empire?"

"Oh, no, I've never lived in the Empire," Tyron said. "I'm from the mountains. I'm Tarxi."

"But the Tarxi don't live in the mountains anymore," Bryony said. "We came down more than twenty years ago, and we don't even call ourselves that these days. We're just energy mages now."

A fierce light came into Tyron's eyes. "Some of the Tarxi might have deserted the tribe and no longer have the right to call themselves by our name. But those of us who were loyal remained. We have been biding our time, preparing, building our strength." His chest puffed out. "They were waiting for me to grow up and come into my power."

"Some deserted the tribe? Surely you mean most?" Darius asked. "I remember someone once mentioning that a few of the most stubborn Tarxi refused to rejoin us. But it can't have been a great number."

"We are few but mighty," Tyron said, the pride clear in his voice.

Captain Vincent cleared his throat. "I was part of the delegation to the Empire just before you started at the Academy." He nodded toward the sofa. "With Prince Jareth. While I was there, I spoke with a couple of people who were part of the hunting party which rediscovered the Tarxi. I had always been curious about that particular incident and questioned them extensively. I even met Amias, the Tarxi intelligencer who brokered peace."

"Tarxi intelligencer?" Jareth asked, just as Bryony said, "Oh! Amias!"

They looked at each other.

"I don't know about any intelligencing," Bryony said, "but Amias is something of an unofficial leader for the energy mages."

Tyron spat onto the carpet. "Traitor!" he muttered, but we all ignored him.

Vincent nodded at Bryony. "Back then, he was a young man, and he claimed that the small faction who hated the flatlands and wanted revenge had seized control of the Tarxi. He had infiltrated their number and joined them on their incursion down into Ardann so he might have a chance to make contact with us and secure a peaceful return for the majority of his people."

"But what happened to the leaders who remained behind in the mountains?" Darius asked with a creased brow. "Why was I never briefed on this?"

Vincent shrugged. "It's considered ancient history now. We've had peace for over twenty years, and no one has seen or heard a thing from those who stayed in the mountains. With the majority of their people gone, most assumed the remaining members must have perished in one of the particularly harsh winters which followed not long after."

"We are survivors," Tyron said. "Especially my father. He is their leader."

As soon as he said the word, *father*, I felt something stir inside him. I had maintained my connection to both him and the composition which currently controlled him, so I felt it instantly.

I gasped. Everyone looked at me, but I couldn't take the time to explain.

"Take control," I said, reaching for this new burst of energy which had been lying hidden, waiting for a trigger.

Even as I wrested control of it, it was already reaching for Tyron, trying to completely drain his energy. My mind raced as I thought how to redirect it. It was an unusually strong and determined composition, turning away from Tyron to quest for someone else when I blocked its access to him.

In a panic, I whispered an apology and directed it toward all of us.

Several cries of alarm rang out, and Vincent reached for his weapon.

"No! Just wait," I said.

A moment later, its energy had been expended.

"What just happened?" Darius barked out. "Something attacked my shield."

"And mine," said Jareth.

"I'm sorry," I said. "But Tyron just triggered a composition that tried to drain his strength. I had nothing else to do with it, so I had to redirect it to all of us. That way its strength was diluted enough to leave everyone tired but unharmed. It all happened so fast."

I gave an especially apologetic look to Bryony, Vincent, and Elsie, who hadn't had shields to protect them.

"Thank you for that," Tyron said, in a conversational voice. "I wondered if my father might have ordered such a thing placed on me. His right-hand commander is greatly skilled at stealing energy."

I took a deep breath, still shaking from the rush and the fear, as well as the energy that had been stolen from me. We had obviously reached something important, which meant we needed to redirect the conversation back to where it had stopped.

"Your father is the leader of the remaining Tarxi?" I asked. "And you grew up in the mountains?"

Tyron nodded. "The mountains make us tough and strong. And soon we will be strong enough to sweep down and rule over all the flatlands, as is our birthright."

"Your birthright?" Darius asked, his voice and body stiff.

"Anyone with power like ours is born to rule," Tyron said. "Why do you think we were banished in the first place?"

Bryony gasped. "Your ability is the reason the power mages banded together and banished all the energy mages all those generations ago. It scared them."

"And no wonder," Jareth muttered.

"There used to be more of us," Tyron said, matter-of-factly, "but now it's just my family."

"I wonder how that happened," Captain Vincent muttered, disgust in his voice. Louder, he said, "Amias claimed that the leader of the Tarxi had seized control of his people. It's why they fled under cover of secrecy, waiting until they knew the might of the flatlands was willing to shelter them. I guess we now know how he seized control."

"But it's been twenty years," Darius said, looking at Bryony. "Why haven't any of the energy mages among us told us the truth?"

She held up her hands. "Don't ask me. I've never heard any of this. My mother told me about the stubbornness of some of the Tarxi who didn't want to change their thinking or let go of their bitterness, but I never suspected something like this."

"You're too young to remember," Tyron said. "You weren't there. And of course your mother could not tell you the truth, or anyone else either. My father isn't like me. He can't implant such complex thoughts and controls. But he can influence many at once and hold on to the sliver of their energy for years beyond counting. Every Tarxi who knows of his existence and his gift is bound to him still, forced to silence on this one issue."

My mouth fell open. "All those people? For more than twenty years?"

Tyron grinned. "Unlike me, he doesn't have to stay close to them to constantly renew his working." His chest puffed out again. "But unlike me, he can't control them in such a complex way. He couldn't come here and do what I have done. And so he bided his time, he waited for me to come into my full power, and then he picked the place where I could cause the most damage."

His shoulders slumped. "If I could have torn Kallorway apart from within, drawing it into conflict with Ardann in the process, nothing would have been more perfect. When my father sweeps down from the north, the Empire would stand alone. And once it was consumed, Ardann and Kallorway would also fall. And a new empire would rise from their ashes. One which acknowledges energy mages as the true rulers."

His voice was ringing by the end of his speech, his eyes shining. How many times had he listened to his father deliver similar such addresses to his few remaining faithful? Promises of the future to get them through the winter cold.

"I thought the remaining Tarxi were few in number?" Darius asked. "How exactly is your father going to sweep down and overwhelm two kingdoms and an empire with a handful of mountain-dwellers—no matter how strong their abilities?"

"A handful of mountain-dwellers?" Tyron chuckled. "No, even he couldn't do that. But you're forgetting, my father has been planning this for twenty years—since my birth."

"I told you he was twenty," I muttered to Bryony.

"He is no longer in the mountains, but in the north of the Empire where he has been slowly binding people to himself for years."

"For years?" Darius sounded skeptical. "Word would have reached us by now if that were true."

"Why?" Tyron asked. "My father takes only the tiniest sliver of their energy and holds it in himself. Nothing in their life need change at all."

"He's been holding on to that much energy for that many years?" I shifted uncomfortably as I considered how that would feel. "I don't care how tiny a sliver he's taking from everyone. If he's succeeded—it must have driven him mad by now."

Tyron shrugged. "Who can discern between madness and genius?"

"I can," Bryony muttered.

"But what is the point if nothing about them changes?" Darius asked, his sharp gaze not having left Tyron as he focused on the most crucial issue.

"Nothing changes now because we haven't wished to draw attention to ourselves," Tyron said. "Nothing changes until the day he commands them to rise up and fight, and they find they cannot disobey. I can control thoughts, but he can bind actions. My father will sweep down from the north with a vast army at his back."

A crash followed by the sound of smashing china made us all swivel around. Elsie, who had quietly returned at some point, was staring at Tyron, the breakfast tray she had fetched having slipped from her nerveless fingers.

"So it's to be war after all," she whispered. "War and bloodshed for everyone."

CHAPTER 23

*C*aptain Vincent would have sent for the Head of the Armed Forces immediately and started amassing Kallorway's own army. Thankfully Darius's cooler head prevailed.

Tyron, it turned out, had been given until Darius's coronation, which wasn't until graduation. His father—whose name was apparently Conall—would not permit Darius to be crowned. But after waiting so long, he was content to give his son until then to find a way to disable Kallorway.

"So as long as we don't reveal we've discovered Tyron's ability, we have time," Darius said. "And don't forget, Conall thinks Tyron can't talk without activating that fatal composition Verene disabled. He thinks he still has the element of surprise, but we're the ones who have it, and right now that's our only advantage. We can't throw it away."

Instead of calling for his army, Darius drew on Bryony's energy to create a communication composition strong enough to reach the Sekali capital. The second communication composition —with a direct line to my aunt—I offered him from my own supply.

"This is not a threat only to Kallorway," he said. "We must discuss together how to stand and fight."

"But those are innocent people in that monster's army! They don't want to fight for Conall," Elsie cried, before clapping her hand over her mouth in horror at having spoken in such a way to Darius.

"I know," he told her gravely. "And that is why great deliberation is needed."

I wasn't there when Darius used the communication compositions, but whatever he conveyed was enough to bring emissaries from both courts at speed.

In the meantime, we all continued to attend classes, maintaining the illusion that nothing had changed. Even Tyron, now bound by the composition Darius had developed to bind Jareth, took his usual place. His own redirected working had ceased to function against him, and he no longer falsely thought of us as friends. Instead he moved about the Academy in total silence, his face an impassive mask.

I had thought the earlier waiting hard to bear, but this was worse. It had only actually been two days, however, when I put my foot on the first step of the great staircase and heard a familiar voice call my name. Whirling around, I saw my mother in the double doorway of the Academy, her face lined and tired, but her arms stretched wide.

I raced across the entranceway and flung myself at her. My father wrapped his arms around us both.

"It's so good to see you, Verene," Mother said, when we at last disentangled ourselves.

"When Lucienne said she needed someone she trusted to go to the Kallorwegian capital as quickly as possible, we couldn't volunteer fast enough," my father added.

I wiped at my eyes, wondering when they had started to leak. The sight of their familiar faces, and the feeling of safety they had always given me, had hit me harder than I expected.

"I didn't know it would be you coming," I said.

"Then you know what this is about?" Father asked gravely. "We know very little other than that it sounds serious. Extremely serious."

"It is. As serious as it could possibly be." I glanced around. "But we can't talk about it here. The utmost secrecy is required. In fact, Aunt Lucienne may have partially chosen you to come because you have an excuse to be here."

"And how did you become embroiled in such a business?" Mother asked, concern on her face.

I hesitated, biting my lip. "That's far too tangled a story for me to even begin. I know Darius has called for representatives from the Sekalis as well, so I'll leave it to him to tell you both at once when you all reach Kallmon."

My parents exchanged a look.

"Where is Prince Darius?" Mother asked, her voice brisk.

"We've just finished the meal, so he may be up in his suite already." I looked around, wondering who I should tell about my parents' arrival.

But I only had to wonder for a moment before Zora appeared, bowing low to them both.

"Prince Lucas, Princess Elena, forgive us for not being ready to greet you properly."

"Don't think of it," Mother said. "We have come unexpectedly and without ceremony." She squeezed the arm she still had around my shoulders, as if I was the purpose of her visit.

"If you will follow me," Zora said, "I have a suite prepared for you. Unfortunately Duke Francis is otherwise engaged at present, but he has asked me to let you know that he and the king-elect will be ready to leave with you for Kallmon at first light."

My father raised his eyebrows but didn't protest. Together we followed Zora across the entranceway and up the stairs. When we walked past the door to my suite, I pointed it out to them, and my mother insisted we stop so she could poke her head inside.

"Very nice," she approved. "Far more luxurious than the accommodations I had in my Academy days."

"But not dissimilar from mine," Father said, with a hint of humor in his voice.

Elsie appeared from behind her screens, her face freezing at the sight of my parents. She dropped into the deepest curtsy I had seen.

"Your Highnesses! I wasn't expecting…"

"I'm sorry to disturb your night," Mother said in a friendly voice. "I suppose you must be Elsie."

Elsie's eyes flew to me, and for a moment I had the same thought I guessed must be in her mind. Had Stellan told our parents about her? But my mother continued, and we both relaxed.

"I must admit, it has eased my mind to know my daughter has an Ardannian to keep her company and care for her needs." She gave a nod to Zora. "Not that I doubt the capability of your Academy, of course, but there is nothing quite like a piece of home."

"Very true, Your Highness," Zora said, while Elsie curtsied again and muttered something inarticulate.

I suspected she had imagined the moment of meeting my parents a hundred times—but I was sure she'd never imagined it happening so unexpectedly.

I continued on with my parents to the guest suite prepared for them, and then asked permission to go and fetch Bryony.

"She'll never forgive me if she misses you entirely," I said.

"Of course," Father said, but I could read in my mother's eyes that she was suspicious of my rush to have someone else join us.

But there was too much that couldn't be said to allow for easy conversation now, and it was true that Bryony wouldn't want to miss them.

Another round of hugs and exclamations greeted Bryony's arrival, and then my Mother grilled us both on our instructors and lessons for a few minutes. But they had both had an exhausting journey from Corrin and were faced with another full day of travel starting early the next morning, so Bryony and I both insisted on not staying long.

I slipped out of bed the next morning in time to wave them off. My eyes lingered on Darius, as well, but we had no chance for private communication. As well as the three of them, they were joined by Duke Francis, and escorted by Captain Vincent and a squad of the Royal Guard.

After they left—in the early dawn before any other trainees or instructors were up to see their departure—Jareth explained that the Sekali representatives were to meet them in Kallmon. The job of guarding Tyron had been handed over to Jareth, while the care of the Academy itself rested with Senior Instructor Alvin.

And so another round of waiting began. It was officially spring now, but it was hard to enjoy the warmer weather, just as it was hard to even think about exams. What plans were the delegates in Kallmon making? How did they intend to combat Conall's threat?

I went through classes in a daze, Bryony, Jareth, and Tyron always by my side. But despite always being surrounded by people, the Academy felt strangely empty without Darius's presence.

Our year mates noticed something was amiss with our small group, but they all seemed to put it down to Darius's absence. There had been some mild speculation at the beginning about what had taken him and the duke from the Academy, but most trainees seemed happy to accept it was royal business and seek no further. Upcoming exams no doubt helped that distraction, becoming the increasing focus of most conversations.

In the evenings, Jareth and his constant retinue of trusted guards always withdrew immediately after the evening meal, no doubt hiding the fact that Tyron remained with them at all times. But Bryony had taken to joining me in the library while I vainly tried to focus enough to do some study.

On one such evening, a number of days after my parents had come and gone, she stood looking out the window at the grounds below. I was curled up in an armchair, carefully ignoring the open book beside me.

"It's awfully blustery out there," Bryony said. "Even for spring. I suppose we're in for a storm."

I stretched and yawned. "That must be why it's so dark already." Even as I said the words, the first drops of rain splattered against the glass. "Come on, be honest. Can you see at least a little of the appeal of this place? And why I always preferred it over early morning training out in the yard with you?"

Bryony shook her head with a reluctant smile. "I never made you train in the middle of a storm." She glanced around at the little nook we'd found for ourselves this evening, the lanterns around us glowing merrily. "I will admit it's pleasant enough, though."

The window rattled, and she shivered. "I'm definitely glad not to be out in this."

I thought I heard the sound of running feet and looked up, but a loud crack of thunder drowned out any other noise.

"Do you hear something?" I asked Bryony, just as a crashing noise reached us, as if someone had collided with a shelf of books.

I frowned and started to scramble out of the chair, just as Elsie careened around the corner of the nearest row of shelves.

"Princess!" she cried, as soon as she caught sight of me.

I jumped the rest of the way to my feet, but she leaned over and put her hands on her knees, trying to catch her breath.

"What's going on?" Bryony asked. "Are you all right?" She looked between the bookshelves, as if she expected to see someone chasing after Elsie.

But when Elsie recovered her breath enough to speak, she didn't address either of us. Straightening, she shouted loudly.

"Over here, Captain! I've found them!"

Captain? I started forward. Had the group from the capital returned?

But the sound of pounding feet preceded the appearance of Captain Layna, not Captain Vincent.

I looked between her and Elsie. Clearly something had distressed them both.

"What's going on?" My hand flew to my throat. "Not bad news from home?"

Layna shook her head. "The trouble's much closer than that, I'm afraid, Your Highness. With the duke gone, and Captain Vincent, I didn't know what to do, but Elsie said we should come to you." She gave me a piercing look. "She seems certain you can help."

"Help with what?" I asked.

"It's this storm," Elsie gasped. "It isn't natural."

"Not natural?" Bryony turned back to the window. "What do you mean?"

"That's a hurricane brewing out there," Layna said grimly. "One laced through with enough power to tear this Academy down."

CHAPTER 24

"*B*ut how? Who?" My mind flew to Tyron, but he couldn't manage something like this while bound to Jareth.

"I don't know any of that," Layna said. "But can't you feel it?"

I stared out the window, focusing on the storm. Now that I was paying attention, I could see what she meant. Power shimmered all through the swirling wind. A flash of lightning was followed by a window-rattling crack of thunder.

My mind raced. "Where's Instructor Alvin? He's supposed to be in charge of the Academy with the duke away."

"He and the wind working instructor have taken the third and fourth year wind worker trainees out there." Layna pointed at the window.

Bryony put her hand over her mouth, looking at the storm outside. "Isabelle is out there right now trying to fight that?"

Another flash, another crack of thunder, followed by something that sounded terrifyingly like a scream.

"I don't think they're going to be able to stop it," I said. "Once a storm reaches this level of natural momentum..." I winced. "A whole team of experienced wind workers couldn't stop the one on the coast."

Layna gave me an odd look. "But Prince Darius could?"

I didn't answer or meet her eyes.

"We have to try to help." I hurried down the closest row of bookshelves, not stopping to see if the others were following.

I reached the front of the library to find both the library head, Hugh, and his wife, Raelynn, comforting a dirty, disheveled girl I didn't recognize. She was wearing the dark green uniform of one of the Academy servants and was too distraught for me to follow her words.

"I'll get my healing bag," Raelynn said, rushing in the direction that led to Hugh's office.

"Which of the tunnels is it?" Hugh asked, clearly trying to restrain his sense of urgency in order to calm the girl enough to get answers out of her.

"The main one," she gasped between sobs.

The mild-mannered library head responded explosively with a word I'd never heard him use before.

I slowed to a stop. "What's happened?" I asked, looking between the girl and Hugh.

"This storm has torn up one of the outbuildings that house the servants. Those in the building escaped the destruction into the main tunnel connecting with the Academy. But it sounds like a large piece of debris must have hit right above the tunnel because there's been a cave in. And now a number of people are trapped down there."

"And if the tunnel's gone, that means anyone else still in the other outbuildings is stuck as well," Elsie said in a horrified voice from behind me. "We have to do something."

"Of course we will," Hugh said. "We can't just leave them there."

I bit my lip, trying to force my brain to think faster.

"No, we have to help, of course, but..." I moved closer to

Hugh and lowered my voice. "Have you felt this storm? Are you aware it's not natural?"

Hugh pulled back, his worried look turning to horror. "An attack on the Academy? And while the duke is away!"

I nodded. "Apparently Alvin and the wind working instructor have taken the third and fourth year wind worker trainees out to face the storm."

"Trainees?" Raelynn asked, arriving with her healing bag secured over one shoulder. "But they don't have the experience or expertise to face something like this!"

"What's the alternative?" Hugh asked. "Let the storm destroy the Academy and all of us with it? They have to try."

"But they're just children," she cried.

I shook my head. "Third and fourth years aren't children. And there's no time to think of that now. People need our help."

Raelynn nodded, a look of determination coming over her face.

Bryony pulled at my arm, dropping her voice as low as she could to still be heard over the storm.

"And what about Jareth? Does he know what's going on? What if Tyron is involved in this somehow? What if this is all an effort to free him?"

I gulped. I hadn't thought of that. I looked from Layna, to the terrified servant, to Hugh and Raelynn, and finally back to Bryony's worried face. I couldn't be everywhere at once, but I wasn't alone either.

"Raelynn, I know you'll need to save your energy for anyone who's been injured in all this, but Hugh—do you have enough creator knowledge to clear the tunnel once you get there?"

His energy levels seemed high enough, at least, and he had a senior role at the Academy, even if it was running the library. He must have expertise in something.

Hugh nodded and patted a pocket in his robe which presumably held parchment and pen. "I can get the tunnel clear."

I turned to Elsie. "Can you gather any servants already here in the main building? Send any who are able-bodied to help Hugh and Raelynn. They may need some manual help clearing stones, and I'm sure some of those trapped inside will need assistance getting the rest of the way through once a path is cleared."

A stubborn look crossed Elsie's face. "I'm not leaving you, Princess Verene."

I shook my head. "I'm going out into the storm, Elsie. You can't come with me."

"I'm not staying behind," she repeated.

"But what about Hugh and Raelynn? They need help."

"I can do it," the girl who had brought the news said. She sounded shaky, but both her face and voice had calmed. I looked at her doubtfully for a moment, but she met my eyes, not backing down.

"Very well." I gave a curt nod. I had seen it before. Some people just needed clear leadership, and the knowledge that someone was doing something, to enable them to regain their capacity to function.

I turned to Hugh. "I'm going outside. I'll make sure no more debris hits the tunnel from the top. We can't afford to lose you and Raelynn as well."

Hugh didn't waste time arguing that I was a child who needed protecting. He just nodded and ushered the servant girl out of the library ahead of him, already murmuring more precise instructions to her.

I looked at the small group of us left. "Layna, you're with Bryony. You need to find Jareth."

Layna looked at me with a similar light of rebellion in her eyes as Elsie had just shown. But I straightened and gave her my most commanding expression. The sounds of the storm were already growing louder, and the occasional ominous creak could be heard from the Academy itself. We didn't have any time to waste.

"This is of the utmost importance. You must find and help Jareth. I don't know how many guards are left given so many went with Captain Vincent, or how many might be trapped by the tunnel collapse, but if you can find any others, take them with you."

I gave Bryony a solemn look. "You understand that we can't afford to lose Tyron." I gripped her arm. "But stay alive, Bree. Don't do anything reckless."

She nodded, her face utterly serious for once. "I'd tell you not to do anything reckless either, but you're going out in that storm, so there doesn't seem much point. But do stay alive, Verene."

I glanced at Elsie. "This is your last chance. You could go with Bryony, or run after Hugh and Raelynn. You can help without leaving the Academy."

She shook her head. "I'm not leaving you, Princess. I've seen you face down a storm before, remember. If you get too absorbed, you'll need someone there to watch over you."

Bryony and Layna had started moving but weren't yet out of earshot, and the last I saw of them was Layna throwing me a measuring look over her shoulder as she left the library. If we all survived this night, she was going to have some questions that would be hard to avoid answering.

I took off running, Elsie close behind me. We almost slid down the stairs in our haste, dashing across the entranceway to the large doors, now closed. I pulled on one, but it resisted me, the wind outside lending it added weight. Elsie stepped up beside me and together we managed to pry it open enough for us to both slip through. It slammed closed behind us with a noise almost as loud as the thunder.

Instantly the wind whipped around us, snatching our breath and pulling at our clothes as if it would lift us into the air entirely. Rain battered against us, and within several breaths we were both completely soaked. I gasped at the shocking cold, but I didn't have the luxury to think about my own comfort.

"We have to go around the back," I called to Elsie, but out here the storm was too loud for speech. I gestured around the Academy, and she nodded.

We moved as fast as we dared, hugging the side of the building to shelter somewhat from the wind. By the time we had made it halfway around the Academy, the storm already seemed noticeably stronger. If it was in the process of growing strong enough to rip up the Academy itself, we wouldn't be around to see it. We would be long gone before that happened.

We rounded the final corner of the Academy to confront a scene of devastation. It was hard to see in the semi-darkness, but the frequent flashes of lightning illuminated the open patch where the wind workers usually trained. Now—just as during class—it was filled with swirling wind, but this time the wind carried enormous chunks of broken stone, torn from the Academy outbuildings which were less able to withstand the force of the storm.

In the center of the space stood a clump of people, most of them in white robes. To my relief, they seemed to be protected by a bubble of power. I watched a large stone bounce off the open air a few feet above their heads. All of them looked upward, and most had compositions in their hands. The ground around them was littered with torn scraps, and several of them sat on the ground, hunched over parchments, their pens flying furiously.

Elsie tugged at my sleeve, pointing toward the ground, and in a rush I remembered the task I had come out here to do. Or one of them anyway. I nodded at her, grateful already for her presence, and then pulled her sharply to one side as a large chunk of stone went flying past us, colliding with the Academy building itself.

I reached out with my senses, trying to ignore the ferocity of the storm. I searched through the ground until I found a bright huddle of energy created by many people standing close together. Searching further, I identified several more people hurrying toward the motionless mass. Their trajectory gave me the location of the tunnel, and I moved further along the building wall to get closer to it.

As I moved around a large bush, I caught sight of the damage to the tunnel. An enormous chunk of masonry had smashed into the earth, leaving a large crater in its wake.

Another stone crashed to the ground, only a few feet to one side, the whole ground shuddering. The energy sources that must be Hugh and Raelynn were well away from the Academy now, and I needed to protect the tunnel long enough for them to clear it and get everyone out. But I had no power of my own to draw on.

I cast around frantically, my mind latching on to the power that still laced its way through the storm itself.

"Take control," I screamed into the wind and felt myself connect with the closest working.

The first thing I noticed was how familiar it felt. The mage who crafted this composition had also crafted the ones that fed the storm on the coast.

"Amalia, it's Amalia," I shouted at Elsie, but from the blank look on her face, she couldn't hear me over the sound of the wind.

But I didn't have time to worry about that now or wonder how she could still be under Tyron's influence. Her working pulled at me, wanting to do what it had been shaped for—whipping the wind into a greater frenzy.

A piece of stone went flying past, and I pushed the composition toward it, directing the wind to send the stone flying up and over the wall of the Academy to land safely in the empty land on the other side.

"Take control," I cried again, not waiting for it to land, and seized on the next composition.

Within moments, I was sucked fully into the deadly dance being performed in the air above my head. I lost all sense of time, and even the cold that wracked my body with shivers retreated beyond my awareness. All that existed was me, the compositions I seized, and the debris I snatched away with their power.

Thanks to my efforts, a second bubble of calm air now surrounded the wind workers, and the tunnel route saw no more hits. Twice I felt Elsie tug at my body, pulling me away from some chunk of stone or flying vegetation small enough to have slipped through my efforts. But I had no time to concern myself about such things. I would have to trust her to keep me alive while I grabbed at composition after composition.

How many of these had Amalia worked? How long had she been building toward this effort—no doubt inspired by her work at the coast? But there she had been going for sheer size—her work taken and amplified by the natural forces already building. Here she had created this storm from almost nothing, whipping it into being until it gained enough momentum to take on a life of its own.

She had concentrated the power, targeting it on one small spot and creating devastating force as a result. But if I could remove all of her compositions, the efforts of the wind workers should be enough to tame the storm this time around.

I grabbed another working and another, swaying on my feet as I directed the power they held away from the storm. I didn't know if my unsteadiness was from exhaustion or the wind, but it didn't matter. I kept working.

More time passed, and I started to wonder if the wind sounded calmer and less ferocious. When I reached for a new composition now, I had to reach further, searching one out in the chaos before me.

At some point the debris over the tunnel shifted, and many of the balls of energy moved, disappearing off toward the Academy. But a few still remained—being treated by Raelynn, perhaps?

I took control of another composition, but when I looked around, there was nothing flying through the air to direct its power toward. With a twist, I sent it spinning in the opposite direction to the prevailing wind, its power soon burning out in the futile effort.

"I think you can stop now," Elsie said, and it took me a moment to realize I could hear her. There was no doubt now the storm was calming.

I looked at her and blinked. Were there two of her? When did that happen?

But a moment later my vision was restored, my gaze captured by a line of red running down my arm.

"I'm sorry," Elsie said, guilt in her voice. "I didn't get you out of the way of that one in time."

I shook my head. "But you did get me out of the way of the others. That's what matters. It's just a cut." But I swayed again, adding blood loss to the list of possible causes for my unsteadiness.

The huddle of wind workers were still focused on the remnants of the storm, all of them looking worn and exhausted, but none of them hurt due to their shield. And now that the wind had died down and the rain nearly stopped, more white and silver robes were emerging from the Academy. I hoped some of them were healers, come to scour the outbuildings for the wounded, and some creators, ready to reverse the damage done by the storm.

But I wasn't interested in staying around to find out. My work here had been completed which meant it was time I disappeared from view before someone started asking questions. And besides, the night wasn't over.

"Amalia. It was Amalia." I pulled Elsie back around the corner of the building, and she slipped a shoulder under one of my arms, half-supporting me. I managed to stumble my way back into the entranceway of the Academy—the doors now standing wide—before I had to stop.

I pulled a stack of parchments from one of my pockets and thrust them at Elsie. "Here. Find the one for cuts."

She rifled through them while I swayed again. Diving back into my robe, I produced yet another composition, but I didn't hesitate before tearing this one myself. I closed my eyes as the stream of new energy hit, the initial moment of discomfort easily overwhelmed by the relief of feeling my strength returning. I was too drained to experience the almost euphoric boost that came when I received energy while almost full myself, but it was still pleasant enough to make me sigh and close my eyes for a moment before pushing them back open and surveying the room with increased interest.

"This one!" Elsie cried, pulling a parchment from the stack and thrusting it into my hands. "Here, you check it."

I scanned it briefly. It was indeed a composition for healing cuts, so I ripped it through without wasting further time, flicking my fingers toward my wound.

I winced and groaned as the flow of blood stopped, and my skin knit back together. But I gritted my teeth, knowing it would be over soon. There was no point wasting a precious pain relief composition on something so short-lived.

Elsie breathed a soft sigh of relief when she saw my arm healed and whole again.

"Amazing," she whispered, and I wondered if she had ever seen a healing working before. But when she looked up at me, her face was all business.

"What now?" she asked.

"Now we find Amalia."

CHAPTER 25

"*A*malia? I thought you'd freed her from Tyron's influence." Elsie looked confused, and I couldn't blame her. I was confused myself.

"I don't know how he could still have his clutches in her, but I recognized those compositions out there in the storm. They were from the same source as the ones at the coast, and Tyron definitely said those came from Amalia. It's been quiet for a long time. We thought Tyron was waiting for a strategic opportunity, but it looks like Amalia was just taking the time to build up enough compositions."

"So she's still following his instructions?" Elsie asked.

I spread my arms wide. "She shouldn't be. He let go of her energy days ago." I frowned. "And besides, why now? If Tyron wanted to destroy the Academy, I would have thought he would do it while Darius was here."

"Unless his purpose has changed. Maybe this was all to free him, like Bryony said."

I bit my lip. "That's the most frightening possibility. We have to find Bryony and Jareth."

A number of trainees and servants had appeared, milling around the entranceway in a babble of voices and questions. I pushed my way through them, heading for the stairs. Several called to me, but I ignored everyone, too intent on my mission.

It took barely a minute to race up the stairs and into my own suite. I'd never had a reason to test the protections on the main door to Darius's suite, and I didn't want to risk it now. Instead I thrust aside the tapestry and ripped open the door behind it.

Tumbling into the room, I stopped short. There were more bodies here than I had ever seen in the space before, the room almost uncomfortably full. Almost everyone I saw had drawn swords, and they stood in a rough circle, all of their weapons trained on a single person.

Tyron sat calmly on a sofa in the middle of it all, although I caught him glancing toward the window with a strange expression on his face. If I didn't know better, I would have thought it was confusion.

When I arrived so unexpectedly, Elsie tripping over my heels, everyone in the room turned in my direction.

"Verene!" Bryony cried at the same moment as Layna said, "Your Highness!" Relief colored both of their tones, and even Jareth looked pleased to see me mostly unharmed.

Layna had managed to recruit a number of extra guards on top of the two who always remained with Jareth and Tyron, and it was entirely clear that no escape attempt had been made by either Tyron or an outside associate.

"Is everyone all right?" Jareth asked.

"Several of the servants' outbuildings were destroyed," I said, "and their main tunnel collapsed. But Raelynn and Hugh went to help them. And Alvin and the wind workers were able to stop the storm."

"You see." Jareth thrust his sword uncomfortably close to Tyron's neck, an ugly look on his face. "Once again, your plans have failed."

"As I have been trying to tell you since Bryony barged in here, this is no plan of mine," Tyron said. "After all, I'm trapped in this building with you and would rather not have it torn down around me."

"No one came for him?" I asked. "There wasn't an escape attempt?"

Reluctantly Jareth shook his head. Clearly he had been hoping for some action, and a chance to release some of the pent up bitterness and anger he carried from Tyron's years of control.

My forehead creased. "But it doesn't make any sense..."

Tyron's eyes latched on to me, bright and curious. "You know who created the storm."

Reluctantly I nodded. I didn't want to give him the satisfaction of answering, but there wasn't time for games. Not while the perpetrator of the storm was still loose.

"It was Amalia." I looked at Jareth and Bryony. "I recognized her compositions."

"Senior Instructor Amalia?" Layna gasped. "But why would she do such a thing?"

"Well, I would have said him." I pointed at Tyron. "But..." Frowning, I whispered, "Connect," and plunged into his energy.

He stiffened, staring at me, but I ignored him as I raced quickly through all the corners of his ability before muttering, "End."

I shook my head. "He definitely doesn't have control over her anymore."

"Of course not." Jareth sounded offended. "How could he? I, of all people, know how effective Darius's binding composition is."

"No," Tyron said slowly. "My power over Amalia ended days ago. How very interesting..."

"Interesting isn't the word I would use," Bryony snapped.

Tyron gave her a contemptuous look. "Well, of course not. You're always thinking with your heart instead of your head."

"You could do with some more heart," I said heatedly, but Layna called my attention back to the most relevant point.

"But where is Amalia, then?" she asked.

"I've never had the impression she was the type to sacrifice herself," I said. "If she intended to pull down the Academy, she must have had an escape plan."

"The tunnel!" Elsie cried.

"I thought it collapsed?" Bryony looked confused.

"The main one collapsed," Elsie said, "but that's not the one I meant. There's an old unused servants' tunnel that leads all the way out of the walls."

"What?" Layna barked. "How did I not know about that?"

Elsie shrugged. "The servants know."

A gold-robed mage guard cleared his throat. "The captain knows, Sir. And the Kallorwegian guards. But I suppose no one ever thought to mention it to you. The captain always saw it as a potential bolt hole for the king-elect and the duke, if it ever came to such a thing. We check it regularly to ensure it's still secure, but they try to keep word of its existence from the trainees. It makes our job easier if they don't know any alternative and secretive ways out of the Academy."

"You know, I think my father mentioned something about that once," Bryony said. "He used to know every nook and cranny of this place from the years he spent as a sort of groundsman. In fact, I think he used it once to help your parents."

"Can you show us how to get to it?" I asked Elsie.

She nodded. "I've only seen it once, but I think I can find it again."

"I'm coming with you," Bryony said at once.

"And me," Layna added, with a stern note that told me she wouldn't be turned away this time.

But I had no desire to discourage either of them from accompanying me.

"I'm coming as well," Jareth said, fire in his voice.

I frowned at him, glancing at Tyron, still sitting calmly on the sofa. "But—"

Jareth shook his head at me, pulling a parchment from his pocket. He met the eyes of the gold-robed guard who had spoken up about the tunnel, and the man nodded. Jareth tore the parchment and then turned to me.

"Let's go." His tone brooked no opposition, and I wasn't inclined to argue.

Jareth pushed open the door to the corridor, and the four of us followed, leaving the room full of guards to watch over Tyron. I hurried close to Jareth.

"He's trustworthy?" I asked, not knowing the name of the guard he had left in charge.

Jareth nodded. "He's Captain Vincent's second-in-command. That's why I was prepared with a composition to pass control of Tyron to him."

Elsie led us into the bowels of the Academy. We passed through a maze of different passages, at least some of which must have been underground. At one point I felt a rush of cold night air, and the ground around us shone wet for some distance. Apparently this tunnel connected to the damaged tunnel.

Eventually we emerged into a series of subterranean storage rooms full of barrels and crates of various supplies. Hidden in one corner stood a rickety set of wooden stairs that led us upward again. I tested every step, amazed the ancient structure had survived the storm. From there we passed into a hidden passage within a wall.

"There's a door up ahead." Elsie faltered for a step. "But I think there's a lock. I don't have the key. I didn't even think of that."

"However things might have been done in the past, I can't imagine Vincent lets anyone else take charge of the key," Layna said. "Which means Amalia wouldn't have one either."

"If the door's been battered down, we'll know then, won't

we?" Jareth's face looked grim, but an eager note underlined his voice. He would be disappointed if this journey didn't lead to Amalia.

"There!" Bryony pointed ahead to where some twisted wood lay across the passage. As we approached closer, I realized it was the remnants of a solid door that had once guarded the secret exit from the Academy.

We all hurried forward with a renewed rush of energy, bursting out into the cold night air in a clump. The storm had completely cleared now, and the moon shone down, illuminating the scene around us.

What had once been open ground was now littered with chunks of stone, large and small, and uprooted vegetation lay scattered between them. For the first time it occurred to me how fortunate we were that the Kallorwegian Academy had been positioned in such a remote location rather than placed in the center of a city like the Ardannian one. I couldn't have pitched the debris blindly over the wall if we'd been ringed by homes and other buildings.

But I didn't have long for reflection before a flash of movement drew my eye. At the same moment, Jareth gave a mighty bellow and started forward. The silver-robed figure started, half-turning to stare at us before taking off running.

In that moment I recognized Amalia's face. She hadn't been far ahead of us then. She clearly hadn't expected anyone to guess where she had gone, or she would have made more haste with her escape.

Jareth sprinted forward, his sword already drawn, but Layna hung back, instead pulling out a composition. Tearing it, she gestured toward the fleeing figure, and power rushed out to circle her like a lasso. But Amalia's progress didn't slow.

We were all running now, but Layna was still pulling out compositions.

"She's shielded," she ground out between breaths.

Before I could do more than consider taking down her shield myself, Layna had torn a second composition. It released a tidal wave of pure power that smashed down Amalia's shield. The instructor faltered, fumbling in her robe for another shield, but she glanced back while she did so, and her face blanched. The sight of Jareth, nearly on her with a drawn sword, sent her scrambling back into forward motion again.

The hesitation had cost her, however. Layna tore another composition, and this one succeeded in circling and tripping her. Amalia went down hard and didn't rise.

Jareth stood over her, sword at the ready and chest heaving. As we neared, he gave Layna a reproachful look.

"I could have handled her."

"Certainly, Your Highness," Layna said smoothly, and I suppressed a smile.

Jareth might be spoiling for a fight, but Layna had been trained to keep royals from needing to enter into such risky endeavors.

Amalia lay on her back, looking up at us. I was used to her face carrying disapproval and dislike, but now it was twisted into pure hatred.

"Connect," I muttered, diving into her energy in search of an explanation for how Tyron had managed to goad her still. I immediately recognized the feel of her ability, matching it with the compositions that had fueled both storms.

Tyron had been right when he said she had both depth and breadth of skill and knowledge. It was clear how she had won the role of senior discipline instructor. But I could find no trace of Tyron or any other control.

Pulling out, I shook my head at the others. "She seems to be free of outside influence. I can't find any trace of Tyron at all."

"You?" Amalia almost snarled at me. "What good are you for

anything? For three long years I have borne the insult of being forced to include you in my class where you never belonged. And why?" She forced herself into a sitting position, spitting on the ground beside her. "Because you're a *royal* and an *Ardannian*."

"You say that like they're bad words," Bryony said. "What did Ardannian royals ever do to you?"

"Everything!" Amalia snapped back. "They took everything from me!"

I stared at her. "You're from Ardann?"

"No, of course not." She looked disdainful at the idea. "Although what does it matter? Both sets of royals sent their people to die. For thirty years they kept sending them."

"That wasn't Ardann's fault," I said hotly.

Amalia gave a harsh laugh. "Oh, don't fret. I have hatred enough to cover the Kallorwegians as well."

"Who did you lose?" Layna asked calmly, her face hard but a sadness lurking in the background of her eyes. Had she seen this before, then?

"My older brother," Amalia said, suddenly slumping, all of the fight going out of her. "The only person in the world I ever loved —and who ever loved me. He was so tall and so clever, so full of promise. But our family had no influence, and the aunt and uncle who raised us wouldn't have cared to exert it on our behalf if they had. So the king sent him off to the front in place of one of his precious courtlings, to be slaughtered like cattle by Ardannian hands."

She spat on the ground again. "Do you think the king or anyone in power cared that I was left completely alone? Of course they didn't. Each new generation is full of pretty words, but underneath they're all the same. Those who have power cling to it, and the rest of us are left to suffer. Well, I have worked many years to make myself into one of those with power and influence, and I wasn't going to waste my opportunity to pay back everything I have suffered."

Her words vividly recalled our long-ago conversation in law enforcement class. I had wondered then who Amalia thought could not forgive or let go of the past. I hadn't guessed it was her.

Elsie shook her head sadly. "Tyron couldn't have picked a more receptive victim."

I nodded slowly. "How effective his implanted ideas must have been in someone whose mind was already so receptive to them. There was no dissonance at all. So much so, in fact, that when his influence was withdrawn, the ideas had already taken root, and she continued with the plan on her own."

"For years I have served my kingdom despite what they did," Amalia said. "Training their future mages. But you..." Her eyes found me again. "And you..." She looked to Jareth. "And that arrogant princeling, calling himself king-elect, and believing himself above even the Academy. It was time you felt some of the pain I feel every day."

"But why now?" Bryony asked. "Why not wait until Darius was back?"

Amalia's eyes returned to me. "I don't want him dead," she hissed. "I want him to feel my pain."

Everyone around me stiffened and drew closer, as if to form a shield between me and the vengeful Amalia. But she hardly represented a threat now.

"I'm sorry," I said quietly. "I'm sorry you chose to hold on to your bitterness and let it ruin your life. But I had nothing to do with your brother's death, and I will not die to satisfy your revenge."

And with that, I turned and walked away, leaving Amalia bound on the ground, Layna and Jareth standing guard over her. Amalia had been a victim, twice over—once when she lost her brother and then again to Tyron. But she had been the one to allow her bitterness to so warp her mind that she was ready to be tipped over the edge into senseless violence and murder. Tyron had sown chaos wherever he could, but I was finished with the last of his poisonous seeds. The Academy was safe, and it was time to focus on the larger threat. Darius would be back any day now, my parents with him, and we had a different kind of storm cloud looming.

CHAPTER 26

ora rallied the servants, ensuring all the injured received healing from Raelynn and her trainees. A number of those who had been trapped in the dark in the tunnels needed time off to recover from the experience, but in the face of the attack, I didn't hear a single complaint from any mage about a lack of service.

Instead everyone pitched in together, even the first years lending what skill and energy they had to the recovery and rebuilding effort. The creator instructor spent an entire day behind the Academy, leading his trainees as they carefully retrieved all the stone I had hurled away. The next step would be fusing it back in its original places, but that was beyond the skill of all but the most advanced fourth years.

With Captain Vincent and so many of his guards away with Darius, we didn't have enough guards to risk sending Amalia to the capital. Instead she remained under careful guard at the Academy, stripped of all her compositions and kept far from any parchment or pens.

Horror and speculation swept the Academy as news of the identity of our attacker spread, but at no point did I hear anyone connect her with Tyron. As far as the Academy was concerned, she had snapped—driven by her personal grievances alone.

In a strange way, I felt guilty for never having liked her. It made it too easy to blame her and see her as the enemy, without remembering that it had been Tyron's poison that had tipped her over the edge. Disliking someone was no crime, and without his influence planting ideas, she might never have moved beyond that.

The next evening, Darius and Duke Francis rode into the Academy courtyard, Captain Vincent and a trail of guards following behind. They looked like they had ridden hard all day to get back after hearing news of the attack.

When Darius saw me, doing my part alongside the team trying to tidy up the front courtyard, he slid off his horse and strode over to wrap me in his arms. Whispers spread through the other trainees present, but he ignored them.

"You're safe." He held me tight, taking several long deep breaths. "Jareth sent word of what Amalia had hoped to..." His voice trailed off as if he couldn't bring himself to speak it aloud.

"But she didn't succeed," I reminded him. "We stopped her."

"It was you again, wasn't it?" he asked in a quiet voice.

"No," I said. "Once again it was a team effort. Hugh and Raelynn freed and healed the trapped servants, Alvin and the wind workers calmed the storm, and Elsie was the one who helped us find Amalia. I just dismantled her compositions."

He chuckled. "Just."

"And everyone is helping with rebuilding." A note of pride entered my voice. "The Academy can look after itself."

"And that puts me in my place," Darius said with a smile.

But I could see the fatigue lurking behind his eyes, and I couldn't resist reaching up to touch his cheek.

"Has it been exhausting?" I whispered. "Have you worked out a plan?"

He grimaced. "I could more accurately say we have agreed that cooperation is necessary."

My eyes widened. "But you've been gone for days."

He sighed. "The situation is complex—incredibly so. But thankfully we have time. As long as we can keep Tyron's father from getting word that we've discovered the truth about his son, we can take the negotiating and planning time we need."

I sighed and nodded. "Yes, thank goodness for the time." I glanced around and realized everyone else had drifted away—or been ushered on by the guards—and only we remained in the courtyard with Darius's ever-present double guard just out of earshot.

Darius himself didn't even seem to notice our surroundings. "We've closed the discussions for now. The delegates need to return home and discuss these tidings with their sovereigns."

I nodded. "And what about you, Darius?"

"I'm here to help rebuild the Academy, decide what's to be done with Amalia, and then find a way to keep Tyron here over the summer without raising his father's suspicions."

"And do you ever get to rest?" I asked softly.

He laughed. "I wanted to be king, did I not? Are kings allowed to rest?"

"Kings need a team around them, to help carry the load," I said firmly. "Don't forget that."

"People like you?" he asked, but there was a shadow in his eyes when he said it.

I nodded. "I told you I would fight for us, and I meant it. I see hope and a future in Kallorway—and that future is you. As long as you want me as part of your team, I'll be here to help you make a better kingdom."

"I told you at Midwinter I would fight for you, Verene, and I meant it," he said, but his voice didn't match his hopeful words. "But I also told you that I had to be sure I was worthy of you and that you would never regret joining your life with mine and embracing my kingdom instead of your own. The only family I have who truly loves me is Jareth, and when I thought I lost him, I went into a dark place. You're the one who gave him back to me. I couldn't bear to be the one to separate you from your own family. Especially when I know how much you love them and they love you. Giving them up is an enormous sacrifice, and I won't ask it of you without their consent and blessing."

Foreboding filled me.

"What have you done?" I whispered.

"For your family's approval to mean anything, they have to give it knowing everything. If I can convince them that despite all my mistakes, I will always care for you and always be faithful to you, then I know it's true."

"Darius," I said, in a louder voice, "what have you done?"

"I took the unexpected opportunity before me," he said. "Just before I left Kallmon, I went to your parents and told them everything."

I stepped away from him. "Everything?"

"Of course. How else can they truly make a decision about whether they believe me worthy of you?"

"But Darius, I haven't told them about my ability yet."

He froze. "But they're your family. I thought surely by now…"

"I haven't told them anything." I struggled to keep my voice from rising or a hysterical note from creeping in. "Do you think they would have let me return here if I had?"

He blanched. "I thought…"

"How could you tell them? I was always going to tell them myself—I was just waiting for the right time." Anger filled me. "It wasn't your place to tell them my secrets, Darius."

He stepped toward me, horror on his face, but I took an equal step back.

"Verene, I'm so sorry. I knew they couldn't know everything, but I thought they knew about you at least. I thought…"

"Why didn't you talk to me first?" I wailed. "You were so

determined to believe yourself weak and untrustworthy, to blame yourself for everything that happened when I never blamed you at all. And now you've gone and done this, and you really are to blame."

What were my parents thinking right now? They must be furious with me. And my aunt...I couldn't even process all the ramifications of what he'd done. When Jareth had said Darius held himself to a higher standard and was struggling to accept what Tyron had made him do, it never occurred to me he might take such a course as this. He wanted my family to accept him— to accept us—but he might have just destroyed any chance of that. If he felt he couldn't trust himself, he should have come to me, not them.

"I'm so sorry," he repeated, his voice thick with misery. "I really thought..."

A carriage rolled through the gates, and we broke off our argument to turn toward the new arrivals. The door sprang open almost before the vehicle had stopped, and a familiar figure jumped down.

My face paled. "And now I don't know if they'll ever let me out of Corrin again."

Darius grasped at my hand. "Verene, I promise I will never stop fighting for us. I will find a way to prove myself to them."

I shook my head. "I think right now I'm the one they mistrust as much as you. And it sounds like the one you need to prove yourself to is actually you."

I didn't have time to say more before my father had also alighted from the carriage. Both parents bore down on me, and I didn't know what was worse—the anger in their faces or the hurt and disappointment.

"Verene, we are going home. All of us. Now." My father's voice left no room for argument.

But I straightened my spine anyway. "The year isn't finished. I still need to take exams."

"We spoke to Duke Francis as soon as we finished with Darius," my mother said, noticeably omitting Darius's title. "He understands that sometimes urgent family business will call a trainee away."

I considered defying them and declaring I would stay. But the hurt in their eyes pierced my heart. They had never done anything but love and support me—despite my disappointing lack of ability—and I had thanked them by keeping the truth of myself from them. If I stayed now, would we ever find healing?

I glanced at Darius, warring emotions burning in me at the sight of him. I was angry at what he had done and at the lack of faith in himself that had driven him to it. But beneath that, my love still burned hot and strong. But he had said he would not accept me if doing so meant tearing me from my family. He would not welcome my choosing to stay now.

My shoulders sagged.

"Goodbye, Darius," I whispered, barely managing to meet his eyes.

I turned and climbed into the carriage without looking at either of my parents. I expected them to climb in after me, but instead my mother closed the door, her face appearing at the window.

"Wait here," she said. "We'll have Elsie pack your belongings."

She disappeared, and I was alone. The minutes dragged on, and several times I nearly changed my mind and left the carriage. But eventually the door opened again, and when it did, I was still in my seat.

But it wasn't my parents. Instead Elsie climbed in and shut the door behind her.

"My parents?" I asked, struggling to keep any trace of tears from my voice.

"They're going to ride," she said.

A swell of relief filled me at being spared what would have been a tense journey.

"What's going on, Princess Verene?" Elsie asked. "Is every-thing all right at home?"

I could hear the nerves in her voice and knew who she must be worried about.

"It's nothing from home," I said. "It's just that Darius told them everything while they were in Kallmon."

"E…everything?" she faltered, her eyes widening.

I nodded miserably. "So now they're doing what I feared all along and pulling me from the Academy."

"They love you," she said softly.

"I know," I replied, still trying to keep the tears from my voice. "But do they love me enough to let me choose my own life?"

"You just have to believe they do," Elsie said firmly. "Once they've had time to adjust to the idea."

"And what of you?" I asked after long minutes of silence rolled by, each of us looking out our respective windows. I suspected that, like me, Elsie was reflecting on both the year behind us and all that we faced at the end of this journey. "You haven't seen Stellan in a year. Do you still love him? Your future would be easier if you found another sealed commonborn to love instead of him."

I had carefully avoided asking her about my brother all year. Part of my purpose in making her my personal servant had been to give them time and space away from each other.

She laughed, a soft, gentle sound. "A year is far too short a time for me to forget your brother. I only hope he hasn't forgotten me. Although perhaps I should hope he has. His life would certainly be easier without me."

I looked across the carriage at her, reading the misery in her eyes at the thought Stellan might have fallen in love with a mage girl in the last year, but also her determination to let him go if that proved to be the case. She might have been born without power, but she deserved him in every other way.

"How could I—of all people—try to keep a member of my

family away from someone they love because I believe it would mean an easier life for them?" I asked. "I can't promise how my brother will feel, but if he still loves you, then I'm on your side. I'll help fight for your right to be together."

Elsie flushed, her eyes brimming over. "And I don't know what possible use I can be, but if there's any way I can help you get back to Prince Darius, I will."

"You were right to say we have to hold on to hope," I said. "In the face of everything that's coming for us, I think it's all we have. That and each other. And I, for one, choose to believe that's enough. We will find a way to come together and defeat Conall—and in the process, we will find a way to be with the men we love as well."

"After everything I've seen you achieve this year, Princess Verene, I believe nothing is outside your capability."

I shook my head. "No, what *we've* achieved, Elsie. All of us together. Darius said we have time to develop a plan to save everyone from Conall, and he's right. And we have time for our own problems too—all summer in fact. Because nothing is going to stop me graduating from the Kallorwegian Academy next year."

NOTE FROM THE AUTHOR

Read about Verene's fourth and final year at the Kallorwegian Academy in Crown of Power.

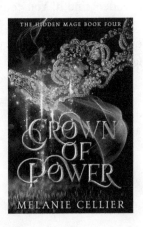

If you missed it, you can also read about the adventures of Verene's mother, Elena, when she attends the Ardannian Academy as a commonborn and becomes the Spoken Mage, starting in Voice of Power.

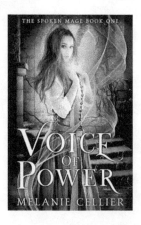

To be informed of future releases, as well as Hidden Mage bonus shorts, please sign up to my mailing list at www.melaniecellier.com.

And if you enjoyed Crown of Strength, please spread the word and help other readers find it! You could start by leaving a review on Amazon (or Goodreads or Facebook or any other social media site). Your review would be very much appreciated and would make a big difference!

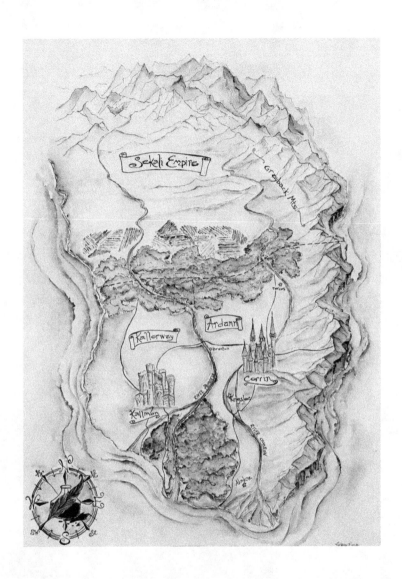

269

ACKNOWLEDGMENTS

As I sit here at the end of 2020, I still find myself marveling at what an unexpected year it's been. It feels impossible to even make a guess at what 2021 might bring. And yet despite all the tumult and pain, I'm so grateful for many things that 2020 has brought, and the Hidden Mage series is one of them. My friends and family are another. I couldn't attempt this writing journey without them, and I only grow more thankful with each book, not less.

To my excellent and reliable beta readers: you are, as always, absolute gems. A big thank you to Rachel, Greg, Priya, Ber, Katie, and Naomi. And, of course, the same to my editors—Mary, Deborah, and my dad.

Thank you to my cover designer, Karri, for always putting up with me—no matter how many drafts and revisions I put us through.

And to my husband and kids, your patience with me—and my lack of chore completion—means an incredible amount. I love you more than words can say.

And the biggest thanks to God, who remains an anchor in the current storms of life.

ABOUT THE AUTHOR

Melanie Cellier grew up on a staple diet of books, books and more books. And although she got older, she never stopped loving children's and young adult novels.

She always wanted to write one herself, but it took three careers and three different continents before she actually managed it.

She now feels incredibly fortunate to spend her time writing from her home in Adelaide, Australia where she keeps an eye out for koalas in her backyard. Her staple diet hasn't changed much, although she's added choc mint Rooibos tea and Chicken Crimpies to the list.

She writes young adult fantasy including books in her *Spoken Mage* world, and her three *Four Kingdoms and Beyond* series which are made up of linked stand-alone stories that retell classic fairy tales.

CPSIA information can be obtained
at www.ICGtesting.com
Printed in the USA
LVHW042141150722
723605LV00007B/159